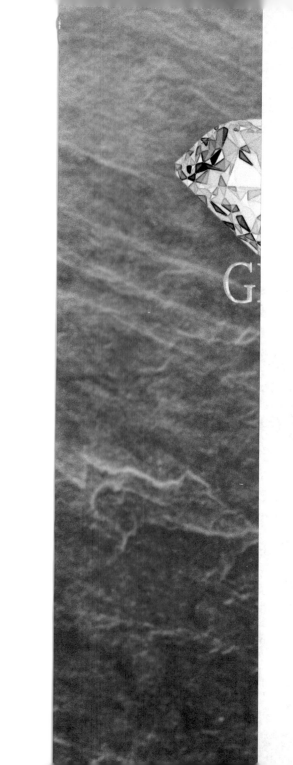

Onyx

FREYA BARKER

ONYX

ISBN: 9781988733906

Cover Design: Freya Barker
Editing: Karen Hrdlicka
Proofing: Joanne Thompson

GEM: a privately-funded organization operating independently in the search for—and the rescue and recovery of—missing and exploited children. Although, at times working in conjunction with law enforcement, GEM aims to ensure the victims receive justice... by whatever means necessary.

Operator Onyx; balanced, strong, a guardian

She's the voice of reason, advocates, and strategizes.

Supporting the team from the background, Onyx rarely goes out in the field. However, when a widespread child exploitation ring is discovered, her particular skill set is needed to get close.

Unfortunately, her boss—a man she's never laid eyes on before—is dead set against her taking the lead. Outvoted, he finds a way to keep her in his sights, risking his own exposure.

It's only a matter of time before the final truth is revealed, and they're forced to face the past and secure their future.

PROLOGUE

I DART ONE LAST GLANCE OVER MY SHOULDER, MAKING sure everyone is still sleeping before I slip out the door and ease it shut.

The only light comes from the yellowed night-light plugged into the wall outside the bathroom at the other end of the hallway. I tiptoe toward it, leaving the girls' dorm room behind. Passing by the only other door, I pause for a moment, listening to make sure there are no sounds from inside. Then I rush ahead and duck into the bathroom.

I don't turn on the light, familiar enough with the layout after spending the past five years of my life in this hellhole. Despite the pitch dark, I know there are three bathroom stalls to my left, a counter with three sinks on my right, and along the back wall six narrow lockers with a shower on either side. That's where I'm heading.

There's no one here—yet. I pick the shower stall on the left and duck behind the narrow privacy wall, just in case someone I'm not expecting walks in.

I feel, rather than hear, someone come in a few minutes later. Nothing more than a slight movement of air as the door to the hallway opens. I hold my breath and wait for the sound of a stall door opening, but it doesn't come. The only warning I get is a slight rustle of clothing a fraction of a second before a familiar voice sounds only inches away.

"Raj?"

I release the air I'd been holding before answering.

"Right here."

Despite the darkness, our hands meet, grabbing on tightly.

"Are you ready?"

The million-dollar question.

I'm so torn about this. Who is going to look out for the others when I'm gone?

The plan is to make our way to Lexington and seek help there, since we know we won't get any here in Lanark. But what if no one believes us? Or worse; what if we get caught before we make it? What will happen to the others then?

"As ready as I'll ever be," I whisper back, shoring up my courage.

"Good." My hand gets a squeeze. "We should get going before someone comes in here. I taped the latch on the kitchen door so we should be able to get out easily."

I nod, realizing right away it won't be visible.

We're supposed to slip out the back and hide in the dumpster right outside the kitchen door, which is scheduled to be picked up every Thursday morning before seven, about four hours from now.

"Now or never," I confirm, feeling a little tug on my hand.

I follow closely, holding on tight as we make our way out of the bathroom and sneak toward the stairs. We both know to avoid the third step down because it creaks, but still wait for a moment at the bottom of the stairs to make sure nothing is moving in the house.

The tile floor of the kitchen is cold under my bare feet. We agreed to leave everything behind, including our shoes. We didn't want to risk dropping or banging something and someone hearing. So bare feet and hands-free it is.

As we inch toward the back door my heart is pounding so hard, it makes my chest hurt. So close now.

When we stop, I hear a soft, *"Shit."*

"What?" I whisper back.

"The door is lock—"

Suddenly the bright overhead lights come on and a voice has my blood freeze in my veins.

"Did you really think we'd let you just walk out of here?"

I didn't resist.

I hadn't resisted since he dragged me out of the house and threatened to make life hell for the girls if I didn't comply. Sacrificing myself was the only way I could think of to look after them.

The fire I had in my heart died a long time ago, and all I'd done since was exist. From one breath to the next, from meal to meal, the only highlight was the drugs that allowed me to disappear.

It may have been weeks or months or years, but when the car stopped in front of Transition House, it sparked a flame that boiled my blood.

I'd been too late for the girls—they were gone, and all I could do was hope they'd be okay—but I could still save myself, and make sure what happened to us can't happen to others.

I STARTLE AWAKE WHEN THE CURTAIN AROUND MY BED IS pushed back, and a nurse walks up to my bed.

"Good morning, soldier. I'm afraid we'll have to change those dressings again today."

I have to shake my head to clear the remnants of those years' old memories. They've been haunting my dreams since I woke up in the military hospital in Germany with no recollection of how I got there.

Perhaps this was my wake-up call.

My second chance to make good on a promise I made almost a decade ago.

ONE

ONYX

"Beverage? Ma'am?"

I turn to find a young kid, little more than a teenager, offering me a tray with a selection of drinks. I smile and select a flute I'm sure holds champagne. I don't plan on drinking it—not when on the job—but having a glass in my hand will ward off being offered one every few minutes. I need to be on my game and could do without frequent interruptions.

The Thoroughbred Charities of America fundraiser is quite the elaborate event. Looking around the hotel's ballroom, I spot a good number of designer outfits among the well-dressed guests as I try to locate the guy I'm supposed to meet. Unfortunately, I have no idea what he looks like.

Hamish Adrian.

Damn Jacob Branch for throwing me to the wolves. I

don't have much experience with covert operations and definitely feel out of my element here. I'm normally in charge of coordination and communications but, in his infinite wisdom, Jacob has decided I should go undercover as a wealthy Pakistani socialite, looking to invest her money in thoroughbred horses.

My contact is a former Canadian horse trainer, who is looking to establish himself in the United States. I wasn't given a physical description for Mr. Adrian, but was assured he would recognize me.

"Ms. Baqri? Onyx?"

The rich baritone has me swing around.

First thing I notice are his dark eyes, aimed at me. My skin breaks out in goosebumps under his intense scrutiny. My eyes drift, taking in the rest of his appearance, but quickly focus back on his eyes.

"That's me. You must be Mr. Adrian?"

I struggle to keep my voice even, shaken by the tight and marred skin creating the appearance of a mask. It's clear some graft work has been done, but the damage from extensive burns is still visible on a large portion of his face and neck. His head is shaved, almost making the scars stand out more.

"Hamish," he corrects me.

Then he extends his right hand, which is missing two fingers and—like the skin on his face—looks badly scarred. I notice he is studying me closely, and I get the sense I'm being tested. Holding his eyes, I take his offered hand without blinking.

Silently I curse my boss for the minimal information

he provided. All I was told is this man is going to lend my cover story credibility.

"Hamish," I echo, tilting my head as I let go of his hand. "I don't detect a Scottish accent."

"There isn't one. I was named for my great-grandfather, a farrier from Dundee who came across after World War I and settled in Canada. I'm a third-generation Canadian."

I suppress a smile at the hint of pride in his voice.

"Horses are in the blood, then?" I observe.

"You might say that." He gestures toward an empty table farthest from the podium. "Let's have a seat."

I lead the way, all too aware of the deep plunging back of my gown. Not my pick—I would've chosen something a bit more modest—but Jacob insisted if I wanted to pull off the cover of a rich socialite, I should start by dressing like one.

He picked the gown.

A sleek, satin, champagne-colored tank dress, hugging my pronounced curves. The color is perfect against my brown skin, but the tight fit would be better suited to someone younger, and definitely skinnier than I am.

"So, how do you know Jacob?" I ask when he takes a seat beside me.

"Shared interests. We go way back."

A rather evasive response, leaving me even more curious. Especially since I'm always in the market for anything I can find out about my boss, who is no more than a voice on the phone to me.

I'm about to push for more information, when a server

walks up with a tray of drinks. I pass, but Hamish selects a Glencairn glass which undoubtedly holds bourbon.

The waiter seems mesmerized at the sight of his mangled hand.

"Thank you," I quickly tell the young man, who startles and rushes away from the table.

Hamish either doesn't notice the awkward moment, or he's accustomed to stares and chooses to ignore them.

"So, I understand you have plans to step into the thoroughbred racing scene," Hamish comments.

I have no idea what Jacob told him about me, so I tread carefully, sticking close to my cover story.

"Yes. I hope to, but I'm discovering it's quite a challenging world to get into."

My objective is to obtain a membership to the Thoroughbred Guild of America. The membership is by invitation only, and so far, I haven't been extended one. Not for lack of trying, mind you.

"A polite way of saying it's an old boys' club," Hamish points out, sitting back in his chair as he unapologetically scrutinizes me. "From where I'm sitting you have a few strikes against you right off the bat. You're the wrong gender, the wrong color, you're too young and too beautiful, and no one knows you."

He seems to recognize my look of disbelief at his blunt observations, and continues before I can voice my displeasure.

"No sense beating around the bush, you should know what you're up against." He takes a sip of his bourbon. "The good news is, I can help you."

He may be right, but his calm arrogance rubs me the wrong way.

"And how do you propose to do that?"

Credit to him, he barely reacts to my snide tone.

"Even though I was sidelined the past couple of years, and have recently moved here, I know this business," he states calmly. "I'm willing to introduce you to it."

"What's the gain for you?"

His grin is a bit lopsided, but it transforms the left side of his face.

"Like I said, I'm new to town, and even though I have a decent reputation in the industry, those who've heard of me only know me by name. I need to reestablish myself in this community. Build up trust, but people aren't that receptive to a face like mine. Having a beautiful woman by my side will make me more approachable. So you'll be helping me as much as I'll be helping you, and trust me, it won't be a hardship."

I'm guessing whatever caused his injuries was the reason for the hiatus from the racing world, and possibly for his choice to rebuild his career here. I can see how connecting with me—or at least my cover identity—might be beneficial to him, but I'm not that sure how he'll be able to help me out.

So...I want to have a little chat with Jacob before I take him up on his offer.

"Excuse me for a minute, please?" I get out of my seat and slip out from behind the table, throwing him an apologetic smile. "I have to find the ladies' room."

I smile and nod at people I pass as I find my way out

of the ballroom. Once in the hallway, I bypass the bathroom and find a quiet corner in the lobby.

"*I wasn't expecting you yet,*" Jacob announces when he answers my call.

"I don't see why not," I retort. "Since you clearly left some information out."

"*Like what?*"

"Well, it might be helpful to know how much—if anything—you told him about my assignment, since he offered to help me out." I'm annoyed and I don't bother hiding it. "Considering I don't know how much he knows, I'm not quite sure what he's offering to help me out with."

Apparently, I raised my voice, an elderly woman passing through the lobby glances at me suspiciously.

"*I haven't told him much. Not because I don't trust him, because I do, but this is your assignment. It's your call how far you want to let him in. I suggest you play it by ear.*"

Next, I hear a click.

Wonderful. He hung up.

Now I'm pissed off.

Is he testing me or something?

Aggravated, I duck into the bathroom to splash some cold water on my face, before returning to the ballroom.

Hamish Adrian is sitting exactly where I left him.

"Okay," I concede, stopping next to him.

He tilts his head back to look at me.

"Okay...what?"

"I'd like to take you up on your offer of help."

He flashes me that lopsided grin before getting to his

feet. Even though I'm not a small woman at five foot nine, I notice Hamish Adrian still has a good six inches on me.

"Excellent. We can begin by getting a little closer to the action."

He places a hand in the small of my back and guides me nearer to the stage where the charity auction is about to start.

I KICK MY SHOES OFF THE SECOND THE DOOR TO THE suite clicks shut behind me.

Much better. I rarely wear heels and I've been on my feet most of the night. Hamish was relentless, dragging me along from one group to the next as he worked the room. Networking, he called it.

During the course of the night, I not only made a few tentative contacts, but was able to learn a little more about my enigmatic guide as well. There were some people who seemed familiar with his name, despite his disappearance from the scene five years ago. In talking to a few of them, I discovered Hamish was seriously injured in a tragic stable fire at a training facility north of Toronto. Whenever someone brought it up, Hamish would swiftly redirect the conversation.

Clearly, he's not comfortable discussing what happened and I'm not going to push it. I barely know the man. Besides, I can do a little snooping on my own. I'm sure I'll be able to find information online. I have to do background searches on some of the industry people I met tonight anyway.

However, it'll have to wait until tomorrow, I don't know how long I'll be able to keep my eyes open.

In the bathroom I pull the pins from my hair, which had been twisted in an intricate updo for the occasion. Letting it fall down my back, I briskly massage my scalp with my fingertips, groaning at the release of tension. Next, I zip out of my dress and change into a shirt and yoga pants.

Padding barefoot into the sitting room, I flick on a light near the courtesy bar, and pick up the remote. Maybe a little TV while I wait for the inevitable phone call.

I'm about to lie back on the couch when a knock sounds at my door. Grabbing my phone, I walk up and squint through the peephole into the hallway.

Hamish is standing outside.

"Is something wrong?" I ask, opening the door.

"I forgot to mention something I overheard earlier," he shares as his eyes seem to take in my appearance. "I'm sorry. I gave you my number but never got yours, and I would've sought you out tomorrow morning, but I have to be on a flight at six thirty."

The man looks distinctly uncomfortable, tugging at the knot of his tie.

"It's fine. You didn't wake me up or anything, I'm still waiting for a phone call. What was it you forgot?"

"Apparently, there's a private auction near Bowling Green in two weeks. The Gilded Bridle. It's thoroughbreds only, and exclusively by invitation, but I think I might be able to get us in. That is, if you're interested."

Absolutely I'm interested. You never know who I might encounter at an exclusive, private auction.

"I am."

"A winning bid at the Gilded Bridle will go a long way to getting your name out there."

And may open some doors which have stayed firmly shut thus far.

I'm going to need to talk to Jacob, I'm pretty sure my expense account won't begin to cover even a starting bid in an auction like that.

"So noted," I tell him.

Then I open my contacts to the number he gave me earlier, and shoot off a text. A muffled ping sounds from his suit jacket.

"Now you have my number so you can get in touch."

He nods, the left side of his mouth twitching.

"I'll call you as soon as I have news."

"I appreciate that, and thanks again for tonight. It was very helpful."

He lifts his damaged hand to his head in a mock salute as he backs away from the door.

"Night, Onyx."

It's not until I turn on the TV, looking for a news channel, it occurs to me I never gave Hamish my room number. We said goodbyes in the lobby.

I have a sneaking suspicion where he might've gotten it, though.

Jacob Branch is my boss, and the owner of GEM, an

organization dedicated to locating and recovering missing kids. Often these children are, or become, victims of sexual exploitation. Our mandate does not end with the retrieval or rescue of the children, but extends to tracking down the predators responsible, and ensuring they receive the justice they deserve.

I am one of the original three operatives. All women, each with their own set of skills. Since then we've added a former FBI agent who was part of a Child Abduction Rapid Response team to our ranks.

I'm normally responsible for planning, communications, and aftercare for victims. For some reason, on this case, I've been forced to the foreground, taking the lead in the field. Not my strength, but my boss is not a fool and I'm sure he has his reasons. He's just not sharing them.

"Jacob," I answer a moment later when my phone rings as if on cue.

"*And?*"

"Your friend was helpful," I admit reluctantly. "I made a few connections I'll check into when I get back to the office tomorrow."

Even though I'm only an hour or so from home, renting a suite in the hotel where the fundraiser took place fits my cover, but tomorrow morning I'm back to being myself.

For now, anyway.

"*Message me the contacts and I can get started with some background research,*" Jacob offers.

I'm too tired to argue and send him the names.

"*Got it.*"

"Jacob? Who is Hamish to you?"

My question is followed by silence and for a moment I think he's hung up on me again, but he surprises me.

"You could say we're brothers-in-arms." Then he adds, *"Catch up with you tomorrow."*

Before I have a chance to respond the line goes dead.

Figures.

TWO

Jacob

"Our target is David Wheeler."

Except, he's supposed to be dead.

"The only heir to his father's multinational shipping corporation—which he promptly sold upon the man's death for billions—made him a rich man. He pretended to be some kind of philanthropist with a focus on charities bene-fiting children and teenagers, but it was a front for his more nefarious activities."

One of his so-called charitable endeavors was Transition House; a group home for disenfranchised youth in Lanark, Kentucky. In reality the home had been a cover for a child exploitation ring.

It was supposed to be a safe haven for kids, but instead turned out to be a place for rich and influential pedophiles to carry out their depraved fantasies without repercussion.

"I don't need to tell you there wasn't—or isn't—a benevolent bone in that bastard's body."

David Wheeler had turned sexual deviancy into an industry, and cruelty into an art.

Two decades ago, Transition House burned to the ground, cause unknown. Three people responsible for the goings-on at the home were reported to have perished in the fire. However, as we recently discovered, at least two of the three survived: Josh Kendrick, the program supervisor, and Dr. Elsbeth Sladky, the home's director. Since then, justice has caught up with both of them, but that leaves David Wheeler still unaccounted for.

"I think, like Kendrick and Sladky, Wheeler survived the fire. And I believe he is still very active."

"I think we all suspect as much," Pearl points out. "But we don't have much more than suspicions and theories, and it looks like the lead you have Onyx chasing is going to be more of a long-term assignment. In the meantime, who knows how many kids are going to fall prey to this guy. Why not put the rest of us to work as well? We all have a vested stake in bringing him down."

The *we* she refers to are the rest of my GEM team, who are gathered in the office.

Opal, the alias I gave Kate Jones, is a marksman and weapons specialist, and has the ability to disappear into the woodwork, making her the perfect undercover operator.

Her husband, Mitch Kenny, is a former federal agent who worked as part of the Child Abduction Rapid

Deployment—or CARD—team. He is the newest addition to GEM.

Then there is Pearl, or Janey Fisher, who ran her own cybersecurity company before joining GEM as our IT expert. She also has impressive martial arts skills that can come in handy.

Lee Remington technically isn't on the payroll, but works with GEM on a consultancy basis. The freelance journalist—and new life partner of Pearl—is a very savvy investigator with personal reasons to delve into anything and anyone associated with Transition House.

And finally, there's Onyx, whose real name is Rajani Agarwal, but her teammates call her Raj for short. With a master's in psychology she worked as a child victim advocate and taught self-defense classes before I convinced her to work for GEM. Onyx brings balance and empathy to the team. She is our case strategist, communications expert, and provides aftercare for the children we manage to rescue.

"I don't doubt everyone is eager to find him and see justice done, but I'm concerned if we all start rattling cages, we'll just alert him. The man had two decades to build himself a new identity, it's gonna take time to track him down."

I look out my office window and watch the dark rain clouds roll in over the Appalachian Mountains. Ever since the deadly flooding last year, people in this region get a little nervous when there's rain in the forecast, but I quite enjoy it. There's something soothing in the steady drum of drops hitting the metal roof panels.

"Why don't I give everyone a bit of an update first?" Onyx's rich, melodic sound has a calming effect. "We can talk about how to go forward after."

"Go ahead."

I get comfortable, leaning back in my chair and putting my feet up on the windowsill.

"As you know, we've been trying to track down a horse," she starts.

I close my eyes and let her voice wash over me.

She briefly recaps the discovery of two missing children on a ranch near Bowling Green not that long ago, and the lead we got as a result.

It was the name of one of the horses stabled at the property that piqued my interest; Pure Delight. The fact it matched the name used for an auction offering underage sex slaves to the highest bidder—one we'd just managed to shut down—could hardly be a coincidence.

I've since been able to trace ownership of the horse to an investment company by the name of Pegasus GLAN. From there it was easy to link the investment company to none other than GLAN Industries. A name by now very familiar to me.

Unfortunately, by the time I was able to make the connections, the horse had been removed from the stable and transported to places unknown. All I have is yet another company name on paper, and although my gut says David Wheeler is behind all of them, I have nothing tangible.

"...trust this Hamish Adrian?"

I'm drawn from my thoughts when I hear Mitch mention his name.

"I vouched for him," I interject, even though the question was likely meant for Onyx. *"I'd trust him with my life."*

"Good enough for me," Mitch returns.

"Apparently, the racing community doesn't trust newcomers—so far I've been *persona non grata*—and I'm hoping Hamish can help with that," Onyx explains. "I need to establish my cover, have at least some credibility, before I start asking questions about Pure Delight, its trainer, or its owners."

I look out on the mountains, listening to the disembodied voices, when I see the window reflects movement behind me. I swivel my chair around and my hand goes to the mute button.

"Sorry to interrupt, but I have to leave if I'm to make my book club meeting. I left your dinner in the oven."

I grin at her. "Thanks, Bernie. See you tomorrow."

Bernice Nelson—my lifesaver—the woman who has had my back for the past fifteen years.

When she's gone, I unmute the phone and just catch Opal asking, "...need from us?"

"Jacob?" she prompts.

"We need to find a property with stables to fit Onyx's cover story. A suitable house, staff quarters, and preferably with an exercise track." I was up last night trying to figure out how best to ensure I can keep Onyx safe. *"I'm going to need you to handle that as Ms. Baqri's personal assistant, Opal. Mitch will be acting as her driver."*

"Surely that's not necessary," Onyx protests.

"*Oh, I think it is, for credibility. I don't want there to be any doubt about who you portray to be. If you want to be taken seriously you'll need quality horses. Maybe you can buy a couple at that auction Hamish mentioned.*"

"A couple? Are you nuts? Do you have any idea what kind of money we're talking about? Top quality thoroughbreds start at a few hundred thousand and go up from there," she sputters.

"*I'm aware. I consider it an investment, and who knows, we may have a winner on our hands.*"

"You're insane."

Perhaps I am, but this is what I've worked for nearly half my life, and I'm not going to risk him getting away.

"Or maybe I'm thorough," I counter. "*I want David Wheeler—or whatever name he's using—stopped, and I don't care how much time or money it takes.*"

I hang up before anyone can respond.

Let them chew on that. They should know how dead serious I am.

Onyx

The silence lingered long after Jacob ended the call. Janey was the first to break it.

"For all our sakes, I hope we're not chasing a ghost."

Her words have been haunting me all night.

I can't say I've never wondered what is driving Jacob Branch. As worthy and—dare I say—heroic his intentions for GEM have been, I think I've always known there is something inherently personal at the root of his crusade.

There have been times I've probed, trying to get him to open up, but he's been a master at evading. Yet his comments last night, and the way he spit out Wheeler's name, spoke volumes.

What's been keeping me up is whether it was Jacob himself, or someone he cared for who fell victim to Wheeler. I don't have any illusions the man limited his depraved activities to the kids at Transition House, but I still wonder if Jacob may have been one of them.

Every boy I ever met at the home passes through my mind. Most of them I didn't even know by name, and even if I did, it wouldn't tell me much. I have no idea who Jacob is. I don't know his real name, what he looks like, or how old he is.

I snort. Heck, I don't even know what he sounds like, he's always used some kind of distortion to mask his voice.

Giving up on sleep, I swing my feet out of bed and head for the kitchen. I could do with a hit of coffee. It takes only a minute for my Nespresso to brew some, and I take my mug and my cell phone out on my balcony to catch the sunrise.

Checking my email, I see five different ones from Kate, all links to real estate listings. Wow, she didn't waste any time.

I've only just clicked on the first link when my phone rings.

It's Kate. I put her on speakerphone.

"Morning."

"Did you look at them?"

Kate sounds way too chipper this time of the morning.

"I'm just looking at the first one. What are you doing calling me this early?"

"I figured you were up when I saw you open the email. Anyway, check out the last listing. The one near Four Oaks."

I pull up the final email and click on the link.

"Where is Four Oaks?"

"About thirty miles east of Williamstown. Only forty minutes or so from my place."

Just then the listing pops up on my phone, and my eyes get stuck on the price tag of two point one million.

"Are you crazy?"

"Just look at the pictures," Kate urges. "It's gorgeous."

I shake my head, but I scroll down to appease her.

She's not lying, the place is beautiful.

The large ranch house looks new, or at least newly renovated. There's a second, smaller building that looks like a guesthouse. A good-sized pool separates the two. On the overhead image I see a barn with a riding ring on the opposite side of the long driveway.

An impressive stone gate is partially hidden by a grove of trees blocking the view from the road. Fenced pastures are visible on either side of the property, and at the rear is what looks like an exercise track. Beyond it looks like nothing but woodland.

It fits Jacob's specifications, but that price tag is staring at me.

Among the many things I don't know about Jacob Branch is the depth of his resources. I'm sure they're not infinite.

"It looks fantastic, but that's a lot of money," I tell Kate.

"I'll call the realtor this morning," she offers. "See if there is any wiggle room."

I can't help but grin at her persistence.

"Maybe you should check with Jacob first."

"He'll leave it up to you. You know he will."

Probably, but I'm not about to spend millions of his money without his approval.

"Still..." I insist.

"Fine, but get ready, as soon as we get the go-ahead, we're heading to Four Oaks."

She'll have to get hold of Jacob and the realtor first. There's no rush.

"I'll see you at the office later, Kate."

"Remember to wear something that screams money."

After breakfast and a shower, I'm standing in front of my meager closet, looking for something suitable. It's slim pickings. I'm going to have to buy a few things that fit my cover.

The only thing I can see that comes close to designer is the black leather, knock-off Chanel backpack an ex-lover tried to pawn off to me as real. I'd tossed it to the back of my closet, but it may come in handy now.

I'm going for casual chic.

Old, torn jeans, a white dress shirt and a pair of wedges, my hair loose and makeup heavy, and that fake Chanel backpack slung over my shoulder.

It doesn't exactly scream money, but it'll have to do.

My ancient Subaru Outback definitely isn't in character but when I pull into the parking lot at the office, I see it's already been taken care of.

A grinning Mitch, dressed in all black, is standing beside a shiny black Lincoln Navigator parked in front of the entrance.

"That's what you're wearing?"

Kate appears by her husband's side. She's wearing a pale blue, fitted pantsuit, and her red hair is piled on top of her head in a messy knot. She's looking at me disapprovingly over the rim of a pair of purple glasses she doesn't need. The whole look reminds me a little of Penelope in *Criminal Minds*.

"Evidently," I point out.

"Well, it's too late to do anything about that now," she grumbles. "We need to hustle; the real estate agent has another potential buyer coming at noon."

"Did you talk to Jacob?" I check with Kate as Mitch opens the Navigator's rear door for me.

She rolls her eyes.

"Yes... He wants me to do a live-video feed of the property tour."

It's clear she's not happy with it.

"Can't expect the man to drop two mil sight unseen, Kate," Mitch points out.

She darts me a sharp look when she climbs in behind me.

I wisely keep my mouth shut.

THREE

Jacob

I sip my bourbon while trying hard to keep my cool as I listen to Miles Graham voicing his concerns.

"I'm not sure this is a sound investment. The real estate market has been slow. Besides that, I'd really recommend some kind of contract before you drop those kinds of funds into an employee's account. Three million dollars is a lot of money."

I take a deep breath before responding.

"To the best of my recollection, you are not my financial advisor nor my lawyer. If I wanted advice, I would have called one of them. You, however, are my banker, which is why I contacted you to transfer the funds. Now, if this is a problem, I can always take my business elsewhere."

I dislike having to play that card, but I have better

things to do with my time than spending it arguing with him about the way I choose to spend *my* money.

Of course, the threat had its desired effect, and Miles quickly assures me the transfer will not be an issue and he was simply looking out for my best interests.

As soon as the call ends, I hit replay on Opal's live feed I recorded this morning. I still can't believe it took her less than twenty-four hours to come up with something suitable.

The Four Oaks farm was a good find. It's fairly new, built in place of the original farmhouse in 2011, and the stables were added at that time. Modern luxury without being ostentatious. It took me all of two minutes to decide, especially after finding out how private it is.

The farm is not why I'm replaying the feed, however. It's the occasional views of Onyx as she moves in and out of focus while checking out the place.

Her gleaming, dark hair is loose, falling down her back and almost reaching the pronounced curve of her ass. I get occasional glimpses of a smile and the distinct, white streak in her hair, as she turns her head to look at Opal. She looks relaxed, seems comfortable moving through the rooms.

Yeah, Four Oaks suits her, which makes paying the slightly inflated price on the property well worth it. The fact the farm had been vacant for a few months already, and the owner was eager to unload it, meant they were agreeable to an accelerated process.

I pick up the phone and dial my lawyer, instructing him to draw up whatever paperwork is needed to facilitate a closing date less than a week from today. To his credit, the only question he asks when I tell him whose name should be on all paperwork, is whether I'm sure. A simple *yes* is enough, and he assures me he'll have all documents ready by Friday.

Finally, I pull up Onyx's number. She should be home by now.

She answers right away.

"I was just about to call you. I think you made a mistake."

"How so?"

"I just got a notification from the bank. Why the hell are you sending me three million dollars? That's almost a million too much."

"You're going to need it for the auction. This is about inserting yourself into the racing community. You can't do that by sitting on the sidelines. You'll need to have a vested stake in the game if you want anyone to believe you're the real deal."

"Is the auction a go? Because I haven't heard anything yet."

I probably should've let Hamish inform her of that, but the cat is out of the bag now.

"I'm sure he'll call. I had him on the phone earlier to discuss his consultancy fee when he mentioned about the auction."

"Shouldn't I be discussing his fee with him? I thought you were letting me manage Hamish."

Shit. I did tell her it was up to her how much she wanted to involve him.

"You're right," I admit grudgingly. *"Call it force of habit. Although, he may not think anything of it since he seems to think we're an item. He asked me as much."*

"And... I trust you disavowed him of that notion, correct?"

I love it when she gets on her high horse. Her tone becomes brisk and haughty, and even though I can't see her, I just know her nose is up in the air.

She has no idea how sexy she sounds.

"I felt it was more useful to leave him guessing. In case he gets any ideas."

"You are my boss, not my father, or my social convenor, Jacob."

For once it's she who abruptly ends the call.

I guess I must have pissed her off.

I lean back in my chair, lift my feet on the desk, and hit replay on my phone. I feel a smile pulling at my mouth when I catch a glimpse of her flowing hair on my screen.

Onyx

"Here. Try these."

I take the fistful of hangers and close the curtain.

I'm not a fan of shopping but there was no holding back Janey—our resident fashionista—when Kate told me once again I needed new clothes.

Janey wasted no time dragging me to Cincinnati, where *"...all the good stores are."* My feet are sore from tagging behind her up and down Vine Street, hitting every designer boutique in our path. She is not showing any signs of stopping so I'm going to have to put an end to this torture. Soon.

"Don't we already have a pair of black pants?" I ask her, holding up what looks to be a pair of black jeans.

"Those are dressy, these are casual. Try them on."

I roll my eyes at her curt response. Hardly the most mature reaction, but it relieves my frustration a bit. Although Janey's bossiness isn't the only thing annoying me. There appears to be plenty getting on my nerves the past day or two.

That's not me. I'm normally even-keeled and not usually flustered, or stressed, and I rarely get bent out of shape over something. I'm supposed to be the calm one, the peacemaker, but I can feel it won't take much to set me off.

This assignment is wreaking havoc on my inner balance.

"Janey, this is the last pile of clothes I'm trying on. No more, I'm done."

I wait for her objection, but she surprises me.

"Fair enough. I have to get home anyway. Lee is on his way to pick up Ricky for a visit and I still have to get the guest room ready."

Ricky is a teenage boy, from an abusive home, Janey and Lee befriended when they were investigating a youth nature program not too long ago.

Thanks to their intervention, Ricky is now living in a good foster home, but Janey and Lee stay in regular contact.

The last item I try are the jeans, and they fit like a glove when I slip them on. I add them to the pile hanging over the door of the dressing room.

"That's the last of the yesses," I tell her.

"Okay, you get dressed and I'll get them to start ringing these up."

I'm hopping on one leg, trying to get my jeans on, when my phone rings. I give up on the jeans, dig the phone out of my bag, and check the screen.

It's Hamish calling.

About time, I was starting to wonder if he changed his mind about helping me. I've been tempted to call him a few times, but am glad I restrained myself.

"Hamish."

He comes back with, "Onyx," amusement clear in his tone.

It irks me a little.

I put the phone on speaker, set it down on the bench, and start putting on my jeans.

"What is it I can do for you?"

"Nothing right now, but you may want to free up your calendar for a week from Saturday. We have an invitation for the Gilded Bridle."

There's a load of expectation in the silence that follows his announcement, and I'd look like an ungrateful bitch if I didn't respond with gratitude. So, I swallow down my bad mood and plaster on a smile.

"That is brilliant news. Where is it going to take place?"

"Drake Stables, it's about fifteen miles south of Bowling Green, and belongs to—"

"Peter Drake. Yes, I've heard of him. His horse won the Kentucky Derby four or five years ago? What was it? Bourbon Belle?"

"You did your homework. Yeah, that's him. I was wondering if you have some time this coming weekend to go over the auction catalog and do some strategizing?"

"Actually, I'm moving into my new place this weekend. I found a horse farm not far from Williamstown with immediate availability," I share, grabbing my bag and stepping out of the dressing room. "It has beautiful stables and even an exercise track."

"Wow. You don't mess around. Well, I'd love to see the place, make sure you have everything you need, because with a bit of luck you may be coming home with a horse or two in the very near future."

Yikes. He makes a good point.

I know very little about horses or their needs. I suppose I'll need a stable hand or something, and of course I can do some research myself, but it would be nice to know I at least have what I need. Even though this is only a temporary setup, it has to be a credible operation.

Here I thought I was on top of things, but I'm suddenly feeling woefully unprepared.

"That might not be a bad idea," I consider.

"How about the use of an extra pair of hands this weekend? I can help with the move, check out the facility, and we may be able to find some time to sit down and go over the auction."

"*Who is that?*" Janey mouths when I join her at the cash register.

"Hamish," I whisper with my hand covering the phone.

My instinct is to check with Jacob, but I may not always have time to run things by him first. I'm going to have to start calling some shots myself.

Taking my credit card, I slide it across the counter to the store clerk.

"You know, it was just a thought," Hamish backtracks.

He clearly took my prolonged silence as rejection.

"No-no, I...uh...I actually think it's a good idea," I quickly set him straight.

The clerk turns the handheld terminal to me, and I suck in a deep breath when I see the amount displayed. I hold up a finger, asking her to wait a moment.

"Hamish? I'm just finishing up something here, but I'll send you the address and you can let me know when you think you'll be there."

"Of course. We'll be in touch," he agrees and ends the call.

Tucking my phone back in my purse, I focus my attention on the bill.

"Six thousand dollars?"

"Five thousand eight hundred and seventy-three fifty, to be precise," Janey corrects me, reading the amount off the terminal.

"For a pair of black jeans and a few tops?"

I scan the contents of the two large shopping bags on the counter.

"Actually, you have those same jeans in olive green, then there's the plum pencil skirt, and the silk watercolor kimono," the clerk contributes, listing items I distinctly recall dropping on the reject pile.

When I toss Janey a look, she shrugs her shoulders.

"You asked for my help for a reason, and you need those in your wardrobe," she states unapologetically.

I don't even bother reminding her she's the one who insisted I needed her expertise. It'll go in one ear and out the other anyway. It's probably less painful just giving in and paying.

Resigned, I nod at the store clerk.

"Ring it up."

Ten minutes later I get into the passenger side of Janey's Traverse and kick off my shoes.

"So...this Hamish...what do you really know about him?" Janey asks as we wind our way out of the parking garage.

"Not much, other than he's a horse trainer from Canada, but Jacob knows him. Called him a brother-in-arms."

"Sounds like they served together. I wondered if Branch could be military or former military."

I glance over at her. "It's possible. I'm sure that's where the term came from, but I've also heard it used simply to describe good friends."

"Still, do you think giving him your new home address is wise?"

I bite off a grin. How times have changed.

I've always been the cautious one, taken on the protective older-sister role, so this is a new experience.

"It's not like I intend to date him, Janey. He is part of my cover."

I feel her gaze on me and turn my head to meet her eyes.

"But do you trust him?"

Do I?

I know Jacob does, and I don't believe for a second he'd ever put me in harm's way. Besides, no red flags go up for me when I interact with him, and I'm generally a good judge of character.

My gut tells me Hamish is safe.

FOUR

Onyx

I haul the last of the boxes from the back of the Navigator and carry them inside the house.

There wasn't really that much to bring, since Jacob arranged for rental furniture. Most of my belongings are staying in my apartment, and all I've brought with me is my personal stuff, shoes and clothes, as well as the contents of my fridge and kitchen.

I like cooking, I find it soothing, and it helps me connect with my heritage in a positive way. So, I need my own stuff; my spices, my knives, my pots, pans, and dishes. I really look forward to cooking with them in this state-of-the-art kitchen. It makes the one in my apartment look like a children's play set.

Mitch and Kate were here earlier with a load, but they had to leave. Jacob called with a new report of a missing nine-year-old boy from Frankfort, only a little over an hour from here.

A lot of our efforts and resources are currently going toward chasing down David Wheeler, but that doesn't mean we don't assist where we can when a child goes missing. After all, rescuing and protecting children is the ultimate reason each of us signed up with GEM. An opportunity to perhaps find some justice for what was done to us, and saving other kids from a similar fate.

A knock sounds, followed by a voice yelling, "Hello?"

I guess I left the front door open.

"Coming!" I call out, making my way to the entrance hall.

A burly man in a ball cap and T-shirt sporting the logo of a moving company stands in the doorway.

"We have a delivery for..." He consults the clipboard in his hand. "Baqri?"

"You have the right place. I'm Onyx Baqri."

"Nice to meet you, ma'am. I'm Bruno and my partner is Wayne; he's opening up the truck. It's a full one. I think we'll just start unloading into a central spot. Maybe the living room?"

"Sure, yeah. That works for me."

There's plenty of room. The foyer opens up to a great room at the center of the single-story home, housing living, dining, and kitchen spaces. It makes sense to distribute furniture from there.

I follow Bruno outside to take a peek at the furniture, when a dark green, dusty Dodge Ram comes rolling up the driveway. The driver is wearing a ball cap and shades, but I know it's Hamish.

He mentioned he'd do his best to be here before noon. I'm relieved, because glancing into the back of the truck, we're going to have our hands full. Especially with Mitch and Kate called out on a case.

As the movers start hauling the first pieces off the truck, I walk over to where Hamish is getting out of his vehicle.

"You found it."

"I did. Nice place."

He tosses his cap and glasses on the dashboard of the truck and closes the door, throwing me a lopsided smile. He looks so different in old jeans and a well-worn, long-sleeved shirt, but it suits him. In daylight, his scars are a little more pronounced, but I also see his eyes are a beautiful hazel. I didn't notice them that night at the hotel, they looked brown in the artificial light.

Hazel eyes are rare, and I've only ever encountered one or two others with that color.

A memory stirs, but I force it back. Some things have to stay buried for the sake of my sanity.

I catch myself staring and quickly cover it by gesturing to the house.

"I'd give you a tour, but as you can see my furniture just arrived, so I'm afraid I'm going to have to deal with that first."

"Of course. Put me to work."

Hamish doesn't seem to notice the looks he's getting from Bruno and his sidekick. Or if he does, he chooses to ignore them and simply grabs the next piece of furniture off the truck and hauls it inside. I'm not sure I would be that gracious.

The extra hands definitely help, and unloading the truck goes much faster than I thought it would. The great room is pretty full and, in my head, I've already started allocating certain pieces to the different rooms. A few things are wrapped or in boxes, and look like they may need to be assembled, but I assume the movers will take care of that.

"Could I get you to sign this?" Bruno hands me the clipboard.

It's an itemized list, and I quickly scan the content before I sign the papers and hand them back. To my surprise, he gives a wave and starts walking out of the house. I rush after him.

"Excuse me. You're leaving? What about the stuff that needs to be put together?"

He shrugs, looking apologetic. "We unload the truck, ma'am, that's all. We have another order waiting for us at the warehouse that needs to be loaded and delivered this afternoon."

The men climb into the cab of the truck and drive off down the driveway.

"Well, that sucks," I mumble.

"Hey, I'm still here," Hamish announces behind me. "I even thought to bring some tools."

I turn and watch him walk to the back of his truck, where he takes out a tool bag.

"Let's get this done."

It takes a while before I can see the house starting to take shape. Lunchtime has long since passed, and my stomach is growling.

"Are you hungry?" I ask Hamish, sticking my head around the door of the guest room.

He's working on the third and final bed. The king in the main bedroom is done, and so is the one in the guesthouse.

In the meantime, I was able to get the master suite set up. My clothes are put away in the walk-in closet, the bed is made, and the bathroom is ready for use. This way I at least have a place to crash tonight.

"I could eat," he answers, wiping his brow with his sleeve. "I can go pick us something up if you'd like?"

"I can whip us up Chicken Kahari in the same time it would take you to get to Williamstown. Do you mind if it's a bit spicy?"

"Not in the least."

By the time we sit down to eat at the massive kitchen island, dusk is setting in.

"Mmm. This is really good. What's it called again?"

"Kahari." I drop my spoon in my bowl and twist in my seat to look at him. "Look, I'm sorry, I didn't mean to keep you this late. My friends were supposed to be here helping as well, but they were called away on an emergency."

"It's not a problem."

"I'm sure you have better things to do," I insist.

"Actually, I don't. Although we do still have to go over the auction catalog. Discuss expectations, budget, timeline, and all that boring stuff. We can't go into that auction unprepared."

I'd almost forgotten about that.

While I clear away the dishes, he heads out to his truck to put away his tools and grab the information on the Gilded Bridle. I set about brewing a pot of coffee, I have a feeling I'm going to need it.

"Would you care for a coffee? Or something else to drink?" I ask when Hamish walks in.

"Coffee is good."

He sits back down at the kitchen island, pulling a pile of papers out of a manila envelope. By the time I sit down beside him, he has several documents fanned out in front of us.

The first one he shows me is a list of all horses up for auction, thirty-eight in total. He explains the listings are a mix of yearlings and horses of racing age, which I guess means two and up.

Each line starts with the hip number—which is like a lot number—the name of the horse, then names of the sire and dam, followed by the agent, and finally an amount Hamish explains is the minimum bid.

"Wow. You weren't kidding. Pricey."

The amounts on the list range from sixty-seven thousand to two hundred and fifty thousand dollars.

"For each hip number there is a separate form, listing the horse's pedigree three generations back, as well as their and their offspring's winnings. At the bottom it lists the horse's own race record if applicable."

I grab the top sheet of the pile of papers he indicates

and scan the listed names, numbers, and abbreviations. It might as well be Sanskrit; it means little to me. I drop the form back on the stack.

"So how do we decide which horse to bid on?"

"That's where your motive comes in. What is your timeline? Your objective?"

He looks at me expectantly, which has me squirm in my seat. I'm not sure how to answer him. My motive is justice, my timeline is urgent, and my objective is to find and bring down a predator with a long and vile history of sexual crimes against children. But I can't tell him that.

Or can I?

He's proven to be trustworthy, has come through on his promises and, in addition, has spent all day helping me get my house in order. It almost seems wrong to continue deceiving him.

Jacob did tell me it was up to me.

The decision made; I waste no time.

"Before we get into that, I should probably give you some background."

"Background? Okay."

He swivels on his stool so he's fully facing me, a curious expression on his face.

"Are you familiar with the nature of Jacob's business?"

"GEM? Yes, I'm familiar. Why?"

"Because I work for him."

He sits back a little and runs a hand over his shaved head.

"You don't say?"

"For almost four years now. All of this..." I wave my hand around. "...is part of my cover."

"Your cover," he echoes.

"The money, the farm, the horses, even that ridiculously big SUV out there—none of it is mine. The work I normally do is mostly in the background: planning, communications, counseling," I ramble uncomfortably. "This is the first undercover assignment Jacob has sent me on, and I'm afraid I'm not cut out for the required deceit."

"Don't count yourself out," he interjects with an edge. *Ouch.*

I suppose I had that coming, but he doesn't really seem that upset. At least he hasn't marched off yet, which I'm considering to be a good sign.

"So explain to me how thoroughbred racing is relevant to missing children?"

I'm a bit hesitant to share too much, but Jacob did say he trusted this man with his life.

"We're trying to find a predator who is responsible for the trafficking and sexual exploitation of a large number of children and adolescents over the past twenty-five years or more. We have reason to believe this man has connections to the racing world."

I watch as his nostrils flare and a muscle starts ticking in his jaw.

"Connections, how?"

"We think he's behind a company called Pegasus GLAN. That company is listed as the owner of a horse by the name of Pure Delight."

"Pegasus?"

"Have you heard that name before?"

He grabs the stack of papers and starts shuffling through them. When he finds what he's looking for, he turns one of the sheets toward me. It has a check mark in the top right corner.

The name of the horse on the pedigree form means nothing to me, but what Hamish is pointing at is right below.

CONSIGNED BY CHOICE RACING, AGENT
FOR PEGASUS GLAN

"I want to buy this horse," I blurt out, glancing at the name at the top. "Arion's Moon. I want to buy him."

My blood is buzzing with excitement. This could be the introduction I've been looking for. If this works out it would be a huge break.

"It's actually a filly," Hamish corrects me. "But it just so happens she's one of the two horses I had earmarked."

"Good, because I want her."

"Then I suggest you check your budget because she's had a very promising first year of racing. I have a feeling you won't be the only one bidding on her, so she's not going to go cheap."

I do a quick mental calculation of the money left after the purchase of the property and all related fees, which I guess is just shy of eight hundred grand. I have no idea if that's going to be enough.

"I should probably give Jacob a call," I announce, sliding off my stool and walking to the dinner table where I left my phone.

"Yeah, I should get going anyway. I have a bit of a drive ahead," Hamish announces, getting up and gathering the papers.

A bit abrupt, but I can't forget I dropped quite a load on the guy. He may need some processing time.

"Oh, yes, of course." I tuck my phone in my pocket and follow him to the door. "I really appreciate all your help. You were a lifesaver today."

"Gladly done, and thank you for dinner," he adds with one hand on the door as he turns to me. "I'll be in touch."

I'm trying to read his eyes as they hold mine, but after a long moment he turns on his heel and heads outside. I stroll out on the front step and watch him walk to his truck, wondering if this will be the last I'll see of him.

For some reason that leaves me with a heavy feeling in my chest.

I step back inside when he calls out.

"Hey, Onyx!"

I turn my head to see him standing by the open driver's side door.

"Tell Jacob to expect a call from me tomorrow. I've got a bone to pick with him."

FIVE

JACOB

"Morning."

Bernie throws a look over her shoulder when I walk into the kitchen.

"You look worse than you sound," she observes dryly. "Late night?"

I rub my face with my hands, still feeling the grit in my eyes.

"You can say that again. I don't think I got more than three hours."

I perch a hip on one of the kitchen stools, and rest my forearms on the counter. Bernie slides a mug of coffee in front of me.

"I suppose you want breakfast?"

I manage a grin for Bernie, who is mostly bluster. She loves caring for me, and I'm not complaining. She's the closest I've ever come to having a mother.

"I wouldn't say no to a couple of eggs."

She rolls her eyes dramatically.

"Bacon?"

"Of course."

While Bernie goes to work on my breakfast, I sip my coffee and plan my day.

After the phone call from Onyx last night, I spent a frustrating time looking into Pegasus GLAN and Choice Racing, their agent.

I already knew Pegasus was a dead end. Set up as an LLC and hidden under several layers of dummy companies, I'd finally been able to trace it back to GLAN Industries. A familiar name by now, since that company has been linked to several cases we uncovered of despicable crimes conducted against children.

Unfortunately, GLAN Industries is a dead end itself. The address for the company is a condemned warehouse marked for demolition along the Tennessee River in Paducah. The only tangible entity connected to the company is a law firm in nearby Mayfield, but they're not likely to reveal who their client is.

The agent acting for Pegasus GLAN, however, could be a viable source of information. At some point, someone connected to Pegasus must've contacted them about representation.

I spent the bulk of my time looking up everything I could on Choice Racing, until I couldn't keep my eyes open anymore. I'll do some more poking around today, maybe get Pearl to do a little more in-depth research into their finances. There has to be a money trail somewhere.

A call comes in just as Bernie slides my breakfast in front of me. When I pull out my phone, she narrows her eyes on me.

"I didn't just cook that for you to let it get cold," she warns, as she sashays out of the kitchen to give me privacy.

She knows the drill.

Mitch's name is displayed on my screen and I answer through the voice changer app on my phone. I put it on speaker so I can eat and talk.

"Hope you're calling with good news."

Mitch and Opal are helping in the search for nine-year-old Alex Crocker, who was supposed to ride his bike home from baseball practice early yesterday morning. The ball field is only two blocks from the house, and practice was over at nine. According to the coach, who saw Alex ride off on his bike, he headed in the direction of home. The boy never arrived.

"Not really. We found his bike in a gully, covered with some branches."

"Someone trying to hide it," I conclude. *"He was taken."*

"Looks like it. I just wanted to give you an update, since it looks like this is a little more involved than locating a missing child."

"Was CARD called in?"

CARD is the FBI's Child Abduction Rapid Deployment team Mitch used to belong to. We frequently work side by side or in concert with the team, which is headed by Matt Driver.

"They're en route."

"*Good. Keep me up to date.*"

"Will do. Opal is worried about leaving Onyx without support though."

"*I've got Onyx. You guys focus on finding Alex.*"

I finish my breakfast and take my dishes to the sink when Bernie returns and bumps me out of the way. I move to the coffeepot to refill my cup to take to my office.

"That didn't sound good."

I glance over at Bernie, who is purposely not looking my way as she washes my few dishes.

It doesn't surprise me she overheard, and it doesn't really matter, I trust her implicitly. It's not like she doesn't already know the kind of work GEM does, but she rarely —if ever—talks about it.

"It isn't. Looks like someone made an attempt to hide the boy's bike."

She shakes her head.

"It never ceases to amaze me the kind of evil that's out there."

"That's why we do what we do, Bernie."

"And noble as your crusade is, I worry about you. You are your work. You have no downtime, no social interaction whatsoever, and no personal life."

"You know why that is."

Bernie is the only person in the world who does. She was there when I had to claw myself back from the edge, patiently waiting for me to battle back my demons. Calmly stood by as I got my life together, and encouraged me when the idea for GEM was born.

She also has no problem calling me out when she sees fit.

This, apparently, is one of those times.

"That's not healthy, J," she states with a concerned look on her face. "There is no reason why you can't continue the important work you do, and have a life at the same time. We're only granted one."

"Don't you worry about me, Bernie." I put a hand on her shoulder and bend down to give her a kiss on the cheek. "I'm doing fine."

That's my way of saying *back off.*

It's been difficult enough to live this life of hiding, of secrecy and deceit. I've second-guessed myself many times in recent years, but unless and until every loose end is tied up, this is the way it needs to be.

Grabbing my coffee, I head for the office, when I hear Bernie mutter behind me.

"Bullshit."

"I'LL WORK ON IT WHEN I CAN."

"That's all I can ask."

With Onyx getting the farm in order, Pearl is the only one in the office and already has her hands full providing support for Mitch and Opal. Time is ticking for Alex Crocker, so our focus has to be on him.

But that doesn't mean we can't have someone doing a little probing for me.

"Pearl, do you know if Lee is currently busy with something?"

Her significant other, Lee Remington, is a freelance reporter whose investigations into Transition House and its sordid legacy have run parallel to my own. His motivations differ from mine, but our objectives are the same.

Like I did with Mitch, I offered Lee a place with GEM, but he declined. I get it, he has his own path to follow, but he did convey a willingness to work with us on a consultancy basis.

"I don't think he's actively working on a story. He was dropping his daughter off at her mother's place this morning, but he should be home by now. Why don't you give him a call?"

"I will."

Lee *is* home, and doesn't have anything pressing on his schedule when I ask.

"What do you need?"

"I wonder if I can interest you in doing an article on an exclusive thoroughbred auction? At least pretend to?"

"Is this connected to David Wheeler?"

"Pegasus GLAN is listed as the owner of one of the horses up for auction."

"The same company listed as Pure Delight's owner. Hell yes, I'm in."

I catch him up on the information we have available so far, and forward him a digital copy of the auction catalog.

"It's at Drake Stables? As in Peter Drake?" Lee wants to know.

"That would be the one," I confirm. *"Do you know him?"*

"I interviewed him once, briefly, right after his horse won the Derby."

"That might come in handy."

At least it could provide a point of connection for Lee to get a foot in the door. He knows better than anyone how to get people to talk, and no one has reason to suspect a journalist asking probing questions. It's par for the course.

"What I'd like to know is, has there ever been a repre-sentative of Pegasus GLAN at any of Arion's Moon's races. That's the filly's name. Apparently, she had good results in her first racing year, so there may be photographs or video of the race or from the winner's circle. And also, is any representative supposed to be at the auction? I would imagine the agent, Choice Racing, might know. If you can get a name, or a face, even better."

Lee chuckles.

"You don't ask much, do you?"

"We're close, Remington. I can feel it. We need to finesse this. He gets one sniff of someone looking at him twice, and he'll crawl right back under that rock he came from. We won't find him again."

"You know I won't fuck this up," Lee promises, suddenly dead serious. "That bastard was responsible for my mother's death. I want him as badly as you do."

Remington's mother was part of the housekeeping staff at Transition House. She was killed in a car wreck. Police at the time ruled it as an accident, but Lee had good reason to doubt that ruling. Back then the Lanark PD was about as corrupt as can be, and we've since discovered its chief was complicit in the atrocities that took place at the home.

"*I know you do. I wouldn't have asked you otherwise.*"

I feel good about Lee's involvement. The more information he can dig up, the better it is. I'd feel better if I could send Onyx into that auction prepared for what—or whom—she might encounter.

She answers on the second ring.

"Jacob?"

I close my eyes and breathe in through my nose. It happens every time I hear her voice, that tightness in my chest.

Sweet torture.

"*I brought Lee on. He's going to do a little digging for us.*"

"That's actually not a bad idea. People expect a journalist to stick his nose where it doesn't necessarily belong."

"*Right. Well, I just wanted to give you a heads-up.*"

"I appreciate it. Hey, by the way, have you heard anything about that missing boy?"

Of course she would ask that. I was hoping to avoid that topic, I don't want her distracted.

"*They found his bike under some branches in a ditch.*"

I hear her inhale sharply. "Oh no. Any leads on who might've taken him?"

"*They're working on it.*"

"If you need me to—" she starts, but I cut her off.

"What I need is for you to focus on your case."

I realize that may have come across a bit curt.

"So noted," she asserts before I have a chance to apologize.

Then she promptly hangs up on me.

Again.

SIX

Onyx

"Do you have lodging organized?"

I'm trying to put on makeup, while eating a piece of toast, and of course Jacob picks this moment to call. A quick glance at the clock tells me I have less than ten minutes before Hamish gets here.

It's my own fault, I should've packed last night. I didn't think it would take this long to try and decide what clothes to bring. In my defense, I've never been to an exclusive thoroughbred auction. I have no clue what to expect, black tie or barn casual. There's also supposed to be a dinner after the auction I needed to plan for.

In the end, I went with both the black and the olive jeans Janey made me buy, as well as a couple of tops. I tucked a pair of high heels in my bag so I can dress it up if I need to. For anything else my brand-new, embroidered, square-toed, low-heeled, western boots will have to do.

"Hamish booked us rooms at the Hyatt," I tell Jacob.

"Good. What time is he picking you up?"

"Any minute. Look, I should get going, I need to get ready. I'll check in with you tonight, okay?"

"Right. We'll talk later."

I'm not sure what's gotten into Jacob this week, he's been like a mother hen, micro-managing everything. Normally he delegates to me and assumes it gets done, but now it's almost like he doesn't trust me.

Now is not the time, but I plan to take it up with him at some point.

Shoving the last piece of toast in my mouth, I stuff my toiletry bag in my overnight tote, and make my way to the kitchen. I barely have time to quickly wash my plate and coffee cup, when I hear a vehicle coming up the driveway.

The only person I've seen since Hamish left last Saturday was Janey, who wanted to see the farm. I've spoken with Hamish a few times, planning for this weekend. When his knock sounds at the door, I suddenly feel nervous. I'll blame it on the upcoming events, and not on the anticipation of seeing him again.

I won't lie, the man fascinates me. The psychologist in me wants to dig around behind his carefully guarded exterior. The taut skin on his face makes it hard to read expressions, and his voice doesn't really betray emotions.

I have to laugh at myself, the last thing I need is another enigmatic man in my life. One is more than enough.

Shaking off the jitters, I open the door for him.

"Morning."

I return, "Morning," as I step aside to let him in. "Have you had breakfast?"

"I have, thanks. Is this your bag?"

He points at my tote.

"Yes."

"Is that it?" he asks, picking it up.

"Yup."

"You travel light."

"It's just for two nights." I shrug and walk into the kitchen, aiming for the coffeepot. "Coffee?"

"Can we make it coffee to go? I wouldn't mind getting on the road. I want to make sure we don't miss the auction preview this afternoon."

"Absolutely."

They've only allotted a one-hour window for the pre-auction viewing, which isn't a lot of time, and I definitely want to be there for it.

I grab two travel mugs from the cupboard and fill them. Then I follow Hamish outside, locking the door behind me.

"Sure you're all right taking my truck? I had it cleaned."

He opens the passenger side door for me, and I dart him a look.

"I'm not *actually* a spoiled heir, I just impersonate one. My real vehicle is an ancient, rusting Subaru, I'm sure I'll survive in your giant luxury truck."

He shakes his head and drops it down, not quite hiding a little smile, as I climb into the passenger seat.

From here to Bowling Green is a little more than

three hours, maybe this is an opportunity to learn a bit more about Hamish. I wait until we turn onto the highway.

"So...how did you become a horse trainer? What drove you?"

I glance over and find him looking at me from the corner of his eye. Then he slides them forward again.

"Are we playing twenty questions?"

"Not really. I'm just making conversation."

The last thing I want is for him to start asking me difficult questions. I'm not ready to answer any. I may never be.

"Okay, uhh...I guess I always liked horses. I more or less rolled into it."

Not exactly a very illuminating response, but it's a start.

"Do you ride?"

"Sure I do. You?"

"I wouldn't say I ride, per se. I have sat on a horse before, yes."

I don't tell him I sat on one for about two-and-a-half seconds before I landed on my ass on the ground.

I feel his eyes on me.

"Why do I get the sense there's a story there?"

"It really wasn't that memorable. But I do like horses. They seem intuitive and gentle animals."

"Most are, but like with people, every now and then you encounter an asshole."

My train of questioning has gone off the track a bit,

but before I have a chance to reroute, Hamish takes the lead.

"What about you? How did you end up with GEM?"

I try for a lighthearted response, "Jacob has a good sales pitch."

Hamish chuckles. "Touché. I guess neither one of us likes to answer questions."

I grin. "Maybe we should stick to simpler topics. You know, favorite movie, food, music, stuff like that."

"*Dances with Wolves*, pad thai, and eighties rock," he answers without hesitation. "Your turn."

I don't have to think too hard either.

"*Good Will Hunting*, sushi, and a little bit of everything."

"I forgot about that movie," he shares, nodding his head. "Robin Williams was the teacher, right? Great actor and one of the greatest comedians."

"Agreed. Although...it may be a toss-up with George Carlin."

During the remainder of the drive, we find we have more than a few things in common. We talk about the upcoming auction, about stuff we enjoy, listen to music, and time flies by.

What we avoid discussing are our respective pasts, which is surprisingly liberating in a way. Like traveling without luggage.

Still, I feel like I have gotten to know Hamish a little better.

"We're here," he announces.

He turns right onto a long, tree-lined drive with fields

on either side, bordered in white fencing. The private road curves up and when we crest the hill, a sprawling horse farm comes into view.

"Wow. That's stunning," I comment, taking in what can only be described as a mansion, and the half dozen whitewashed buildings arranged around it. More white-fenced fields—some holding horses—cover most of the valley.

"Big operation," Hamish contributes.

My eyes are trying to take everything in while he navigates us to one of the larger buildings. Several vehicles are parked outside and a simple black-and-white sign on the large barn doors reads 'Viewing.'

Suddenly butterflies take up residence in my stomach and my hands get clammy.

"Ready?"

I glance over at him.

"I suppose."

"We'll go in, keep a low profile, and say as little as possible. We can talk when we're back in the truck."

He's out of the truck before I have my seat belt undone, and comes around to open the door for me.

Hamish hands the invitation to a guard, just inside the barn, who waves us through. The center of the large building features an indoor exercise ring, with horse stalls lining the walls on either side of it.

A silver-haired man approaches us, an air of propriety about him as he smiles and holds out his hand to me.

"Ms. Baqri, I'm so pleased to meet you. Peter Drake."

I guessed as much already. Taking his offered hand, I return a smile.

Showtime.

"Pleasure is mine. Can I introduce Hamish Adrian? Hamish has been kind enough to lend me his expertise."

"Ah yes, Mr. Adrian, I believe I saw you at the TCA fundraiser a few weeks ago. Canadian, right? I believe you worked with Bob Diego's horse, Little Secrets?"

It's a not-so subtle way to let us know he's done a bit of research.

"Many years ago, yes."

The older man narrows his eyes on Hamish.

"You were gone from the racing world for several years after your unfortunate accident. I was under the impression you were retired."

"Not quite."

Drake appears to wait for a more elaborate answer, but none is forthcoming as Hamish calmly stares him down.

"Well." Drake turns his eyes on me and aims a tight smile. "I shouldn't hold you up any longer, I'm sure you're eager to have a look around. Starting from the right, the horses are stabled in order of hip number. The auction will take place in the exercise ring and starts at one tomorrow afternoon. I hope you find what you're looking for, Ms. Baqri."

"Onyx, please, and thank you for your hospitality."

Hamish simply nods at the man, places his hand in the small of my back, and steers me toward the first stall.

"What was that?" I whisper when we're out of earshot. "Pissing contest?"

"Posturing," he grumbles. "Ignore it."

We slowly walk around, occasionally encountering another buyer, but other than the exchange of acknowledging nods, there are no other interruptions. Hamish points out a few horses—in particular a yearling he thinks may have potential and would be worth putting a bid on—and then finally we get to Arion's Moon's stall. She'll be up halfway through the auction.

"Why not save her 'til last?" I want to know.

"Probably because people are likely to hold on to their money until her number comes up, and low-bid on everything else. The way they set it up is all yearlings go up first, and race-age horses after," he explains.

I lean over the stall door, taking in the sleek, gray-dappled filly. I'd noticed someone standing off to the side, keeping an eye on the horse, and I'd love to chat with him. Arion's Moon has her eyes on me and slowly lumbers in my direction, testing the air with flaring nostrils.

"Hey, pretty girl," I mutter, reaching out a hand.

When she sniffs my fingers cautiously, I turn my head to the young guy standing guard.

"Is it okay if I touch?"

He shrugs. "Knock yourself out."

I lightly scratch under her jaw and she takes another step closer, butting her nose under my arm.

"You've got the touch."

I turn my head at the unfamiliar voice, to find a

second man—this one wearing a sports jacket and an ascot tie—standing beside the groom.

"She's normally a high-strung filly," he adds, indicating the horse.

"She seems sweet. Are you her owner?"

I notice Hamish is keeping his distance while I chat these guys up.

"Ha, no. I represent the owner," ascot guy clarifies as he steps closer. "I'm an agent with Choice Racing."

"Oh, I see. That's interesting. Do you represent other owners or just this one?"

Ignoring the horse for a moment, I focus my attention on the agent, leaning my arm on the stable door.

"Only Pegasus for this auction," he volunteers.

"Doesn't Pegasus own that horse..." I snap my fingers. "What's the name...Pure Delight, that's it."

He nods. "Yes, he does."

He does. Singular.

"Do you usually represent the same owners?"

"Often." He reaches out a hand. "Oliver Doyle."

"Onyx Baqri. It's lovely to meet you," I gush, shaking the man's hand. "You'll have to excuse me for the questions. I'm rather new to the racing world and am finding I have so much to learn. It's very helpful talking to someone much more seasoned like yourself."

I can almost see his narrow chest puffing up with self-importance.

"Well, I have over twenty years experience in the business. I don't mind sharing what knowledge I have." He pulls a business card from his pocket and hands it to me. "Perhaps we could share a meal at some point. Unfortunately, I'm busy until after the auction. My owner is arriving tonight."

It's hard not to show a reaction when I really want to pump my fist.

"Oh? He's coming for the auction?" I ask as innocently as I'm able to.

"Yes, he should be there, despite the fact he doesn't like to socialize. He tends to keep a low profile."

Oliver pointedly glances at his watch.

"I'm sorry, I should let you go. I've taken up enough of your time," I'm quick to apologize.

"Not at all, although I do need to get going. Will you be bidding tomorrow?" he asks.

"Yes, I plan to."

"In that case, I wish you the best of luck."

With that he marches off, and I join Hamish who, I'm sure, has been listening in from farther down the aisle. I flash him the business card.

"Smooth," he mumbles under his breath.

"I saw an opportunity..."

For appearances' sake we stopped at the remaining stalls, checking the other horses on the auction block. We encounter two men coming in just as we're heading out.

One of them is Lee Remington.

I shouldn't be surprised, Jacob warned me he'd called in Lee's assistance, but it still startles me to see him here. To Lee's credit, he shows no recognition at all, his eyes barely skimming me when he walks right by me. Hamish's grip on my elbow tightens as he steers me out the door.

"Are you okay?" he inquires when we get to his truck.

"Yeah, I'm fine."

I'm not sure Jacob wants him to know about Lee's involvement, but I'm keeping it to myself for now. Luckily, he doesn't push.

"What's next, hotel? Or do you want to grab a bite first?" he suggests when he gets behind the wheel.

Having skipped lunch, I'm ready for an early dinner, but I should probably give Jacob an update while it's all fresh in my mind.

"I wouldn't mind a bite, but first I want to touch base with Jacob."

I already have my phone out and dial his number. It rings five times when a generic voice tells me to leave a message. I don't bother. He'll see I've called and get back to me.

We end up at The Bistro, a restaurant a few blocks from the Hyatt where we're staying. Hamish orders lamb chops and I try a bowl of voodoo rice, which is delicious and spicy.

Conversation is surprisingly casual and easy, and by the end of the meal my cheeks hurt from smiling so much. I can't remember the last time I've been this at ease with a man.

When he walks me to the door of my hotel room, I'm not in the least concerned. Not until I catch the look in his eyes when I turn to tell him goodnight.

Then I realize I might be in trouble.

SEVEN

*J*ACOB

I fucked up royally.

But before I can chastise myself further, my phone rings.

"Onyx, you've got something for me?"

I listen to her take in a deep breath and blow it out.

"I met the agent today. Oliver Doyle of Choice Racing. He approached us at the auction preview. I'm sending you a copy of his business card now."

"Anything interesting?"

"I think so. Apparently, there's a single representative of Pegasus GLAN and he intends to be present to watch the auction tomorrow."

"He'll be there?"

"That's what the agent said. I just wish we could have some more eyes on this place. The auction is supposed to take place in the indoor exercise ring. We weren't able to go in there today, we were confined to the stables in the outer hallways. Walking around I noticed multiple entrance and exit points into the building. Large barn doors at the front as well as the rear, and a side door about halfway down either side. It's going to be impossible for me to keep an eye on all of them."

"I'll get in touch with Lee. See where he is going to be tomorrow."

"I actually saw Lee today. Almost ran into him as we were leaving. He was with a heavy-set guy—I'm guessing late forties, early fifties—he was wearing a straw cowboy hat that had seen better days."

"Sounds like Hank Wilson, Drake's right-hand man," I suggest.

Pearl had been able to send me some general background information on all the known players, and included—if available—were pictures. I'd gone over the images with a fine-tooth comb, looking for anything I could identify, but nothing stood out to me.

"I'm not even going to bother asking how you know that," she comments, sounding a bit annoyed. "You'll probably leave me guessing anyway."

Definitely annoyed.

"Okay, I'll bite; what did I miss? Something is clearly bugging you."

"No. It's nothing, it's fine."

"But?" I prompt.

"No buts. I'm just tired, that's all."

I don't believe it for a minute, but I'm not about to challenge her, she obviously doesn't want to elaborate.

Nevertheless, I can't resist asking, *"Everything okay with Hamish?"*

There's a distinct pause before she responds.

"Why wouldn't it be?"

Bingo.

"No reason," I tell her quickly. *"Why don't you get some rest? I'll get Lee set up to take pictures of anyone showing up for the auction tomorrow."*

"All right," she concedes.

Then she ends the call and I instantly feel the loss of her voice.

I lean back in the chair and rub my hands over my face. I'm losing my focus and I can't afford to, not at this point in the game. I've come too far, sacrificed too many years, and invested too much work into bringing every last one of these sick bastards down to blow it now.

Personal feelings will have to wait. It's the whole reason I set up GEM the way I did. Using code names and staying anonymous ensured a continued level of separation, making for a more effective and professional work environment. Feelings only blur the objective, but it's been damn lonely all these years.

I dial Lee, who answers right away.

"You're calling for an update," he guesses.

"That would be correct. I hear you managed to get into the preview today, Onyx saw you. What did you get?"

"Drake's manager likes his bourbon. Turns out he also gets chatty when he drinks, which he did plenty of over dinner."

"I'm sure you made good use of that."

"You better believe it. I'm sending you a list with names of most of the invited buyers."

A notification pops up on my laptop and I click on it.

"The few bits of industry gossip he shared, I added to the corresponding name on the list."

"I've got it. Anything on Pegasus?"

"He was able to give me the name of the trainer who works exclusively for Pegasus, Brian Haley. And apparently, he refers to his boss as Mr. A. That's all I have."

"It's more than we had. Onyx was able to connect with the agent and found out from him Pegasus GLAN is just one man."

"Mr. A?"

"Possible. In any event, it looks like whoever it is plans to be there during the auction tomorrow. I'd like pictures of anyone coming in or out of the farm. We know Wheeler is hiding behind a fake name so that doesn't help us identify him, and he likely has an altered appearance, but there are some physical markers you can't change. Is there a discreet place you can set up with a camera?"

"I've been told no recording devices or cameras, but I'll see what I can do. I'll be inside with Hank, observing in the background."

"Any visuals you can get would be helpful."

"I'll do my best. Any more news on the boy?" Lee adds.

My insides twist at the mention of Alex. It's been a week since he went missing and, despite GEM and the CARD team's involvement, there's been no sign of him since his bike was recovered.

"No. Nothing."

"Shit. That's not good."

He's right, it's not.

"It isn't, but we have good people who will keep looking for him. Getting back to what we were talking about, let me know if you have something for me to look at."

"Will do."

I hang up feeling guilty. Maybe I should have had everyone work on finding the boy, but it's my job to keep the big picture in mind. If we can take down Wheeler, we could prevent God knows how many children from harm.

I always thought once we brought justice to every last remaining predator from Transition House, I would be done. I'm starting to realize I'll never be done. Our work over the past years extended far beyond my original objective, and I can't just walk away from that.

What's more, I don't think any of the others can either.

Onyx

This is ridiculous.

I'm agonizing about what I'm going to wear for the auction tomorrow, when I really should be sleeping.

Disgusted with myself, I grab a random outfit from

the bed and drape it over the chair. I stuff the rest of the clothes I had spread out on the bed back into my bag.

Then I take my time getting ready for bed, but as soon as I lie down my mind goes to what had me out of sorts in the first place. Or maybe I should say who...

Hamish.

Those eyes, I swear I could read the need in them. Then when he reached out and brushed the backs of his fingers over my cheek, I leaned forward, placing a hand on his chest.

It was as if my touch burned him. He jumped back so quickly, I almost stumbled forward. Without a word he turned and headed down the hall to his own room. I was mortified.

I'm no less embarrassed now. And confused. I'm supposed to be the intuitive one, the empath, and I don't understand how I so completely misread him. Or did I? I mean, I know I may be out of practice, but he did caress my face, which is not exactly a platonic gesture. How should I have interpreted that any different?

This is going to make things even more strained and stressful tomorrow, especially if I'm going to lie here mulling about it all night.

Annoyed with myself—and with him—I flip the covers back and swing my legs out of bed. I pull on my jeans, shrug into my jacket to cover my sleep shirt, and grab my card key from the nightstand. I'm already halfway down the hall when I realize my feet are bare, but I'm not turning around now.

I knock on his door, listening for movement inside,

but I can't hear anything. It's ten thirty, would he be in bed already? Or maybe he went out.

Turning around, I'm about to head back to my room when the door behind me abruptly opens.

"Onyx?"

The first thing I notice is he's wearing a short-sleeved T-shirt, leaving his arms exposed. It's not just his hand and face, but his entire right side that appears to have been damaged in that barn fire.

It throws me off enough it takes me a minute to realize he's waiting for me to explain why I'm here.

"I need to know, what was that, earlier?"

"Not sure what you mean."

He glances over my shoulder and pulls me inside his room, just as a couple passes us in the hallway.

"I'm sorry, that's bullshit, Hamish. You didn't accidentally stroke my cheek."

His mouth opens, but then snaps shut again. He drops his head down, shaking it.

"I spent all night beating myself up for misinterpreting what happened, but there was no mistaking that touch. What is going on?"

"Nothing. Call it momentary insanity. It was inappropriate and I was out of line."

"I don't even know what that means. What are you trying to say?" I probe him.

I'm standing right inside the door, watching him as he walks over to the bed and sinks down on the edge.

"I had no business touching you. I'm here as a favor to

a friend and to help you catch a sick, pedophile bastard. This is not the right time."

He lifts his head when I take a few steps closer, stopping right in front of him.

"Why did you touch me?" I insist.

"You're pushy, do you know that?"

"I'm aware," I admit easily. "I get that way when communication is not clear. Blame the therapist in me."

He sighs deeply, tilting his head slightly as he looks up at me.

"I like you. I'm attracted to you. That's why I touched you. Hell, I was about to kiss you. Is that what you wanted to hear?"

A smile pulls at the corner of my mouth.

"Yes, because that means I did not read you wrong."

I lean down, place my palm against his scarred cheek, and lightly brush his lips with mine.

"And you're right, this may not be the right time but that doesn't mean there won't be."

Then I walk out of the room, smiling at a woman I pass in the hallway. In my room I shrug out of my jacket, strip off my jeans, and dive straight under the covers.

I'm gone before my head hits the pillow.

EIGHT

ONYX

"Ma'am?"

I almost missed the young kid with the Drake Stables shirt and ball cap. I was too busy looking around and getting my bearings.

"Your name?" he asks.

"Onyx Baqri."

He hands me an auction paddle with the number eight.

"You'll find the corresponding number on the back of your assigned seats."

"Thank you."

When we arrived, we were directed up a set of stairs to a semi-circular gallery overlooking the exercise ring below. Stools are arranged side by side along the railing with a second row behind it. The wide, shelf-style banister doubles as a bar-height table, a tray with a jug of water and glasses placed on top every two or so feet. A program, notebook, and pen are left on each stool.

When I look down the gallery, I note only three spots taken.

"Looks well organized," Hamish comments softly behind me.

"I know."

I'm glad we got here early. It gives me a chance to observe most of the other buyers as they come in.

Jacob's call woke me up this morning. It was a short call, he was just checking in, but it left me feeling a bit guilty. Jacob has always just been a voice on the phone, but I can't help feel he and I have had some kind of connection. Something...more than simply a relationship between boss and employee.

That's probably why the memory of last night's visit to Hamish's room felt a little like betrayal this morning.

I was just pulling on my boots when Hamish knocked on my door at nine. I'd already had my shower, was dressed, and was ready for a proper cup of coffee and some breakfast.

Seeing him wasn't as awkward as it could've been had I not gone over to clear the air last night. We ended up eating at the breakfast bar in the hotel dining room, and conversation was easy and geared toward the auction.

I sit down in the front row while Hamish takes the stool behind mine, assuring me he can easily see over my shoulder. I would've felt better with him beside me, but seating was set up this way for a reason.

I'm nervous, I won't lie.

When we arrived, I had to fill out a form which asked for my address, phone number, and banking information. That made me a little uneasy and my hands were shaking. I'm handling more money than I ever have before and it's not even mine. I had to bring a cashier's check for fifty-thousand dollars made out to Gilded Bridle Auctions, as a security deposit. If I win a bid, I have fourteen days to transfer the funds into the seller's account, after which my deposit will be returned, and we'll be able to take possession of the horse. If I don't honor my bid, I lose the fifty thousand.

So yes, I'm a bit jittery, although Hamish doesn't seem worried at all.

Only ten more minutes before the auction is supposed to start and barely half of the sixteen buyers have arrived. So far, I'm the only woman here, which is probably why I can feel eyes on me at all times.

To my left I see a gentleman I met at the fundraiser come in. He is handed a paddle as well.

"What's his name again?" I ask Hamish on a whisper.

"Gordon Chen," he returns under his breath.

Then he gets up from his stool when the man approaches.

"Ms. Baqri, Mr. Adrian, pleasure to see you."

"And you as well, Mr. Chen," I respond with a smile.

"It promises to be an exciting afternoon," he comments, scanning the ring before returning his eyes to me. "I wish you the best of luck."

He's already moving past us before I have a chance to mutter, "The same to you."

By the time the first yearling is led into the ring, sixteen prospective buyers—some with a guest—have filled the gallery on either side of us.

It's definitely an older crowd. I'm guessing the average age is probably in the fifties with a few exceptions, myself being one of them. Hamish and I both get our share of stares, but I don't let them bother me. Let them look.

Unfortunately, no one I've seen so far has raised any flags. What I remember from Wheeler is that he wasn't particularly tall—maybe five ten—he was fair-haired, had light eyes, and he was husky. Of course, other than his height, any of those identifiers can be changed. Still, I'd like to think, regardless of any changes to his appearance, I'd be able to recognize him.

Maybe it'll be his eyes, his voice, the way he walks, or some distinct mannerism that gives him away. It may trigger memories I've successfully suppressed for many years, but I'm willing to go there if it means finally taking David Wheeler down.

I focus on the pretty yearling being led around the ring below. It isn't one I'll be bidding on. Hamish suggested I sit the first few out to get a feel for the process. I'm supposed to bid on the yearling with hip number nine, just to let everyone know I'm a serious contender. Of course, the horse I'm really interested in is the dapple-gray filly, Arion's Moon, but she's not up until later in the program.

It isn't until the fifth horse is auctioned off, I begin to follow what the auctioneer is saying. I try to catch the bids, but those are challenging to pick up on as well.

Sometimes it's just a flick of the wrist or a jerk of the chin to alert the auctioneer.

When hip number nine is up, I sit on the edge of my seat, my paddle at the ready.

"Relax," Hamish rumbles. "You look like you're about to jump over the railing."

I feel his hand lightly on my shoulder.

"See if someone else bids first," he reminds me.

The opening bid is set at sixty-eight thousand, which is more than I used to make in a year. We agreed beforehand I wouldn't go over eighty so I'm a bit shocked when the bids reach seventy-five in no time flat. When the auctioneer calls for seventy-six, and it looks like there are no other bids, I raise my paddle.

"Seventy-six to the lady." He points his hammer at me. "Can I have seventy-six five?" He nods at someone to my left. "Seventy-six five bid. Can I have seventy-seven?"

I wait for a moment to see if anyone else is bidding before I lift my paddle again. This time I glance to my left to see who started bidding against me and recognize Gordon Chen. He catches my eye and winks as he signals the auctioneer again.

Asshole.

"He's bidding you up," Hamish whispers.

I figured as much, but two can play that game.

This time when the auctioneer calls for a seventy-eight-thousand-dollar bid, I flash my paddle right away, making it seem like I'm eager. Predictably Chen tops my bid by five-hundred dollars.

We do it twice more, bringing the bid to eighty thousand on the nose. However, this time when Chen tops my bid, I glance over, calmly lay my paddle face down in front of me, and wink back at him.

A few chuckles go up in the gallery as Chen pretends to tip his hat.

"Well done," Hamish compliments.

I don't bother hiding my smirk as I turn my attention back to the ring below, but some of my newfound confidence disappears again as the next several horses are auctioned off.

When hip number sixteen is called, I keep my eyes on the area behind the auctioneer where I've noticed people come and go every time a new horse is led in. I figured they were probably the owners or agents.

As the young guy I saw at the filly's stall yesterday brings her in, I catch sight of Oliver Doyle but no one else appears to be with him. Looks like the owner is a no-show after all.

Disappointment washes over me, but I don't get much of a chance to wallow in it, since the auction of Arion's Moon is underway.

Hamish had suggested I put in a few bids early, figure out how many were interested, and then pull back to give the impression I was out. Then when bidding slowed down, I'd go back in with an amount ten thousand over what was last called. If it works, the hope is others aren't comfortable with that big a jump and will bow out. If it doesn't, I have carte blanche from Jacob to make sure I walk away with the winning bid.

Either way, I will have drawn attention from whoever is behind Pegasus GLAN, which is the objective.

As predicted, the bidding is stiff on the filly, the numbers going up by five-thousand-dollar increments. Already we're heading toward four-hundred thousand when I hear Hamish behind me.

"Four others left bidding. Time to back away."

When the auctioneer glances my way, I give my head a little shake, passing on the bid, which is quickly picked up by another. Once four hundred and fifty thousand is reached, only two are left bidding, and the pace has slowed down dramatically.

"Wait for him to start calling," Hamish mumbles.

When I see one of the buyers indicate he's done, I close my fingers tightly around the paddle. The moment I hear, "Four-hundred and seventy-five thousand, going once, going—"

"Five-hundred thousand," I call out, jamming my paddle in the air.

My blood is rushing in my ears as the adrenaline pumps and I can barely hear what the auctioneer is calling.

It's not until I feel Hamish squeeze the back of my neck and hear him say, "Congrats," I realize our strategy worked.

Down below I catch sight of Oliver ducking out of the ring, a white-haired man right behind him.

Dammit, I didn't get a good look at him.

Before I realize what I'm doing, I'm on my feet and moving.

"Where are you going?"

"Bathroom. I'll be right back."

I shoot him a quick smile and head for the stairwell. The young guy is still guarding the top of the stairs.

"Where can I find the bathroom?"

"Down the stairs and to your right. It's by the side entrance."

There is no one in the hallway when I come downstairs. Instead of going right however, I turn left, toward Arion's Moon's stall.

I'm about three doors away when I hear voices coming from her stall that stop me in my tracks. One voice I recognize as Oliver's, but it's the other that has the hair at the back of my neck standing up. I press my back against the wall, my hand clutched to my chest. I try to catch my breath as my heart races and my head spins.

"...any information you can find. I expect you to report in back at Grandview tomorrow."

"You're leaving now?"

"I am, and I'm taking Jason with me."

I glance to my right when I hear a stall door open and catch the young stable hand stepping out, the white-haired man right behind him. I hold my breath until I see them turn away from me. As they start walking toward the rear doors, the older man places his hand on the back of the young guy's neck.

A shiver runs down my spine and I quickly turn the other way, back to the stairs.

"Is everything okay?" Hamish asks when I slide back in my seat.

That's not a question with an easy answer.

"We'll talk later."

I LEAN MY HEAD BACK AND CLOSE MY EYES THE moment I get into the truck.

"Onyx?"

"Just give me a minute."

I hear the engine start and wait until we begin moving away from the farm before I open my eyes.

"I need to call Jacob," I announce, pulling out my phone.

"Hold on one sec, don't leave me in the dark here. You looked like you saw a ghost back there."

"Something like that." I inhale deeply and blow out a breath. "I think we found Wheeler. I caught him talking to the agent downstairs."

"You saw him?"

"More like heard him."

"Are you sure?"

"Positive. That's not a voice I'll ever forget."

I can feel his eyes on me and turn to look at him.

"You know him," he concludes accurately.

"I was living in a youth home. David Wheeler was a benefactor."

I give him some time to let it sink in, I'd rather not spell it out. Luckily, it doesn't take him long.

"That's how you know he's a predator. You were a victim," he bites off.

I nod, looking away from his angry eyes.

"One of them. I wasn't the only one, there were more of us at the home, and who knows how many since then. He was reported to have perished in the fire when the home burned down many years ago, but we recently became suspicious he may have somehow survived."

The truck suddenly swerves onto the shoulder.

"What the hell are you doing?"

"Turning around," he snarls, the knuckles of his hands white as he clenches the steering wheel. "What do you think I'm doing? If that bastard is there now, I—"

I reach out and stop him with a hand on his arm.

"He's already gone. He left minutes before I came back up to the gallery."

Hamish drops his forehead between his hands on the wheel.

"Did he see you?"

"Wheeler? No. At least not when I went downstairs. He may have caught sight of me during the bidding, but even if he did, there's no way he knows who I am."

It's highly doubtful he'd recognize me after twenty-four years. I was a skinny teenager, I didn't have a white streak in my hair, and it was never really me he was interested in anyway.

I give his arm a gentle squeeze.

"Do you think we can go to the hotel now? I want to have a shower, put a call in to Jacob, and order in room service."

He lifts his head and glances my way.

"Are you okay?"

I could lie but there doesn't seem to be a point.

"No," I tell him honestly. "It stirred up a lot of old crap, but I'm sure I'll be fine."

He lifts his right hand off the wheel and reaches out to gently touch my face, mumbling, "Soft, and yet so strong."

Then he abruptly pulls his hand back and steers the truck back on the road.

"While you call your boss and have your shower, I'll pick up some dinner."

That's kind of him but I really just want to veg in my pj's and maybe find something distracting on TV. My emotions are too close to the surface right now. Anyone says one nice thing to me and it'll all be bubbling over.

"I appreciate the thought, Hamish, but I'm not sure I'll be good company."

The corner of his mouth quirks up.

"That's fine. I'll just be dropping off your sushi."

Tears well up anyway when I realize he remembered my favorite food.

NINE

JACOB

"*Grandview?*"

I glance out the window, watching a taxi pull into the parking lot below.

"Yeah, I'm sure that's the name he used. I should've remembered it last night, but I was pretty shaken up."

"*Understandable. Do you know what he was referring to?*"

"I'm pretty sure it was a place. He told Oliver Doyle to report back there today."

"*I'll look into it,*" I promise her. "*You guys are heading back this morning?*"

I watch the same taxi drive out of the parking lot. He probably dropped off a fare.

"That's the plan, although I haven't heard from Hamish yet. I may go knock on his door in a minute."

"*Can you hang on one sec? I have a call coming in.*"

I switch to the incoming call, hit speaker, and put my phone down.

"*Lee, what do you have for me?*" I ask as I grab my jeans off the chair and pull them on.

"Pictures. Sending them through now. Pay special attention to the last set. White hair, older guy. Arrived with a driver in a black Cadillac Escalade and was dropped off around the back. Left again half an hour later with a younger guy in tow. I snapped what I could. There are one or two of the vehicle, where you can see part of the license plate that might be helpful."

"*Appreciate it. I'll be in touch. I've got someone on the other line.*"

I switch back to Onyx as I tuck my shirt in my jeans.

"*That was Lee. He got some pictures yesterday he's sending to me. I'll forward them to you. Call me when you've had a chance to look at them.*"

I end the call and shove my feet in my boots. Then I sit down in front of my laptop and open up my email. Lee's message is at the top with a link to a Dropbox folder, which I quickly forward to Onyx.

Next, I click on the link and scroll down to the last set of twelve images. The first one doesn't show much, just a grainy image of someone sitting in the back of the SUV. The next few are shots of the white-haired man getting out of the back seat, but it doesn't really show his face. It looks like Lee changed his vantage point because in the next picture the man is coming out of the rear barn doors with a younger guy, who looks like he's barely twenty years old. The young kid's face is partially obscured by the bill of his ball cap, but you can see the older man's face clearly.

I've never seen it before.

The next few images must've been shot in quick succession since they show the two men walking to the vehicle and opening the back door. There is something about the way the old guy has his hand around the back of the kid's neck that has every hair of my body stand up.

I can almost feel the pressure of fingers digging in.

The sharp knock at the door almost has me jump out of my skin. I quickly snap my laptop shut and shove it in my bag.

"Door's open!"

Onyx

The face doesn't stir any memories.

Now that I'm over the initial shock of hearing his voice, I'd hoped seeing his picture would be a visual confirmation, but I can't tell if it's him.

"What's wrong?"

I glance over at Hamish, whose eyes remain on the road.

"You keep staring at those pictures on your phone."

"I'm just thrown by the fact I could've sworn it was his voice I heard, but this isn't the face I remember."

It's making me question what I think I heard.

"And now you're starting to doubt yourself," he assesses correctly. "Appearances aren't that hard to alter, but you can't change a voice."

I know he's right, but I'd feel a whole lot better if there was something or someone else who could confirm the old man is David Wheeler. I'd hate to be wrong.

"One of my colleagues—Pearl—she has a face-recognition software that takes certain measurements on a face, like the distance between the eyes for instance. Those are also supposed to be unchangeable."

She'd also need a decent old picture of Wheeler to compare to, but I'm sure we have a bunch of those on file somewhere.

"Call her," he prompts.

"Let me try Jacob first, he may have already asked her."

I dial his number but I'm getting kicked straight to voicemail. Instead of leaving a message, I try Janey next. She answers on the third ring.

"I'm in the middle of something."

Janey has a tendency to be abrupt but that's simply the way she operates. She's almost painfully straightforward, which easily puts people off, but I know she doesn't mean anything by it. I've long wondered if Janey is on the spectrum. She certainly has some of the earmarks.

"Okay, I'll explain in an email, but check as soon as you have a moment."

"Sure."

Immediately the line goes dead.

I quickly forward the image Lee took showing Wheeler's face with an explanatory note. It's quite possible Jacob already asked her to run the image through the program, but I'd rather ask her twice than not at all.

"How do you feel about grabbing some breakfast?" Hamish asks. "Unless you have to get back to Four Oaks in a hurry?"

"It's Sunday, there's not a whole lot I can do until tomorrow anyway. I could eat," I admit.

Jacob mentioned last night he wants me to hold off on finalizing the purchase of Arion's Moon until we have a chance to gather some more information. I will need to visit with a lawyer Jacob says he'll arrange for me, because apparently buying a horse isn't that much different from buying a house. The process is very similar with money as well as title transfer being handled by an attorney, after which arrangements can be made for the actual transfer of the horse.

Which reminds me, I still have to hire a stable hand or something because I can't expect Hamish to be there all the time, and I don't have a slightest clue how to look after a horse.

"Denny's okay?"

He points at the familiar sign, visible near the next exit.

"Fine by me."

My stomach starts growling when the smell of bacon hits me as soon as we walk in. Not a surprise, it's already after ten and all I've had is the watery coffee the little machine in my room made.

The place isn't busy at all as a waitress shows us to a booth by the window. Despite his ball cap, Hamish has to endure several looks. It's becoming so annoying; I start doling out angry glares to the gawkers. I can only imagine what it must be like for him.

"Morning, my name is Donna. Can I get you a coffee?" the woman asks as she slides menus in front of us.

"Please," we both respond.

She's back a few moments later with a carafe and a bowl with milk and creamers. She flips over the mugs on the table and fills them to the brim.

"Do you need more time?"

"I know what I want," Hamish answers and then turns to me. "Onyx?"

"Eggs Benny for me, please," I order.

I don't even feel guilty, it'll be breakfast and lunch combined.

"I'll have a Philly cheesesteak omelet, and could I have two buttermilk biscuits instead of toast? No gravy."

When Donna leaves with our order, Hamish leans his elbows on the table.

"Did you manage to get any sleep?" he asks, his hazel eyes locking on mine.

I shrug, unsuccessfully trying to lower my eyes, but his won't let go.

"Some. That reminds me," I quickly change the subject. "I never thanked you for the sushi last night."

"No problem. I'll be honest, I was conflicted leaving you alone last night."

"I think I needed a moment though," I explain.

He nods and picks up his mug, taking a sip.

"Not an easy thing, coming face-to-face with your nightmare," he observes.

He's not really pushing, but not exactly letting go either. Oddly enough, I don't mind. He seems genuine in his concern.

"Those are not memories I often pull out of the box. They tend to be securely tucked away. I don't think I was prepared for the impact being confronted with him would have," I admit.

"Not sure that's something you could prepare for," he astutely points out. "How did you end up at the home in the first place?"

I take a fortifying swig of my coffee.

"I shamed my parents."

He doesn't say anything, but simply nods for me to go on.

"My parents came here from Pakistan when I was three years old, an only child. They held on tightly to their culture and religion. By the time I went to middle school, I wanted the freedom my peers enjoyed and started rebelling against my parents' strict hold."

I pause when Donna walks up with a pair of plates, but they're for the couple a few booths over.

"My father caught me kissing a boy in the alley behind our house. It was the culmination with all the other ways I'd disobeyed them that was the last straw for my parents. I was shunned, and my father handed me off to the director of Transition House."

"Wow. That's harsh...and disturbing."

"It is in the western world, but not to my parents. This clash between cultures is not unique."

This time when the waitress approaches it's with our breakfast, and for the next ten minutes or so we focus on our meal.

During that time, I'm trying to figure out what it is about this man that has me talking about things I haven't shared since I was in therapy many years ago. Perhaps it's those warm, hazel eyes that prompt me to open up like this. Every so often, he glances over and I'm curious what it is he sees when he looks at me.

I've barely moved my mostly empty plate aside when Donna shows up with the bill and another carafe.

"You can pay at the cash register. More coffee?"

I reach for the bill, but Hamish beats me to it. He ignores my frustrated grunt and turns to the woman.

"Yes, to go, please."

When Donna walks away, he turns to me.

"Did you ever have contact with them?"

I don't have to ask who he's talking about.

"My mother died three years after I left, but I saw my father once. He turned his back so I didn't try again. He's since passed as well."

It's surprising how little I feel, talking about my parents. There was a time I worried perhaps there was something wrong with me—that I was cold—but the truth is I've given them enough of my grief, my anger, and my pain.

I don't want the rest of my life to be shaped by events I had no power over and cannot change.

The arrival of our coffees to go is a welcome distraction, and I quickly excuse myself to visit the bathroom before we hit the road again. I use the facilities and splash some water on my face before joining Hamish, who has apparently already paid and is waiting by the door.

As he has done every time, he opens the passenger side for me. I get in, buckle up, and notice he's still standing there with the door open.

"It's probably not politically correct to say this, but what was done to you by people, who were supposed to look after you, is fucked up."

He closes the door, heads around the truck, and gets behind the wheel. The engine rumbles to life and the truck starts backing out of the parking spot when it suddenly stops.

Hamish puts the truck in park, grabs my hand and lifts it, and with his eyes on mine, kisses my knuckles.

"And yet here you are...incredible."

TEN

JACOB

I follow the scent of fresh baking into the kitchen where Bernie is just pulling a large tray of cinnamon rolls out of the oven.

"Are you trying to give me a potbelly?"

She looks up.

"Who says these are for you?" she fires back.

"That would be particularly cruel, even for you, Bernie."

I count twelve large rolls she is now liberally slathering with thick icing, and my mouth is watering.

"Oh fine, you can have *one*. The rest are for my book club meeting tonight."

"Didn't you say there were eight of you in that group?"

She narrows her eyes at me.

"There are. What are you getting at?"

I shrug. "Math isn't my strong suit but doesn't that leave four for me?"

She slides a warm, dripping cinnamon roll on a plate and hands it over.

"*One*. Save some for later."

I pour a coffee, grab my plate, and announce I'll be in my office.

"Didn't you say you were heading out again this morning?"

"I will be, I just have a couple of calls to make."

First thing I do when I sit down at my desk is check email and messages while eating my still-warm bun.

There isn't much news, other than some more background information on Grandview Estate my lawyer sent me. It had taken me a while to find the property, which is located near Russell Springs on Lake Cumberland. The place is surrounded by water on three sides, and appears to be quite secluded.

I wasn't able to get much information online, so asked my real estate lawyer to request a title search at the Russell County courthouse, which is what he forwarded to me. Just in time too, since Onyx is supposed to sign the papers and hand over a bank draft later today.

The next step will be arranging to pick up the horse and I would like to know exactly what she'll be walking into. Pearl had been able to run the picture Lee took at the auction through her face-recognition software, and was able to match it to an old image of Wheeler with an accuracy of close to eighty percent. Good enough for me, but

I've decided I don't particularly like the idea of sending Onyx anywhere near this man.

My phone vibrates with an incoming call. It's Mitch, so I answer through my app. My stomach clenches, worried this may not be good news.

"Tell me."

Mitch doesn't waste any time.

"Alex Crocker was found this morning. Alive."

"You're kidding me?"

"Nope. We looked into the boy's uncle, whose behavior at the searches raised some red flags. Found out he was let go from the elementary school where he worked as a janitor for inappropriate behavior. He owns a hunting shack in the hills twenty miles north of Frankfort, where we found the boy. He wasn't in great shape, but he should recover."

"Physically," I specify. *"There's no saying if he will psychologically."*

"Valid point," Mitch concedes. "Anyway, just wanting to give you an update. We're about to head straight home to catch up on some sleep, unless there's something urgent?"

"No, nothing. I'll get you guys caught up after you've had a rest."

After I get off the phone, I check the time. I'm already running a bit late and I still have to check in with Pearl at the office. There's no time to look over the information the title search produced, so I forward the email to Onyx.

"Is there anything urgent you need from me?" I ask Pearl when she answers the phone.

"No, there isn't."

"*Good. I'll be out of reach. For emergencies, send me a text.*"

I end the call, gather my dishes, and head for the kitchen, which is empty. I find Bernie in the laundry room folding sheets.

"I'm off," I announce.

"Are you going to be home for dinner?" she wants to know.

"Don't count on it, otherwise, I can look after myself."

She snorts and rolls her eyes. In response, I loop an arm around her shoulders.

"Granted, not as well as you do," I concede. "But I won't starve."

"Fine, take those leftover cinnamon buns with you, but don't eat them all yourself, share."

"I will." I grin. "You're the best."

I follow her into the kitchen where she puts three pastries into a plastic container and hands it to me.

Ignoring her grumbling, I kiss her cheek, grab my keys and ball cap off the table in the hall, and head out.

Onyx

I blow a strand of hair from my face, and take in the mess around me.

Dammit.

I have a pounding headache and of course I can't find my painkillers anywhere. I've been tearing apart my bathroom and bedroom without any luck. I was so sure I'd seen them in the vanity drawer. Where the hell did I leave them?

Of course now my phone starts ringing in the kitchen. I'd ignore it, but I'm expecting a call back from a potential stable hand.

I leave the mess I made for later and hurry to the kitchen.

"Hello?"

"Is this the Four Oaks farm?"

The voice sounds like a younger man's.

"It is."

"Hi...uhh, my name is Jose Cantu. I understand you're looking for hired help?"

I grab the printouts off the counter to check the name of the guy I left a message for, but it's not Cantu. None of the résumés I have are in that name.

"Yes, I am actually looking for a ranch hand. Where did you hear about the job?"

I turn one of the papers upside down and look for a pen in the kitchen drawer. The first thing my hand encounters is the container with painkillers.

Thank God.

I'm listening with half an ear as I wrangle the lid of the container and shake out two pills.

"...Chen suggested I give it a try."

"Gordon Chen?" I ask as I grab a cup for some water.

"Yes, ma'am."

Hard to believe the guy who tried to outbid me at auction, now suddenly decides to send me help, but it doesn't hurt to hear him out. It's not like the candidates are lining up outside the door.

"Well, why don't you tell me a little about yourself. Background, skills, work experience, that kind of thing."

When he starts talking, I quickly pop the painkillers before picking up my pen and making some notes. It sounds like Jose has quite a bit of experience as a stable hand but is looking to advance his career. He sounds interesting to say the least.

"Listen, Jose, do you have a résumé and reference contacts you can email me?"

"I can do that."

I recite the Four Oaks email account I set up. Then I tell him, once I receive his information and check out his credentials, I'd like to have my trainer talk with him as well, before any decisions are made.

My headache still hasn't cleared up after I end the call, so I go lie down on the couch for a few minutes and wait for the painkillers to take effect.

I must've fallen asleep, because the sound of knocking on the door wakes me up. Swinging my feet to the floor, I give myself a second to gain my equilibrium before I stand up. Thankfully my headache is gone.

I check the peephole to see Hamish standing outside. Quickly disabling the elaborate alarm system Jacob had installed, I open the door for him.

"Did I catch you sleeping?" he asks right away.

"Dozing. I'm sorry, were you waiting long?"

I step aside and wave him in.

"No, I just got here. I ran a little late."

He follows me into the kitchen where I grab the empty coffeepot and hold it up.

"I was going to put on a fresh pot, will you have some?"

"Sure."

I grab my canister of coffee beans and fill the grinder.

"Sorry, it's noisy, but freshly ground tastes best."

"I won't argue that."

I glance over my shoulder and catch him peeking at the handful of résumés.

"Would you mind having a look at those? Oh, and you'll never guess who sent another candidate my way. Gordon Chen."

"Doesn't surprise me. The guy is obviously enamored with you."

I snap my head around, my mouth open.

"How do you figure that? I actually get the opposite vibe from him. I don't think he likes me at all."

I finish setting the pot up to brew and turn around, leaning my butt against the counter.

"I beg to differ; you don't see what we see."

If I thought the comment was about appearance, I'd roll my eyes, but I don't think Hamish was simply talking about my looks. I ignore the little tingle I feel at his words and point at the résumés.

"I made some notes on the back of one of those. I

should go see if the new candidate sent his work history yet."

I slip down the hall to the second bedroom I set up as an office and open my laptop. I didn't really expect him to have sent it already—I simply needed a moment to myself—but to my surprise, I see the email in my inbox. I print it out and briefly glance at it, but I don't really know what to look for.

"Here it is."

I hand him the document and head for the coffeepot, grabbing a few mugs from the cupboard above.

"Did you talk to any of the others?" he wants to know.

"Talked to one guy earlier today, who started by telling me he had a bad back so wouldn't be able to do any physical work," I recount that frustrating conversation.

"Did he explain why the hell he was applying for a physical job then?"

"He was making my headache worse so I cut the conversation short." I slide a coffee in front of him. "I left a message for another guy but so far he hasn't returned my call, and I have yet to contact the third applicant."

"So, this Jose guy and which other one?"

I point out the work history for the other applicant.

"I'll take care of this," he suggests, looking at me with his head tilted, "while you get ready."

I look down at myself to find I'm still wearing the sweats I put on for comfort this morning. I grab my coffee and hustle to the bedroom.

Normally I wouldn't care, but Hamish is here to take me into Lexington. I have an appointment with a lawyer to finalize the purchase of Arion's Moon. Not in my wildest dreams could I have imagined being the owner of a thoroughbred racehorse. Of course, it's really Jacob's horse, but it will be in my name. At least for the time being.

Signing the paperwork today means I need to make sure I'm ready for the horse. Hamish is coming because we'll be picking up a horse trailer and making a stop to pick up some last minute supplies.

I clean up the mess I made earlier, grab a pair of designer jeans, pull on a slouchy sweater, and shove my feet into my favorite boots. In the bathroom, I quickly brush on a little mascara and tinted lip balm. It's going to have to do.

"I like this Jose," Hamish announces when I return to the kitchen. "He seems like he knows what he's talking about and definitely has the experience. I also got hold of Joey Vernon who, as it turns out, is not a guy but a woman and I like her too. In addition to being an experienced hand, she's an exercise rider as well, which would be an added benefit."

I drain my cup and put it in the dishwasher. Hamish hands me his as well.

"So what are you suggesting?" I ask.

"Hire them both. We can check a few more referrals first, but I think that's the way to go. The horse will need daily care that really requires more than one person anyway."

I glance at the clock.

"We have a little time. We could split the referrals

between us. If those check out, we can invite both of them here. Like a meet and greet, get a sense of them in person."

I'm going to have to try and figure out the staff quarters on the other side of the exercise track. I'm pretty sure the building is not set up with a men's and women's section. We may need to make some adjustments there.

"Here, you take Joey's," Hamish suggests as he hands me one of the printouts. "That way you can get a sense of her. I'm going to give Gordon Chen a call, find out what prompted him to send Jose Cantu this way."

His voice has a definite edge when he talks about Chen. I wonder if his suggestion that man has more than a professional interest in me is prompting him to make that call.

Or maybe I'm reading too much into it. I'm finding myself more and more drawn to him, with an attraction that goes much deeper than the surface. Life has left its scars on all of us. Some of them perhaps more visible than others. The ones Hamish wears don't detract from the man I'm getting to know.

Just like the lack of a physical presence hasn't kept me from feeling a special connection with Jacob.

If there is some greater being orchestrating our lives, they have a cruel sense of humor. I haven't had feelings for a man since I lost the one who had my heart completely. Not for lack of trying though.

Yet here I am, suddenly drawn to two men—friends, no less—and I'm caught in a situation where I can't walk away from either of them, and guilt is a constant companion.

Lovely.

I'm sure whoever is up there is having a laugh on me.

With my phone and Joey's résumé, I duck into my office for some privacy to make a few calls. When I return, Hamish is just ending a call.

"Any luck?" he asks.

"You're right, she sounds good. I was able to get hold of both references and they spoke highly of her. Her last employer said he regretted seeing her leave."

"I'm sure he did, since he was apparently a cheap bastard paying her less than her male counterparts," he explains. "She told me she asked for equal pay and was brushed off, so she quit."

I like her already.

"There will be no gender distinction in wages here," I state firmly.

Hamish grins, "I figured as much."

"What about Jose?" I inquire.

"Yeah, sounds legit. Chen said he worked for a friend of his, who recently retired and sold off his horses. The friend sent Jose to Chen, who didn't have any openings and suggested calling you."

"Great. So we can set up a day and time for them to come here," I suggest.

"Call them from the road. We've got to get going."

"Okay, give me one sec."

I take down a couple of travel mugs and fill those with the remaining coffee, handing one to Hamish. Then I grab my purse and the résumés, and follow him as he heads for the door.

"You washed it," I observe as we walk outside and notice the gleaming truck.

"It needed it."

He clicks the locks and opens the passenger door for me.

"Oh, shit, I forgot," he remembers, grabbing a container from the seat.

He waits until I'm buckled in and hands it to me.

"Have one. Best cinnamon buns you've ever tasted."

ELEVEN

JACOB

"Sorry I missed your call. My physical therapist is here, torturing me."

I grin when I hear a protest go up in the background.

"No worries. How are you?"

"You mean other than being subjected to cruel and unusual punishment for any and all inadvertent insensitive comments I may have made over the course of my marriage?" More background protests from Laura, his wife *and* his PT. "I'm good. Maybe a little bored. When are you coming back up here?"

"Once this case is settled, and I'll bring a bottle of the best Kentucky bourbon money can buy as a thanks for your help."

Help is an understatement. I've relied on more than just this man's expertise to guide me in my quest to bring down David Wheeler. He offered me his knowledge, his connections, and his reputation, without asking what I needed it for. He knows what I do is good work and that's enough for him.

I'd do the same for the guy I'd spent almost a month beside in a hospital room in Germany, after our unit was ambushed by insurgents fifteen years ago.

"Not going to say no to that, brother. How are things going anyway? Did you get everything I listed?"

"About to. I'm just waiting for the paperwork to be finalized. Then we can make arrangements for the pickup."

My eyes are fixed on the door, keeping watch for whoever walks out.

"Have you looked into a companion pony for the filly?" he asks.

"Working on it. But what I was calling you about is to see if you've ever heard of a Morton Ackers?"

"Ackers? No, can't say I have. Why? Who is he?"

"He owns a place called Grandview Estate. It's a large property with a main lodge, several guest buildings, stables, a track. It's big. Apparently, several racehorses are stabled there at any given time."

It was a long shot, but I had to try.

"Never heard of it."

I catch sight of the door opening, but it's an older couple coming out of the building. My eyes start following them into the parking lot when I notice someone coming outside behind them.

"Hamish? Sorry, I've gotta go. I'll get back to you."

I hang up, just in time for the passenger door to open.

"It's done."

Like every other time I've been in her presence, every nerve in my body goes on alert. This woman has that effect on me. Her smile is like a punch in the gut and I struggle to keep an impassive mask in place.

She waves a folder in my face.

"Signed, sealed, but not quite delivered."

"Was anything said about the actual transfer?"

"He said the agent would get in touch with me to schedule a pickup."

I nod, start the truck, and drive out of the parking lot.

We're in downtown Lexington and the roads are gridlocked due to construction and volume. It's going to take a frustrating while to get out of the city. Traffic starts getting heavy around three o'clock and tends to last until at least six.

It's even more frustrating sitting in traffic, next to a woman who haunts my dreams but is out of reach.

"I'm starving," Onyx announces.

"Afraid I'm all out of cinnamon buns." We ate those on our way here. "I can stop somewhere if you'd like?"

"Can we hit up a drive-thru? I don't really want to stop; we still have stuff to do."

"Sure. We're going to pass a couple of fast-food places up ahead. Take your pick."

She wants Rally's because of their milkshakes so that's where we stop to pick up burgers and shakes. I can't remember the last time I had a milkshake—probably in my much, much younger years—but it's pretty tasty.

Eating while driving is not normally something I'd

recommend, but in stop-and-go traffic I can make it work. Not a huge fan of the cheeseburger, but I'm finding everything seems to taste better when in Onyx's company.

She's currently driving me crazy with her occasional little moans and grunts of enjoyment. It calls up mental images that are also not advisable when operating a vehicle and are more suited for visualization in the shower. I strategically drape a napkin on my lap.

It isn't easy to continuously deceive her—or any of the others for that matter—but I have my reasons for wanting that degree of anonymity. I question whether any of them would be working for me if they knew, and the work we set out to do is too important.

I'm taking a risk, working side by side with her, but we each have our reasons for wanting to bring Wheeler down.

"I feel better now," Onyx declares, crumpling up her food wrapper.

I watch from the corner of my eye as she leans back in her seat, crossing her hands over her stomach, before she turns her head my way.

"I'm assuming you've pulled a trailer before?"

"I have."

It wasn't a horse trailer exactly, but I don't think it makes that much difference. At least I'll have a chance to tow it a few times without the precious cargo inside.

"That reminds me," I add. "We need to talk about one or more companion ponies."

"Companion ponies?"

"Ponies, you know...small horses?"

I grin when I catch her glaring at me.

"Don't be a smart-ass, Hamish. I know what ponies are, I'm just not sure what a companion pony is."

"Horses are not loners by nature, thoroughbreds are no exception. A companion pony is like a support buddy for the horse, both at their home base and on the road. They travel with the horse and often double as a lead pony to keep the thoroughbred calm right before the race."

"And Arion's Moon needs one?"

"She'll need a companion, yes, and it's safer to have more than one," I inform her.

"Does Jacob know this?"

I turn my head and look at her.

This is the part I fucking hate; lying to her.

"He is aware, yes."

Onyx

I'm not going to lie, I'm excited about having a couple of cute ponies roaming around.

Maybe we can add some goats, plus, I've always wanted a dog.

I shake my head and remind myself this is not my farm, Arion's Moon is not my horse, and this is not my life. It's a temporary situation and when the time comes,

I'll be heading back to my apartment where animals are not allowed. If I don't stop fantasizing, I'll cause myself heartbreak.

"How did you find them?" I ask Hamish, who was back again first thing this morning.

He hitched the trailer we picked up yesterday to his truck, and we're on our way to look at a pair of ponies at a farm one county over. It's going to be another busy day. The prospective stable hands are coming this afternoon, and I still have to figure out how to give Joey some privacy in the dorm.

"Through a contact. These two come as a pair, so the owner was looking for someone willing to take them both. The horse they were companion ponies for died unexpectedly a few weeks ago."

It's a nice drive through the hills, only half an hour or so. An older gentleman is waiting in front of a barn, waving us over when we drive up to the farm. Hamish rolls down his window as the man approaches the truck.

He does a little double-take when he catches sight of Hamish but covers it well.

"The turn is a little tight here. It's easier if you loop around the back of the barn."

We do as instructed, and Hamish parks the truck with the back of the trailer close to the barn doors.

Eager to see the ponies, I'm out of the truck before he has a chance to open the door for me. I walk up to the man and hold out my hand.

"Onyx Baqri. Nice to meet you."

"Likewise," he states a bit gruffly. "Neil Myers."

His hand is calloused and grabs mine firmly.

"Morning, Neil. We spoke on the phone yesterday," Hamish says behind me.

"Yes. I brought the ponies inside for you to have a look."

I'm almost giddy with anticipation when he opens the large barn doors. Not exactly two cute Shetland ponies, but I love the look of the two beauties poking their heads over the side-by-side stalls.

"They're Paints," I observe, instantly drawn to the black-and-white patched horses.

"They are, both geldings," Neil confirms. "They're known for being calm and even-tempered, which makes them well-suited as companion or lead ponies."

I walk up to the one on the right, already angling his head toward me. I hold out my hand and his soft lips brush lightly over my palm, looking for a treat.

"I don't have anything for you," I mumble.

"His name is Murdoch," the owner shares. "The other one is Buck."

As I pet Murdoch, his buddy nudges my arm with his nose, so I give him some attention as well.

"I can bring them out so you can have a proper look at 'em," Neil offers.

No need for me, I'm already sold, but Hamish clearly needs more reassurance.

I step back as Neil opens the stall door for Murdoch and hooks a lead on his halter. The horse waits patiently in his stall while Neil puts a lead on Buck as well. Then he guides both horses to the middle of the aisle.

Hamish approaches and runs his hand along Buck's neck and down his front leg, lifting it up. I'm not sure what he's looking for, but he does the same with the other three legs, before checking the horse's mouth and then his back end. Next, he moves to Murdoch and puts him through the same scrutiny.

"How old did you say they were?" he asks the older man.

"Buck is seven, Murdoch is five years old."

"And you're asking twenty-eight thousand for the pair."

Neil confirms with a nod.

"Seems a little steep," Hamish comments.

"Not if you consider you're buying two experienced lead horses, who have been tried and tested out on the track. They also make for great trail horses. My grandkids ride them."

"Twenty-five."

The old man narrows his eyes on Hamish.

"Twenty-seven and not a penny less," he fires back.

Before Hamish has a chance to piss the man off more, I intervene.

"Sold. Twenty-seven it is."

Hamish throws me an exasperated look I ignore. Instead, I turn to Neil.

"Let's get this finalized."

It turns out buying a couple of companion ponies is much less involved and complicated than buying a race-horse was. It's not even noon when we drive away from the barn, Buck and Murdoch in the trailer behind us.

"I could've gotten him down to twenty-six, given a chance," Hamish grumbles.

I shake my head. He's no different than most other men I know; everything becomes a competition at the expense of common sense.

"Nickel-and-diming an old man over a thousand dollars is a waste of time. Especially after spending an easy half a million dollars on a racehorse."

He opens his mouth, intending to protest I'm sure, but apparently thinks better of it.

"Besides," I try to mitigate. "He did throw in their tack."

"Those saddles are falling apart."

"They're not that bad, and they'll serve us just fine."

For the next several minutes it's quiet in the truck until Hamish breaks the silence.

"Did you ever ride?"

"A horse? I sat on a pony once when I was a child, that's about it. It wasn't really something common when I was growing up, and of course there was nothing like that when I was living at Transition House. I love them though, they're so majestic and yet seem so gentle."

"I can take you. Teach you. You have horses now. And tack," he adds with a lopsided grin.

That grin gets me every time. Because of the scarring, his face is like a mask and not very expressive. However, when he grins like that, laugh lines fan out from the eye on the unmarred side of his face, letting his personality shine through.

"I think I'd like that. But I should probably check with Jacob to make sure my medical insurance is up to date."

I'M STANDING BY THE GLASS DOORS, LOOKING OUT AT the stables in the rear, where I just see Hamish disappear.

"What do you think?" Kate asks, sidling up beside me.

"They both seem nice and capable, but let's see what verdict Hamish comes back with."

Mitch dropped Kate off about ten minutes after we got back with the horses. He went on to Lexington to meet up with Sawyer, his daughter.

Having Kate arrive when she did was perfect timing, giving a little more credence to my portrayal of wealthy socialite when Jose and Joey got here. I'm well aware it's a role I'll have to be mindful of at all times, once they move here. Although, for how long that cover is necessary, remains to be seen.

"You like him."

My head snaps around. Kate is scrutinizing me. Or at least it feels that way.

"Sure, I like him. What's wrong with that? He's a decent guy, has been very helpful. In fact, he's gone out of his way to—"

I'm cut off when Kate puts a hand up to my face, palm out.

"Whoa, Nelly. It *was* an innocent statement, but you just elevated it into a friendly inquisition. Give me all the dirt."

"There's no dirt. Nothing worth mentioning."

"So, there *is* something," she persists.

I should've known she's not that easily put off, Kate is as headstrong as they come.

Part of me thinks maybe I should tell her. Of all people, Kate and Janey know me, just as I know them. We share a traumatic history, one we were all able to recover from, but also all have lingering hang-ups from.

"Can I venture a guess?" Kate offers.

"Be my guest."

It's not like I'm going to stop her anyway.

"You're conflicted because any feelings for Hamish would be a betrayal of the torch you've carried for Jacob. On top of that, feeling something for Jacob is safe, because he's a voice on the phone. This guy is real, flesh and bone, you can touch him, feelings for him might actually develop into something real, and that scares you."

My first reaction is to snap at her.

"You'd think it was you with the psychology degree."

I know I'm lashing out because her analysis is painfully close to the truth. Of course it's immediately followed by a deep sense of shame at my reaction.

I, however, *am* the one with the degree, but what is it they say? Healer heal thyself?

"Close," I admit. "It does feel like a betrayal."

"Of who? Of Jacob, or Nathan? Or both?" Kate probes. "Do you know how ridiculous that sounds? I mean, I know there's some kind of connection between you and Jacob—we all do—but you've never actually met the man. And Raj, Nathan has been dead for over two decades."

"I'm aware of that," I whisper.

I can still feel the boy, who was supposed to be my future, brutally ripped from my arms.

Kate puts her hands on my shoulders, looks me in the eye, and gives me a little shake.

"Honey, do you really think he'd want you to restrict yourself to half a life?"

TWELVE

JACOB

I'm exhausted.

Driving over an hour each way almost every day is getting old fast.

I'd forgotten how energy consuming simply being among people can be. Normally, most of my time is spent at home, in my office, working. Surrounded by computers.

I stumbled onto e-trading when I was still in the hospital in Louisville. With little else to do, I simply kept an eye on the meager savings I'd invested. With a lot of time on my hands, some common sense, and a whole lot of luck, I was able to build those modest savings into a decent portfolio.

I did well over the years, took crazy risks that sometimes failed but more often succeeded. When I'd amassed more than I'd need in my lifetime, I stuck most of it in blue-chips and other safe stocks, invested some in real estate, and handed my portfolio to a financial manager.

Then I started putting my plans for GEM into effect.

Fifteen years of work with a single goal in mind to the exclusion of everything else. The funny thing is, now that I'm so close to reaching that goal, I'm almost scared for it to be over. Because with the truth fully exposed, I could lose all that ever meant anything to me.

"You look like hell."

I blink open an eye to find Bernie standing in the doorway.

"Thanks. Tell me what you really think." I take my feet off the desk and sit my chair up. "What are you doing still up, Bernie?"

"I'm old, I don't need that much sleep. And also, I was watching Jimmy Kimmel and was just turning off lights when I saw your office lights still on."

Bernie is approaching seventy, but she's far from old. Still sharp as a tack and not much escapes her. Of course, it helps her apartment is in the opposite wing of the house, right across the courtyard from my office. I should've had blinds put up.

She sits down in one of the club chairs on the other side of the desk, facing me with a stern look on her face.

"You know you're going to run out of juice at some point, right?"

I drag a hand down my face and sigh.

"We're close, Bernie. So close."

Her expression softens.

"I know. I'm just worried at what cost, my friend. What happens after?"

Trust Bernie to almost pluck the thoughts from my head. I guess after taking care of me for almost fifteen years—seeing me at my worst, watching me claw back from the dark abyss I was sliding toward—she's intimately acquainted with my demons. All of them.

"GEM will continue doing the good work. For every predator we've taken out, another pops up. The work is never-ending."

"Fair enough, but what about you personally? Or maybe I should ask what about her?"

She knows my heart. Hell, she knows my entire sordid history, which is why she pinpoints with great precision the most tender of spots.

During those long, sleepless, dark nights, when pain and misery breathed new life into old trauma, she sat beside my bed, held my hand, and listened.

She stayed in touch when I was sent home. Then, when she returned to the U.S. a few months after that, she looked me up, and ended up staying. Bernice had no relatives to speak of, never had children, and we became each other's family.

"I'm keeping my distance. She may never have to know."

It's hope speaking, not conviction.

I know Bernie doesn't agree, but I'd rather stay part of her life at a distance than allow myself to get close and risk losing her completely.

"The moment you decided to come out of hiding—

even using a fake identity—you set that wheel in motion. It's inevitable someone will find you out eventually," she foreshadows.

"Then I'll have to deal with it as it comes, but you know I'm doing this for them as much as I am for myself."

She shakes her head, a gentle smile on her face as she rises to her feet.

"Not as much. More."

She brushes the creases from her blouse as she rounds the desk. Then she kisses the top of my bald head.

"Get yourself to bed, J."

"Jesper Olson's case was in front of a grand jury yesterday."

On my way to Four Oaks, I had to park in a pull-off to call into the office.

"*And?*" I ask Mitch.

GEM had been on the trail of Jesper Olson since he first popped up as a person of interest when Opal was investigating the director of the Youth Center in Lanark. Olson had posed as one of the teenagers, but was in fact bait for a child sex exploitation ring.

He disappeared to the Bahamas, but Pearl was hot on his trail. She tracked him to West Virginia where he worked as a group counselor at a camp for troubled teens, doing much the same thing as before; coercing and exploiting minors. This time with the added offenses of kidnapping and trafficking.

We caught him however, in a joint takedown with Matt Driver and his CARD team, but he never talked.

"They got the indictment. Matt said it didn't take long, but what was interesting was the replacement of the public defender assigned to Olson, by Herbert Rosenberg."

"No way he's financing that on his own."

Rosenberg's firm is located in Louisville and was very recently in the news for their involvement in another child sexual exploitation case involving a prominent Kentucky politician.

"Agreed," Lee contributes. "Unfortunately, we can only guess at who is behind it. Rosenberg isn't going to share who's footing the bill."

"Right. But what I find interesting is the reason behind it. I think it's a safe bet to assume it's Wheeler who is paying for his defense, but why? Olson isn't talking and it wouldn't be much for Wheeler to make sure he never does. We know what he's capable of."

"The only thing that makes sense is if there is a personal connection," Onyx offers.

"The kicker is," Mitch adds. "The next step will be in front of a circuit court judge, who could conceivably grant bail now Olson has a big law firm behind him."

"That would be a travesty," Lee concludes.

Just what I need, another potential loose end. In this case, one we thought we already had wrapped up. Goes to show you can never let down your guard.

"Stay on top of it, and see if you can find anything else that might connect Wheeler and Olson."

Checking the time on my dashboard, I quickly end the meeting. Last thing I want is to raise suspicion if I show up at Four Oaks late.

It would be so much easier if I could find something closer by. Maybe I can get Bernie to look into that.

Onyx

I feel a little apprehensive.

That's a lie. It's really a lot. Enough to make my hands sweat around the leather saddle horn.

As sweet and placid as Murdoch seemed standing beside him, sitting on him I'm suddenly not so sure.

"Relax."

Even Hamish's warm baritone fails to calm me.

"You don't understand. I was little," I explain, "so that fall took forever and left an impression."

"All the more reason to relax this time, because you're not going to fall off."

"How could you possibly know that?" I fire back, slightly panicked as Hamish starts walking Murdoch around the corral.

"Because I won't let it." He turns his head and looks up at me. "Lift your arms."

"What?"

"You have a death grip on the horn, I want you to let go and raise your arms."

"Why on earth would I want to do that?"

He's nuts. My death grip is the only thing holding me in this saddle.

"And you're not helping!" I yell at Kate, who is leaning over the gate, snickering at my plight.

"Because," Hamish drawls, "you're holding on so tight, your ass isn't even in the saddle. You'll never get a feel for the rhythm like that. Now, do you trust me?"

That's a loaded question, given what he's asking of me. Then again, I trusted him enough to share my past with. All things considered, that was even scarier than the prospect of falling off a horse.

When I let go, my butt seems to sink into the saddle.

"That's it. Now relax and let your body follow the horse's gait."

I slowly lift my arms over my head and aim a triumphant grin at Kate. The next moment Hamish makes Murdoch change direction, and I start sliding. I quickly grab for the horn again.

"No, keep them up." He puts a hand on my knee and presses in. "You don't balance with your arms; you use your knees. Squeeze them. Once you're more comfortable in the saddle, you can start using your knees to direct the horse."

After a few loops around the corral, he hands me the reins and takes a step toward the center of the ring. Murdoch keeps going.

"You're on your own."

I fight down the initial panic I feel and actually start enjoying myself. Then I hear the ring of my phone and glance over at Kate, who's holding it for me.

"Can you answer that for me?"

I pull back slightly on the reins, like Hamish told me and, as promised, Murdoch stops.

"Hang on." He walks up and grabs the reins. "Dismounting is the same as mounting, but in reverse."

He talks me through it, step by step, until I'm back on solid ground. It feels a little like stepping off a boat onto shore.

"Hold on one minute, please," I hear Kate answer when I approach her.

"It's Oliver Doyle," she announces, handing me my phone. "I put the call on mute."

"Mr. Doyle, how are you?"

Hamish has his eyes on me as he walks over, leading Murdoch.

"Ms. Baqri. I'm doing well, even better now I have you on the phone. It's so lovely to hear your voice."

I have an instant, physical reaction to that comment. One of aversion. I immediately steer the conversation in a more appropriate direction.

"What can I do for you, Mr. Doyle?"

"Ah, yes. I'm calling to see what might be a desirable time for us to transfer Arion's Moon."

"Where would that take place?" I ask.

"Grandview Estate. The property is near Russell Springs, but I will email you exact instructions on how to get there."

I do an internal fist pump when I hear Grandview confirmed. There was no guarantee the exchange would take place there, but we'd hoped it would.

"That would be helpful, thank you. Perhaps it's easier if you included some preferred dates and times, so I can check availability on my side?"

"Of course. The horse already has a recent Certificate of Veterinarian Inspection if that is sufficient, unless, of course, you would prefer for your own veterinarian to examine her?"

I have no idea what the right answer is, so I avoid answering and buy myself some time.

"Let me see what I can arrange, but I will inform you either way via email."

"Of course, that would be fine. I will send that information to you shortly. It was a pleasure speaking with you," he adds in a saccharine voice.

Yuck.

"Thank you, Mr. Doyle."

I end the call and shiver. I feel like I need a shower.

"Do we have a date?" Hamish wants to know.

"He's emailing some options and details. He did confirm Grandview Estate as the location."

"No guarantee Morton Ackers will be there," Kate points out.

"Maybe not, but I can at least poke around, talk to people, ask some innocent questions."

"Sounds dangerous," Hamish comments, his mouth a line.

"Don't worry, I'll be careful," I appease him. "Doyle

said they already have a veterinary certificate, but if we want, we can arrange for our own vet. I suggest we do that; it'll slow down the process, giving me more time to see what I can find out about this Morton Ackers."

"I can look into a vet," he offers. "Right after we take care of Murdoch. Let's go."

He hands me the reins.

"Me?"

"There's more to riding a horse than getting on. You'll have to at least know how to look after the horse and the tack."

Kate snickers behind me, as Murdoch and I follow Hamish to the stables. I figure it's best to ignore her.

"I can take him, Ms. Baqri," Jose offers when he sees us come in.

I'm tempted, but then I catch the look on Hamish's face, and for some reason I don't want to disappoint him.

"Thanks, Jose, but I'd like to take care of him myself."

We asked Jose to come in first thing this morning, so he could get his bearings and look after Buck and Murdoch. Joey will start closer to when we pick up Arion's Moon, it made no sense to have them both here.

Once I have Murdoch taken care of to Hamish's satisfaction, I head inside to check my email and give Jacob a call. Hamish went to look for Jose to check if he knew any vets he could recommend.

Doyle's email is here, with three possible dates. Either this coming Friday or Saturday, or Tuesday of next week. If it's up to me we'd do this as soon as possible, but there's no guarantee Hamish can organize a vet in three days. First, I should check in with Jacob.

I dial his number and he answers right away.

"Make it snappy. I'm in the middle of something."

Great. He sounds in a mood.

"Well, hello to you to," I snipe back. "I'll do my best not to take up too much of your time, but I thought you'd like to know I just spoke to the agent for Pegasus GLAN, and the exchange will take place at Grandview. We have a choice either this Friday, Saturday, or the Tuesday following."

"Saturday. That gives me a few days to get feet on the ground near Russell Springs. Tuesday is too long a wait."

"What feet on the ground?"

"Pearl's. Backup, just in case."

I could get bent out of shape, but to be honest, I don't mind the idea of Pearl having my back. Maybe we could even smuggle her in with us.

Two sets of eyes see more than one.

THIRTEEN

ONYX

"Lee, dig up anything on Ackers?"

Through the kitchen window, I watch Jose and Joey walk the horses from the stables to the field. Kate is sitting at the island, her phone on speaker so we can both listen in.

"Other than he's elusive? I interviewed Gordon Chen yesterday and he claims he's never met whoever is behind Pegasus GLAN, but I have my doubts on whether he's being truthful. The man is hard to read. I did drop Ackers's name to see if that would trigger a response, but he denied knowing the name. I *was* able to set up an interview with Brian Haley, the trainer, for this afternoon. He was willing to talk about his success working with both Arion's Moon and Pure Delight. We'll see what comes out of that."

"Are you meeting him at Grandview?" I hear Mitch ask.

"No. He's apparently in Lexington today. We're meeting at Carson's downtown."

Janey left for Russell Springs yesterday afternoon already, and Mitch went into the office to pack up some surveillance equipment he's going to drive out there today.

At this point, Jacob has everyone on this case, and the building anticipation is tangible. Hamish and I are supposed to leave early tomorrow morning to get to Russell Springs by nine thirty, which is when we're supposed to meet the veterinarian Hamish organized.

This morning he picked up the trailer to have the tires replaced that were apparently getting worn. He wanted to make sure transporting Arion's Moon would be as safe as possible. Protecting his friend's investment, is what he said. Yet another thing to appreciate in the man.

"Onyx, how do you see this going down? What's the plan?" Jacob inquires.

"No real plan, other than to try and confirm Wheeler is there and, if possible, get an introduction. I have some ideas on how to draw him out, but I'll have to let circumstances guide me. If he's not there, I'll see what information I can glean from his staff, and I'll try to get into the main lodge."

"You are not to take any unnecessary risks."

I roll my eyes at Kate.

"Jacob, are you questioning my abilities?"

It's silent for a moment. Good, I hope he's thinking carefully about what comes out of his mouth next.

"This isn't about trust, Onyx," he comes back with.

"Oh good, because I was about to ask why you gave me this job in the first place."

"I don't want you getting hurt."

"Can I ask you something? I'm assuming you don't want any of us hurt at any time. Did you tell Janey not to take unnecessary risks? Or anyone else for that matter?"

I'm not sure why but he's rubbing me the wrong way today. Perhaps I want him to admit he's singling me out, or maybe I'm secretly hoping he'll acknowledge I mean something more to him than just an employee.

All I know is, I'm frustrated.

The silence that follows drags on long enough for me to start regretting my outburst in front of everyone.

"Forget I said anything," I blurt out. "I'll be careful. I'm sorry, I need to go, I've got a call coming in."

I grab my silent phone, shoot Kate a warning glare, and walk out the back door.

So much for me being the steady one, the balanced one. I must sound like I'm losing my shit. If I don't get a grip, Jacob will have cause for concern.

I walk up to the fence where Buck is grazing the longer grass around the posts. Curious, he lifts his head and nudges the front of my shirt. The moment I lift my hand to stroke his soft nose, Murdoch comes trotting up, jealous of the attention.

"They're taking to you."

I turn to find Joey walking up. She's carrying an armful of hay and tosses it over the fence.

"I'm not so sure," I comment, watching the horses dive for the treat. "They may have just seen you coming." I tilt my head slightly. "How are you making out? First day and all that?"

"Still getting my feet wet. You have a beautiful property here though," the fresh-faced brunette compliments.

I feel like a virtual giant next to the five-foot-nothing woman.

"Yeah." I glance around at the views before turning back to her. "I really lucked out."

"I actually wanted to thank you for offering your guesthouse, but I'm quite used to sharing living space with men. It kinda comes with the territory. Plus, I grew up with four brothers."

"Wow, I can't even imagine what that must've been like. Still, I'd like to make sure you have your own bed and bathroom. The contractor should be here on Monday to start the work."

Joey grins. "I appreciate that. Especially the bathroom part."

She heads back for the barn and I turn toward the house where I see Kate hanging over the deck railing.

When I'm within range she calls out, "Feel better?"

I decide not to grace that with a response until she follows me into the kitchen.

"Much, thank you. Okay, what did I miss?"

"Nothing. Jacob wrapped it up lickety-split after you walked out. I think you rattled his cage," Kate suggests.

"Maybe I should apologize."

I pull my phone from my pocket but Kate stops me.

"Don't. Sometimes guys need to sit on it for a while."

Maybe, or maybe I should lead by example and get over this weird, virtual connection I have with Jacob. It's not healthy for either of us.

Mitch picked Kate up an hour or so ago. He was going to drop her off at home, pack himself a bag, and head out to Russell Springs to meet up with Janey.

Restless, I've been putzing around in the kitchen, cooking enough food for a couple of days, and getting my head right at the same time.

By the time Hamish gets back with the trailer, I am resolved to be open to possibilities.

"Everything go all right?" I ask, opening the door for him.

"Yup. Trailer's good to go, I just came back to drop it off. Before I go, I'm going to ask Joey to bring at least Buck inside tonight, since he's coming with us."

"You're leaving?"

I'm trying not to let disappointment show, but I'd really hoped he'd at least stay for dinner.

"I should probably head home; we've got an early day tomorrow."

He hangs his head a little, avoiding my eyes.

I shrug. "It just seems a little silly leaving now, only to

be back here at the crack of dawn. You're welcome to crash here."

Now he looks at me from under his eyebrows.

"Did you forget you have Joey in your guesthouse?"

I shake my head.

"No, but there are extra bedrooms and bathrooms on that side of the house. We wouldn't have to get in each other's way."

I lose a bit of my nerve when Hamish doesn't say anything, but stares at me intently.

"You know, it was just an idea. Of course you don't have anything with you. Never mind."

"Actually..." He lowers his eyes and seems to stare at his boots. "I always have a change of clothes in my gym bag in the truck."

I bite my cheek to keep from smiling.

Jacob

I must be out of my mind.

Or I will be, after spending the night here.

She threw me for a loop with her invitation. Talk about having a carrot dangled in front of your face. The house smelled amazing—she'd clearly been cooking—and there was something about the way she looked at me. I resisted the temptation and turned her down at first but, like an idiot, I folded like a wet suit, *after* she gave me an easy out.

"Let me guess, you'll be late again tonight?"

Christ, Bernie.

It's a good thing I love that woman.

"I won't be home at all," I share.

"Well, I'll be...it's about time."

Now she sounds absolutely giddy.

"Nothing, Bernie. We have to hit the road early tomorrow morning, so it makes sense I crash here."

"Okay, sure," she returns.

Her inflection makes it clear she's not buying it.

"Not sure what time I'll be home tomorrow but it'll likely be late."

"Don't rush home on my account," she chirps.

"Night, Bernie."

Ending the call, I grab my gym bag from the truck and head back inside.

I don't see her in the living room or kitchen, but there is light coming from one of the rooms off to my left. When I walk into the guest room, I find her making the bed.

She's struggling to get a fitted sheet on the mattress and doesn't seem to hear me coming in. I set my bag down and walk up to the bed to help her.

She startles and promptly lets go of the corner she was trying to stretch over the mattress.

"Oh my God. I didn't hear you come in."

"Sorry, I thought I'd give you a hand," I tell her, quickly adding, "Or better yet, I can take over. No need for you to do that."

"That's okay. If you could just hold on to that corner, it keeps slipping off."

"Sure."

This is a first. It's been a while since I've made a bed, and I've definitely never made a bed with a woman. It's strangely intimate. Or perhaps that's only because I'm doing it with Rajani, and this is coming uncomfortably close to one of my frequent fantasies.

Between us it takes no time at all to make the bed, and it teaches me something about her I didn't know. She's meticulous, making sure to brush out every crease.

"There are clean towels in the bathroom and I left a new toothbrush on the counter."

"Thanks. I appreciate all this."

She suddenly doesn't seem to know what to do with her hands, and nervously shoves them in her pockets. There's something about seeing the normally calm and contained woman unsettled and vulnerable. It makes me grateful for the bed between us, otherwise I might not be able to resist taking her in my arms.

"Right. I should get back to the kitchen. Dinner should be done in half an hour. There's beer in the fridge, help yourself." She's backing out of the room as she talks. "Whenever you're ready."

She almost backs into the door and, at the last minute, swings around and slips down the hallway.

I hit the bathroom, splash some water on my face, and sitting on the edge of the bed check my email. Killing time in hopes it'll diffuse some of the pull I feel, and I'm pretty sure I'm not alone.

Funny, I thought my scars could be a shield for me to hide behind but, as it turns out, after our initial meeting, Raj doesn't seem to see them anymore. It doesn't appear to matter whether I'm hiding behind a distorted voice on the phone, or a disfigured face, somehow, she feels the draw.

And now I'm hiding in the bedroom.

This is ridiculous.

I get to my feet, shove my phone in my pocket, and walk out of the bedroom.

She's stirring something at the stove and turns her head when I approach.

"Whatever that is, it smells amazing."

"Butter chicken, aloo gobi, and I'm just stirring the vegetable biryani."

She turns her attention back to the pan.

"That sounds like a lot of food," I observe.

"I had some time this afternoon, and it keeps well. Some of these dishes are pretty labor intensive so I make it worth my while and cook for a few meals." She flashes me a smile. "I'm about to dish out. Why don't you grab yourself a drink?"

I pull open the fridge and find a few bottles of a nice lager in the door.

"Can I get you something?"

"I'll have one of the ciders." She leans over and points at the top shelf. "Behind the eggs."

I set our drinks on the island and go in search of a glass for the cider, opening cupboards.

"Glasses are in here," she says, pointing at the one

beside her. "And could you grab spoons and forks from the drawer in the island?"

I grab a glass from the cupboard, and find the cutlery where she indicated. I'm suddenly aware how domestic this scene is. It should feel awkward, but it doesn't. It feels comfortable.

"Island or table?" I ask.

"Table."

I move the drinks, pour her cider, and place the cutlery where I think it belongs.

"Sit," she orders, walking up with two steaming plates.

She slides one in front of me.

"Eat."

She doesn't have to tell me twice. I dig in with fervor and the flavors explode in my mouth. This time it seems I'm the one unable to hold back the moans and groans.

Rajani is grinning when I take a sip of my beer and look over at her.

"Sorry," I mumble.

"Don't be. It's flattering to the cook."

"This really is amazing," I compliment her, shoving another bite in my mouth. "Bernie spoils me but this is fantastic."

First, I feel a distinct drop in temperature at the table, before I realize what I let slip.

"Bernie is my landlady," I quickly explain, sticking as close to the truth as I can. "She likes to cook for me, and since I'm hopeless in the kitchen, I don't object."

When she smiles, I know I pulled it off.

"Lucky guy."

"I know it, and even if I didn't, Bernie would not let me forget it."

That leads me to recount a few safe anecdotes while we eat, illustrating the kind of person Bernice is.

"You care for her," Raj observes as she shoves her empty plate aside.

"I do. She mothers me, it's nice. Haven't had a lot of that. She makes me laugh too."

It's too fucking easy to talk to her. If I don't watch it, I'll blow everything. I can't afford to.

For a moment she looks like she may probe me on my comment, but she goes a different route.

"Your landlady sounds like a card."

"She is," I agree.

I escaped that one as well, for now. Knowing Raj, she won't let it go. At some point she'll circle back to it.

Then I get to my feet and collect our dishes, carrying them to the sink, where I quickly rinse them. When I turn around, I almost run into Rajani who is carrying our empties.

"Sorry, the recycling is in the cupboard under the sink."

I step aside so she can get in there, but that's as far as I move. As she straightens, I put a hand on her shoulder.

Her eyes lock on mine and I watch as her pupils dilate. Slowly her hand comes up to rest on my chest.

With my other hand I cup the side of her face.

"Stop me."

She shakes her head and presses herself against me.

I'm not sure what is driving me, but if this is all going to blow up in my face, I'll take this one memory.

Her lips are soft under mine, yielding when I slick my tongue along the seam. I love her mouth; sweet and rich with a hint of spice. For a few moments I lose myself in the kiss. I file everything to memory: her taste, the silk of her hair brushing my hand, her curves, the soft moans, and her fingers clutching my shirt.

It wouldn't take much to move this from the kitchen to the couch or a bedroom, but I can't do that to her. She deserves to know who she's sharing herself with.

With almost superhuman strength, I release her mouth and take a step back. I brush my thumb over her swollen lips and take in her flushed color.

Gorgeous.

"Thank you," I whisper before walking out of the kitchen.

I look over my shoulder when I'm across the living room. She's still standing in the same spot, a somewhat confused look on her face.

"Night, Onyx. I'll see you tomorrow morning."

FOURTEEN

JACOB

One of the worst nights of sleep I've had in a long time.

Mainly because I couldn't stop replaying that kiss in my mind. Over and over again. I finally gave up and hopped in the shower around four this morning. Since then, I've been doing some work on my phone, mainly poring over satellite images of Grandview Estate to get a feel of the place.

What makes it a bit challenging is that parts of the property are fairly densely treed. I can make out most of the driveway, which is rather curvy, to the point where the trees end and it opens up with meadows on either side of the drive leading to the main lodge. The stables and corral are easy to identify, but the guest cabins are difficult to spot under the tree cover.

On the digital blueprints my lawyer was able to

obtain, you could see what the property looked like when it was built. It helps to give a bit of an idea where each building is, but there's no guarantee modifications or additions haven't been made. I wish I had my damn laptop, at least I'd be able to put the satellite image and the blueprints side by side on the screen to make it a little easier.

By five fifteen the battery on my phone is almost drained, so I turn off my data. I can charge it in the truck. I shove yesterday's clothes in my bag, straighten the bed, and go in search of some coffee.

Tossing my bag by the front door, I head for the kitchen. I watched Raj make coffee before, so I know where she keeps the beans. I'm guessing at the quantity I need for a pot, but figure better too many than too few.

The grinder makes a hell of a lot of noise, but since we have to leave in forty-five minutes, I'm not too worried about waking Raj. She probably should be getting up anyway.

I'm just pouring some fresh brew in one of the travel mugs I found in her cupboards, when Raj walks in. I can feel her eyes on my back.

"Morning," she says, leaning an elbow on the counter and grinning up at me.

She's in a far better mood than I expected after blowing her off last night.

"Morning to you. Here..." I shove the mug in her direction and grab another from the cupboard.

"I see you've made yourself at home in my kitchen," she observes. "I think I approve, if it means I have fresh coffee waiting for me."

I glance over at her.

"You know you can get coffee makers that work on a timer, right?"

She rolls her eyes and bumps me aside with her hip, as she reaches for the sugar pot.

"That would mean I don't get freshly ground coffee."

She studies me over the rim of her mug as she takes a sip.

"What?" I ask, a little uneasy under her scrutiny.

She lowers her mug.

"You look a little rough."

I bark out a laugh. "You just noticed now?"

"I'm talking about your eyes. They look tired. Didn't sleep well?"

"Restless."

"Ah, I'm sorry." The little smile tugging at her mouth implies she's not. "I slept like a baby myself," she adds with a shrug.

I'll be damned if she isn't making fun of me.

"Good. I'm glad," I mutter.

She's already opening the fridge when she asks, "Would you like some toast? A yogurt? I can make a quick breakfast burrito too. It'll only take me ten minutes."

I glance at the clock. It's twenty to six.

"If you don't mind making them. I'll hook up the trailer and load Buck in the meantime. That way we're ready to go."

"No, I don't mind."

She stops me, grabbing my arm when I walk past her. Then she hooks the other hand around my neck, goes up on her toes, and kisses me full on the mouth. Before I can wrap my arms around her, she ends the kiss and steps out of reach with a smile.

"See you in a bit."

Then she turns her back and begins pulling stuff from the fridge.

It takes a second for my legs to work, but the moment they do I hustle outside.

What the hell was that?

I was not expecting that kiss, and now I'm starting to think I put something in motion last night that may not be so easy to put a halt to. At this point I don't even know if I want to.

I get in the truck and back it down the drive to where I parked the trailer in front of the stables. When I get out, Joey is already walking up.

"Morning."

"Hey. Would you mind giving me a hand hooking up the trailer?"

"Sure."

With her help it doesn't take much time at all to hook it up.

"Want me to load some hay in the back of your truck?" she asks.

"I can do that. If you wouldn't mind getting Buck ready?"

Ten minutes later, I pull the trailer up to the house. Raj is already waiting outside, her backpack slung over her shoulder, a grocery tote in one hand, and the travel mugs in the other.

"I thought we'd eat on the road," she suggests as she hands me the coffees before getting in the passenger seat. "I wrapped the burritos so we don't make a mess."

"Sounds good to me."

Even if we don't encounter any slowdowns on the way, it'll still take us the better part of three hours, if not more, to get to Russell Springs. The sooner we can get on the road, the better it is.

I wait for her to buckle in before I pull away from the farm.

I'm afraid this three-hour trip is going to feel a whole lot longer than our drive to Bowling Green last week. I can't afford to let down my guard though. Like I said to Bernie, we are so close, I can taste it. I'm going to have to put last night's kiss, but even more so this morning's, out of my mind.

Onyx

I can feel the tension radiating from him.

Maybe I shouldn't have teased him with that kiss this morning, but he was being a tease last night, leaving me hanging.

There had been an intensity to his kiss, a sense of desperation. Initially, I thought perhaps it had been a while for him—hell, it had been a hell of a long time for me too—but then it occurred to me he could have been careful with me because of my history.

Either way, that kiss was something else.

I haven't been a nun all these years, but there's a reason I've kept any encounters to a purely physical level. Without emotional investment, I don't risk making myself vulnerable. For that same reason, kissing is something I've tried to avoid. To me, kissing is infinitely more intimate than straightforward sex is.

I let Hamish kiss me all the same. In fact, I was more than ready for him to. I'd have been ready for more too, except that's when he put the brakes on.

But I'm good with taking things slow. I think it says a lot about him, and the way he sees me.

Still, I feel a hint of guilt, even though I don't think I've done anything wrong. Jacob had every opportunity over the past years to make a move. He held all the cards but never made an effort.

"We're about to drive through Somerset. Do you need me to make a stop?" Hamish asks.

I actually could use a bathroom stop. I shouldn't have had all that coffee and it's been a long drive. Plus, if I'm honest, I'm nervous. My palms are sweating.

"Will we make it in time?" I check with Hamish.

"Close enough."

We stop at a Marathon gas station just outside the city limits. I hustle inside, do my business, and check the cooler for a couple of bottles of water. My eye is drawn to these individually wrapped glasses of white wine. I wouldn't mind tossing back one or two of those for courage.

When I get back to the truck, I hand Hamish a bottle of water.

"I don't know how long we'll be there and how hospitable they are, so I brought you a water. Hope that's okay."

"Water's fine, thanks."

As he gets back on the road, I twist the cap off my bottle and put it to my mouth. I'm chugging it down when I feel his eyes on me.

"Easy. If we have to make another pee stop, we definitely won't make it in time," he points out.

"I should've bought that wine," I grumble, putting the cap back on the bottle and dropping it in the center console.

"Nervous?"

I open my mouth to deny it, but think better of it.

"A little."

He reaches over and gives my hand a squeeze.

"We're picking up a horse, that's all."

I'm about to tell him it's not that simple when my phone rings. It's Janey.

"Where are you?" she asks when I answer.

"Just coming through Somerset. We've got another..."

I glance over at Hamish.

"Thirty minutes," he fills in.

"Thirty minutes," I echo to Janey.

"Good, that gives me time to try and get closer to the lodge. Mitch has an eye on the gate. He'll keep track of comings and goings. I'll keep an eye on you. Text only from here on out."

"Gotcha," I confirm, but she already ended the call.

We'd briefly discussed me wearing an earpiece but decided against it. The risks outweigh the benefits in these circumstances.

The remainder of the drive, I try to regulate my breathing so I don't puke all over Hamish's truck. I barely pay attention to the landscape until Hamish slows down and turns left onto a paved driveway, where he has to stop at an intimidating gate.

A couple of cameras are mounted on both stone gateposts aimed at us on either side. I resist looking around to see if I can spot Mitch and focus instead on the small speaker attached to a steel post on the driver's side.

"Names please?"

"Onyx Baqri and Hamish Adrian."

The gates start swinging open, and Hamish slowly advances until there is enough room for us to go through. The road up ahead curves to the right and disappears into the trees. We can't see anything beyond the trees from here.

"How long is this driveway?" I ask.

"The property spans the entire peninsula, and this is the only road going to the actual lodge, which is located on the tip. So a fair stretch, I'd say three quarters of a mile."

I send him a surprised look.

"You've done your homework," I observe.

He shrugs his shoulders. "I prefer getting a lay of the land so I know what I'm getting into."

Sounds like something someone with a military background might feel the need to do. It would fit with Jacob's brothers-in-arms comment.

Which reminds me, I haven't heard from Jacob this morning, which is kind of unusual. I would've expected a good luck call, or even last-minute instructions.

"Has Jacob been in touch with you at all?" I ask Hamish.

"Just a message last night. Hey, look."

He points up ahead where the trees make way for open fields. On the other side, up on a rise, an imposing lodge comes into view. The entire building appears to have been constructed with massive logs.

"Wow," escapes me.

"Not too shabby," Hamish rumbles.

Only now do I notice the outbuildings to the left of the lodge. There's a horse in the corral or paddock in front of what I'm guessing are the stables, and two men leaning on the fencing, their heads turned in our direction.

"Is that Doyle?" I ask.

"Looks like it."

The agent is not wearing a suit this time, and instead has opted for dark jeans, an ornately embroidered western shirt, and boots that look like they're polished daily. His version of casual, I guess.

The fellow beside him looks a bit more relaxed, more at home in this environment. I wonder if that could be the vet. The man remains where he is, while Doyle walks toward us, waving us to a parking space beside the stables where two other horse trailers are parked.

Hamish has barely turned off the engine when my door is ripped open and Doyle sticks his head in.

"Ms. Baqri, what an absolute pleasure."

"Hello, Mr. Doyle, if you'd give me a minute, I can gather my things and get out."

That appears to fluster him as he backs away from the door. Good. I dislike people getting in my space uninvited. Well, I particularly dislike the agent crowding me.

"Nice slap on the hand," Hamish shares under his breath.

While I tuck my water bottle in my backpack, he's already out of the truck and rounding the hood. As I get out of the vehicle, I notice him greeting Doyle.

"I hope your drive was smooth?" the agent asks, turning to me.

"Very uneventful, thank you."

"Excellent. If you'd allow, I'd like to introduce you to Brian Haley, Arion's Moon's trainer." He turns to Hamish. "Of course, I mean former trainer."

Hamish says nothing, so I jump in with, "We'd love to meet him."

Doyle leads the way to where the other man is leaning against the enclosure, watching our approach.

"Ms. Baqri, I'd like you to meet Brian Haley, head trainer here at Grandview Estate."

"Nice to meet you."

I take Haley's offered hand.

"Nice to meet you as well," I echo before stepping

aside and indicating Hamish. "And this is Hamish Adrian, he will be working with Arion's Moon at Four Oaks."

The trainer narrow's his eyes on the man by my side.

"Adrian? You've gotta be shitting me."

He grabs Hamish's hand and starts pumping it furiously.

Wait a minute, they know each other? I glance at Hamish, who looks a little like a deer in headlights. Why wouldn't he have mentioned something? It's not like Haley's name hadn't come up.

"Damn, man. I was sorry to hear about the accident. It really did a number on you, didn't it?"

Hamish grunts an inaudible response, and darts a glance my way.

What the hell is going on?

FIFTEEN

Jacob

Fuck.

I screwed up. I asked Hamish whether he knew Morton Ackers, but never bothered asking him if he knew the damn trainer.

What are the odds?

Hamish and I are similar in build and even looks, or at least we used to be. Back in the day our commander frequently mistook one of us for the other. I'd gambled that, given Hamish has worked in Canada for fifteen years, and even I have a hard time recognizing myself, I could get away with impersonating him.

I hadn't counted on coming face-to-face with someone who actually spent time with him.

I think I managed to duck and weave my way through the rehashing of an apparent shared time at a training facility near Pocatello, Idaho. I don't think I've ever even been in Idaho. I probably came off as an asshole, which is preferable to being pegged as a fake.

But an even bigger problem is Rajani, and the confused looks she's sending my way. To her credit, she hasn't questioned me out loud, but I'm sure once we're alone, I'll be in the hot seat.

I trail behind as Doyle shows Raj around the stables in a somewhat proprietary way. Other than Arion's Moon, there are three more thoroughbreds in the stables. One is Pure Delight, and the other two I'm not familiar with, but according to Doyle those are owned by Pegasus GLAN as well, and considered up-and-comers on the track.

The facilities are impressive. Clean—kept that way by several stable hands we encounter—modern, outfitted with climate control, and with a high-end, close-circuit security system that allows the monitoring of every individual stall.

It must've cost a sweet penny, and the agent is showing it off with the pride of an owner. It seems a bit excessive for someone only doing a job.

"Oh wow," Raj comments on the view when we step out the rear doors.

We're at a bit of an elevation, overlooking an inlet of Lake Cumberland. It's a beautiful spot, but looking over at the lodge, which sits at a slightly higher level, I bet the view is even better.

"What are those buildings over there?" Raj asks, pointing in the opposite direction.

To the left of us the shore juts out slightly, and

tucked back into the tree line three cabins are visible. The satellite images I reviewed showed partial roofs of several structures, mostly hidden in the trees. None of those were part of the original layout of Grandview Estate.

"Those are guest cabins," Doyle answers readily. "I believe there are six in total."

"Wow," Raj reacts. "Guess the owner entertains a lot."

"I'm not sure but I would assume so."

I make a mental note of the cabins' location. It might be worth sending up a drone later. Or, even better, if Janey found a covert route onto the property, she might be able to use that to get in under cover of night, and set up some minicams so we can monitor traffic in and around those cabins.

The agent leads us around the side of the stables, to show us an entire row of outside stalls.

"These are for the trail horses," he explains, when Raj walks up to one of the half doors and pokes her head inside. "They're out in the field right now."

Raj turns around and leans her back against the stall door.

"I meant to ask you; will I have a chance to meet the owner? I think I just missed him last week at the auction. You did say he was there, right?"

I notice Doyle's eyes darting to the front of the stables.

"He briefly popped in, yes," he confirms. "Unfortunately, I think he's out of town. I haven't seen him this morning."

"Ah, that's too bad," she tells him with a regretful smile. "Maybe I'll have another opportunity."

Damn. I would've loved a chance to face that sick bastard.

We head back to where Brian Haley is keeping an eye on the horse being exercised on a lunge line inside the corral.

"That's enough, Derrick," he calls out at the young guy in the ring. "Take him inside."

Then he turns to us.

"Didn't you have a vet coming?"

I glance at my watch, it's after ten already.

"Yeah. Let me see what's keeping him."

Taking my phone from my pocket, I turn my back and walk a few feet away. When I look at my screen, I see he left me a message.

"It looks like he's stuck behind an accident," I announce when I rejoin the group. "He'll get here as soon as he can."

"That's unfortunate, but these things can happen," the slimy agent volunteers. "Ms. Baqri, could I offer you some refreshments at the lodge while we wait?"

Raj throws me a look and then turns a smile to Doyle.

"That would be lovely."

The agent leads the way and I'm about to follow when Haley calls my name.

"How about you and I use the time to get Moon acquainted with that pony you brought? We can introduce them in the paddock."

I catch sight of Rajani, who is already halfway to the

lodge. I'm not sure how I feel about her going in there alone, but it doesn't seem I have much choice.

"Sounds good," I tell Haley. "I'll go grab him."

Buck doesn't give me any trouble and backs right out of the trailer. He seems glad to be out and I walk him over to a trough of water on the side of the barn to let him have a drink.

He lifts his head when Haley walks out with the spirited Arion's Moon on the lead. I wait until the trainer releases the filly in the corral before I walk the Paint over to the enclosure. Moon neighs softly when she notices Buck standing near the gate. Her nostrils flare and her ears are on alert, pointed forward, and her tail is held high. The only thing moving on her body is an occasional twitch of a muscle on her flank.

Buck bobs his head a few times before stretching out his neck over the railing.

"Let her come to him," Haley suggests.

That's what I thought I was doing, but I'm not getting into a pissing match with a guy who's supposed to know me. I just wish the horse would get on with it. I'd like to go find out where Raj disappeared to.

Finally, the filly lowers her head and stretches her own neck, sniffing the air. When Buck snorts softly, Moon takes a step closer, and then another and another, until they're nose to nose.

"Why don't you let him in."

I unclip the lead from Buck's halter as Haley lifts the latch of the gate. When he carefully moves it back enough, I let Buck into the enclosure. At first the filly seems agitated, but when the Paint calmly begins to walk the inside perimeter, she eventually falls into step with him.

"They're fine," he states.

Then he grabs an armful of hay from a wheelbarrow on the side of the corral and tosses it inside. In no time both horses are side by side, munching away.

"I think Moon will do better with the vet if we leave him in here."

"Sounds good to me."

"Come," he says, lightly slapping my shoulder. "Let's join them inside for a cup of coffee. You don't want to leave any woman alone with Doyle too long. He's a weird guy."

I turn on my heel and start marching toward the lodge, Haley keeps up.

"So, you've had enough of Canada? I thought you went and married a Canadian?"

"We're no longer together. She had a hard time dealing with this."

I indicate my face and silently apologize profusely to Hamish's wife.

The woman is as close to a saint as you can get. There's no way she would leave her husband, who's been wheelchair-bound since the fire. Something he didn't want to advertise. Of course that worked out for me.

The only burns Hamish has are on his butt and legs. A fire had broken out in the hayloft, and he was getting the horses out of the stable when a burning beam came down and landed on his lumbar spine, pinning him to the ground. A couple of guys got the beam off him and dragged him out of the barn, but the damage to his spine was already done.

"Shit, I'm sorry. That's harsh."

"You're telling me."

He opens the door for me and leads me through the massive foyer, past the open door of a kitchen, to a living room at the rear of the lodge with views of Cumberland Lake. I was right, the view is even better from here.

Oliver Doyle is standing outside on the large patio, a phone to his ear.

Rajani is nowhere to be seen.

Onyx

I feel I need a shower.

I sat through twenty minutes of Oliver Doyle self-important babble. It's clear he's looking to score a new client, making sure I understand he will represent clients both in the sale *and* purchase of horses.

The entire time I had difficulty keeping my attention on him, my mind kept on drifting to Hamish, and the fact he never mentioned knowing Brian Haley. He'd actually looked rattled when Haley mentioned his name. I'm not quite sure what is going on, but it'll have to wait until we leave and I can ask him what that was about.

I had to get my focus back where it belonged, and tried getting more information on Ackers. The only thing I managed to get out of the agent was Ackers apparently does not have a family and lives here alone.

When his phone rang, I jumped at the opportunity. He apologized and told me he had to take it, and I quickly asked directions to the bathroom. Already distracted by the call, he waved in the general direction of the hallway as he stepped out on the back patio.

Seeing as he only gave me a general direction, I feel I have an excuse to check behind a few closed doors. I've seen at least three of those on the right side of the foyer. One is a set of French doors to what looks to be a library, but the other two are regular doors.

Behind the central staircase there's a hallway going in each direction. The living room and kitchen are at the rear, a formal dining room right across the hall, all on the left side of the house. I have no idea what rooms are to the right.

My guess would be the powder room is behind one of the doors in the foyer, so I save that for last. Instead, I move down the long hallway to the other side of the house.

My first stop is a pair of French doors to my left. They open up into some type of conservatory with glass walls and roof, letting in bright sunlight. I can't see the entire width of the room so, after checking both sides of the hallway, I carefully open a door and poke my head inside. Despite the modern steel and leather furniture, the room has a tropical feel, with large-leafed plants softening the overall look. Nothing that tells me more about the lodge's owner.

I ease the door shut and move on to the next one, revealing dark wood paneling on the walls and a large pool table under a pair of drop lights in the center of the room. I close that door too.

This brings me to the double doors at the end of the hall. My guess would be this is a study. I'd love to have a peek inside, but the problem is, if someone sees me, I can hardly claim to be looking for a powder room behind a set of double doors. Regretfully, I have to give them a pass.

Two more doors left, one appears to be a supply closet, and I'm just opening the second door when I hear a voice in the foyer, followed by footsteps and the closing of a door. Panicked, I duck into the pitch-black room and pull the door almost shut. Only a narrow crack remains and I can just see the French doors through the opening, but nothing beyond that.

The scent of laundry detergent indicates I'm likely hiding in the laundry room, and I hope to God no one is looking to run a load. To my relief, I can hear the footsteps heading the opposite way, and wait for a minute before slipping back into the hallway.

My heart is racing and I'm hyperalert as I make my way to the foyer. At this point I actually do need the bathroom.

The first door I encounter opens up to a stairway to a basement. A faint red glow can be seen at the bottom and I quickly close it again.

Only one door left, and I quickly duck into the powder room.

I take my time using the facilities to give my heart a chance to get back in a normal rhythm. I check my face in the ornate mirror and a flush of color still stains my cheeks, but there's nothing I can do about that.

I'm about to step out of the bathroom when I hear a set of footsteps walking down the hallway. I wait a moment until they fade, and step into the foyer. I'm about to round the back of the stairway when I hear voices from the far end of the hallway on the right.

When I recognize Wheeler's—or Morton Ackers's—voice, I stop in my tracks and listen.

"...*the hell do you mean?*"

"*I don't think he's who he says he is.*"

That's the trainer speaking, and I know instantly who he's talking about.

"*Why is that?*"

I clearly hear the click of a door closing and I peek around the corner to confirm no one is in the hallway anymore. Then I dart around the staircase and rush down the hallway to the living room.

The first person I see walking in is Hamish.

Or whoever he is.

SIXTEEN

JACOB

Something is definitely wrong.

She has not looked me in the eye for the past hour.

I follow Brian Haley outside where the vet is just driving up in his truck. I'm glad he's finally here. I just want to get Raj away from this place—find out what is up with her—the sooner the better.

"Call me Rob," the vet introduces himself.

He's a younger guy, but doesn't seem to be lacking for confidence. He casually takes charge, ordering Haley and me to tie up both horses. Moon, inside the corral, while I lead Buck around the outside, tying him up so the horses' heads are together but the fence separates their bodies.

The filly is surprisingly relaxed as Rob thoroughly examines her. At some point Raj comes outside, walks up to the corral, but stays on the other side of Buck, and watches what the vet is doing.

Sometime later he asks Haley to lead Arion's Moon around the corral, while he observes. Then he instructs the trainer to bring her into the stable so he can take some X-rays. He goes to his truck and pulls a large, silver, over-sized suitcase from the back and carries it inside.

When they disappear inside, I lean over Buck's shoulder and glance at Rajani.

"Talk to me."

She keeps her eyes averted and shakes her head.

"Not now."

She pushes away from the enclosure and begins to walk past the stables to where a path leads into the trees beyond. I don't know whether I should go after her or whether it's better to leave her alone. Probably the latter, but it may not be safe having her traipse around here by herself. I'm about to follow her when Oliver Doyle comes walking from the direction of the house. I hadn't even realized he was missing.

"Where is everyone?" he wants to know.

"Taking X-rays of the horse in the stable, and Ms. Baqri went for a walk."

He pulls up a carefully manicured eyebrow. "A walk?" Then he looks around. "Where did she go?"

I point in the direction she disappeared, and he immediately rushes after her. They return a few minutes later, at the same time the stable doors open and the trainer leads the horse back outside. The vet is right behind him and leaves his suitcase next to his truck before walking in this direction.

"Give me a minute to review these X-rays," he addresses me. "But everything else so far looks good."

"I'll go wait in the truck," Raj announces, after Rob returns to his vehicle.

I watch her go, knowing we'll have an interesting drive back to Four Oaks. The one good thing is she'll be stuck in the truck with me. If this is coming to a head, I'll at least have an opportunity to explain.

I hope.

Half an hour later, we make our way down the long driveway, Buck and Arion's Moon in the trailer we're pulling. Raj is silent beside me, and I don't have the heart to say anything. I'd do anything to avoid the conversation I know is inevitable, so like a coward I keep my mouth shut.

It's not until we pass through Russell Springs, she breaks the silence.

"Wheeler was at the lodge."

It takes me a second to realize what she's saying, and when it hits, I almost swerve off the road.

"What? You saw him?"

"Heard him talking to someone. He was in an office all the way down the hall at the other side of the house."

"Jesus, tell me you weren't snooping around."

She finally darts me a glance, an impassive look on her face.

"Okay. Then I won't."

The knuckles of my hands on the wheel turn white, I'm squeezing so damn hard. The thought of her poking around with Wheeler in the house sends chills down my spine.

"Who was he talking to?"

"He was talking to Brian Haley." She pauses for a moment before she adds, "About you."

Oh shit.

"At first, I wondered why you wouldn't have mentioned knowing Haley before. Then it occurred to me you seemed as taken aback as I was, which would imply *you* didn't know him. Which was underlined when I heard Haley say he doubted you were actually Hamish Adrian."

"Onyx..."

She shakes her head sharply.

"No. I'm not done, Ha—" She waves her hand in front of her face. "I don't even know what to call you."

She turns to me with tears in her eyes, and I immediately look for a place to pull off.

"I don't want you to stop," she says, guessing my intentions. "Keep driving."

"Okay."

I don't say anything else, giving her a chance to finish what she wants to say. She seems to need to compose herself, making me feel even more like a fucking bastard than I already do, but I wait while she stares out of the window.

"I would've slept with you last night. Jesus...I kissed you. Do you know how messed up that is?" she finally shares.

"Raj..."

She twists in her seat to look at me.

"I struggled. I was torn, being drawn to you felt like a betrayal." She barks out a harsh laugh. "And all the time I was being betrayed. How's that for irony?"

"Rajani...I never meant—"

"Who is Hamish Adrian, Jacob?" she interrupts me.

There's a rest stop coming up and I turn off the highway and find a quiet spot at the back of the parking lot. Then I undo my seat belt and shift in my seat so we're face-to-face.

"Hamish Adrian is a horse trainer in Ontario, Canada, who was injured in a barn fire a couple of years ago. He's also a good friend and brother-in-arms, who gave me permission to use his identity in an important case."

"Glad to know you didn't lie about everything," she scoffs.

"That kiss wasn't a lie. The way I feel about you isn't a lie. What I told you about Bernice wasn't a lie, although she's not my landlady, but manages my house. And for the record, I absolutely hated every lie I did tell you."

She huffs.

"Then why the subterfuge? For more than three years you've been hiding behind technology. But you can show yourself pretending to be someone else? I don't get it. I really don't."

And I don't know how to explain it to her. Not yet. Not until the job is done.

"It was the only way I could get close to you. The only way for me to protect you."

"Then why assign me this job in the first place?"

She throws her hands up in frustration and turns away from me, aiming her eyes out the window, mumbling.

"Jesus, this is crazy, I feel like I've been betrayed by two of you."

Onyx

"I assigned it to you because you were the best possible choice for this particular job."

In other words, he doesn't care to explain. A managerial brush-off if ever I heard one.

I have so many questions, I don't even know where to start.

Actually, I do.

"Would you drive, please? We're wasting time sitting on the side of the road."

Just take me home, where I can hide out with my thoughts.

I feel his eyes on me before he finally pulls out of the parking lot.

"How do you know so much?" I finally ask, adding, "About us, I mean: Kate, Janey, and me. Where do you get your information? Why hire us specifically? Did you live at Transition House? Did you know someone there?"

I snap my head around at him when he doesn't answer. His eyes are fixed forward and his jaw is clenched. When he glances over at me, I recognize regret in his eyes. I don't want to see it, I'm too angry right now, but it's there.

"I promise you, all those questions I will answer...*after* we find a way to take down Wheeler."

"Why not now?" I persist.

He shakes his head. "There's a good reason for that, trust me."

I bark out a harsh laugh.

"Trust you? That's rich."

I focus on the landscape whizzing by outside the truck, nurturing my anger so I don't break down and cry. At least he has the sense to stay quiet as well.

I'm overwhelmed with thoughts and conflicting emotions. How is it possible I am so angry and still feel a sense of relief? Don't get me wrong, the betrayal cuts deep, but I'm starting to understand how it's possible I fell for someone I thought was a stranger as fast as I did. I already knew and was drawn to him; I just wasn't aware of it.

"What about the scars?" I suddenly wonder out loud. "If you weren't in that barn fire, how did you get your burns?"

When I turn my head, I just catch him touching a hand to his face.

"Fifteen years ago, my unit was part of a convoy in

Afghanistan when we were attacked. Hamish and I were lucky. The two of us ended up in a military hospital in Germany."

My hand is pressed against my chest. There is so much more in that response than a simple answer. I'm still trying to come up with something appropriate to say, when he offers more information.

"It's where I met Bernie. She was an army nurse, close to retirement, and spent a lot of dark nights next to my bed. We stayed in touch and she's had my back ever since."

Again, I'm learning a lot more about Jacob than I ever have, and my anger fades under a wave of empathy.

"I'm sorry that happened to you," I state softly.

"I'm not telling you this for pity," he returns immediately, sounding annoyed.

"Who said anything about pity?" I fire back. "I'm expressing empathy for someone I care about. That's not pity."

Silence returns, each of us lost in our own thoughts, but this time it's him speaking first.

"You care about me? Still?"

I glare at him.

"Really? I'm too pissed to answer that right now."

This time, neither of us says anything until we pull into the driveway to the farm.

"Can you drop me off?" I ask him.

"Sure."

He brings the truck to a halt when we get to the

house. I'm in the process of getting out when his voice stops me.

"I realize this may be too big an ask, but I hope you can keep this to yourself for now."

I turn around.

"Why?"

"I don't want to distract the team. I can't risk anything impacting the investigation. We need everyone sharp."

I want to argue. I want to lash out, but knowing my sisters of the heart, they would be upset, not only on their own behalf but on mine as well. It's quite possible it would affect their focus.

"Fine," I reluctantly agree, getting out of the truck.

"Thank you. And, Rajani?"

I pause with the door in my hand and glance at him.

"I'm sorry you had to find out this way. Not that it makes a difference, but I fully intended to tell you every-thing once Wheeler was taken care of."

He's right, at this moment it doesn't change anything, but I actually do believe him. That doesn't stop me from being hurt and feeling like a fool.

He leans his upper body over the center console. "And for the record, I was awake all last night imagining you right there in bed with me."

I'm not going to pretend his words don't have an impact. The blush burning my cheeks would make a liar out of me. Still, I shut the door and walk toward the house, hearing the truck begin to roll toward the stables behind me.

Once inside, I head straight for my en suite bathroom

and run myself a bath. While it fills, I go pour myself a generous glass of wine and set it on the edge of the tub while I strip. Then I add bath oil to the water and get in, grabbing my glass as I lean back.

Funny, I'm usually the one my friends come to for a friendly ear, but now I could use one, I'm not able to call on them. Unfortunately, it leaves me alone with my thoughts and a host of emotions, making me vulnerable to memories I normally keep carefully contained.

I close my eyes against the burning, but it's useless, the tears fall anyway. It's as if old trauma and buried grief create a painful vacuum in my chest. Before I have a chance to stop myself, I begin sobbing uncontrollably.

The lid on my vault of memories seems to have come off and there doesn't seem to be any way to hold the flow back, so I just let them come.

I'm seventeen again, full of hope one moment and paralyzed by terror the next. We were defenseless, our hands tied with the threat of harm to those we cared about. Puppets for him to play out his sick, perverted fantasies.

I remember Nathan whispering to me urgently, telling me to look in his eyes to the exclusion of anything else happening. I held his steady gaze, his face impassive but pain undeniable in his eyes at the ultimate violation.

We'd held out, vowing to wait until after we were free. What should have been a pure and special experience was defiled by David Wheeler. Then with my eyes still holding Nathan's, he was pulled off me and told by Wheeler if he resisted that I would pay the price. He told me if I caused any more trouble, I'd only make life harder for the younger girls.

As Nathan pulled up his pants, he promised me he'd find a way to come for me and the girls, before walking outside as Wheeler ordered. I got off the kitchen table and watched through the window over the sink, as Nathan was forced into the trunk of a car. I hung on to his promise after the car drove off, and cleaned myself up as best I could at the kitchen sink. Then I went back upstairs to the dorm room where I'd left Kate and Janey sleeping, my heart cracked and my dreams squashed.

Three days later, during mealtime, Dr. Sladky announced Nathan had died in an unfortunate accident.

My hope died right along with him.

SEVENTEEN

JACOB

It's been a hellish couple of days.

Giving Rajani space, I've kept my distance from the house. Of course, by my own design I'm forced to keep up the ruse of trainer, and have shown up at the stable every day. Mostly I've let Joey take Arion's Moon through her paces, but I'm in no way, shape, or form qualified to handle this horse. Not even with Hamish on speed dial.

I've also been keeping an eye on construction at the staff quarters, which started yesterday. Raj insisted we need a separate bedroom and bathroom for Joey, which I'm more than happy to accommodate. The sooner construction is done, the sooner Joey can move out of the guest quarters.

I've been toying with an idea, which would require use of the guesthouse. Not for me, but I'm hoping to entice Hamish and Laura to move down here once this case is over. He hasn't worked since his accident and seems convinced his training days are over, but I don't think the fact he's in a wheelchair has to keep him from doing the job he loves. It simply requires creative thinking and perhaps some practical modifications.

The trick will be to be able to show him what is possible, rather than just tell him. All he sees at this point are his limitations instead of his potential. He and Bernie pulled me from a place where I believed I no longer had purpose; I want to return the favor.

Of course, none of that is going to happen until I've done what I set out to do. And until I've come clean with Rajani, and the rest of the team.

"Moon needs to be reshod and earlier I noticed one of Murdoch's shoes is loose. We should get a farrier in," Joey announces when she dismounts the filly.

I guess I'm adding a farrier to my list. Already on there is find a local vet, one who has experience with racehorses.

"I'll get on it. In fact, I'll do it right now."

I walk to the stables where I parked my truck. It is serving as my office for the time being. I get in the passenger side and set my laptop on my knees. I find a farrier located in Dry Ridge, where Opal and Mitch live. His website quotes having worked with one or two well-known racing stables. I leave a message for him.

I'm about to call Rob Sutter, the vet who helped us in Russell Springs, to see if he can refer someone more local to us, when an alert on my phone warns me it's time for the conference call I set up with the team.

I'm eager to learn if we've made any progress. Mitch, Pearl, and Lee are still in the Russell Springs area. Lee is looking to see what information he can get from the locals and following up with the trainer, while Mitch and Pearl are keeping an eye on what is going on at Grandview. Opal is holding down the fort at the office and patching everyone into the call.

"Everyone here?" I start.

"I'm waiting for Janey," Opal indicates.

I persist in identifying the women by their code name, enforcing a distance I feel is still necessary. That distance is already breached with Raj—the proverbial cat is out of the bag—and it feels almost disingenuous to think of her as Onyx now.

"She should be here any minute," Mitch volunteers. "She was just printing something out."

"Lee, can you get us up to speed? I know you didn't have much luck with the trainer, but were you able to get something from the locals?

"A few things. I spoke to the owner of a cabin rental place a few miles up the road, who says he has noticed a large catering truck, a Lexington company, go through the gate onto the property. He says he's seen the truck a couple of times since."

"Check with caterers in Lexington, see if any will confirm having worked at Grandview Estate. If you can't get someone to talk, get a picture of the catering trucks. See if the neighbor recognizes one of them."

"That was the plan," Lee states dryly.

Right. I have to remember this kind of investigating is his bread and butter. Also, there's a reason he chooses to work as an independent, he's not a fan of getting bossed around. Something I do well.

"I'll leave that to you, then. And Olson? Anything there?"

"He has an appearance in front of Circuit Court Judge Severino this coming Friday. Rosenberg must be pulling some strings to get him on Judge Severino's docket this fast."

"Whoever's paying must be in a hurry to get Olson out," I observe.

"GLAN Investments," Pearl's voice comes in. "I just pulled the law firm's financials."

"Jesus, Janey," Raj pipes up.

My eyes are instantly drawn to the back of the house, where I see her standing behind the glass sliding doors, her phone to her ear. I swear I can feel her eyes on me.

"What?" Pearl reacts.

"Onyx means you're taking risks," Lee pipes up, sounding pretty annoyed himself.

"Not really. I had to look back a few years but I thought the name of the firm sounded familiar. I set up their cybersecurity in 2014, so it wasn't too hard for me to circumvent."

"Good work. That's the connection we were looking for."

"Is it?" Raj questions, her eyes aimed directly at me. "It still doesn't explain Wheeler's interest in Olson."

"True. Did we ever do a background check on Olson? Where he's from, his parents, family?"

"I did," Pearl volunteers. "But there really is no history until he showed up at the Youth Center in Lanark. There's a birth certificate naming Britta Olson as his mother, but no father listed. Britta Olson died in a car accident when Jesper was eleven. He managed to evade Child Protective Services, and his whereabouts were unknown until he popped up in Lanark."

"Dig into the mother. See what you can find on her."

"I can do that," Raj offers. "Janey has her hands full with surveillance."

"Fair enough. Okay, next, the cameras. Any luck?"

"Yes. They've been up since last night," Mitch takes over. "Land access is monitored everywhere, but there's a way onto the property along the shoreline. The water is fairly shallow and as long as you stay close to the rock wall, they can't see you from up above. It's a bit of a climb to get up the ledge but there are no cameras fixed on the cabins. I should say, there weren't, because there are now. Ours."

"Excellent. Pearl? Can you patch through the feed so I can access?"

Opal goes over messages that have come in at the office, including a new case of a missing toddler from Louisville. Unfortunately, we won't be able to take that one on.

"Maybe refer them to one of our contacts," I suggest.

"I gave them the number for Invenio Investigations," Opal shares.

Knowing everything is under control, I sign off, so I can have a look at the camera feed. However, first I want to check in with Raj, who still has her eyes on me.

I set my laptop aside and get out of the truck, but when I turn toward the house, Rajani is gone from sight.

Onyx

Call me a coward, but I'm not ready yet.

The moment I see him get out of the truck; I just know he's coming to knock on the door.

It's my own fault for gawking at him. I'm not sure what I was hoping to accomplish, but staring at him did not give me clarity.

The therapist in me feels this ongoing need to pick my emotions apart. All it does is make me even more confused. Heart and head seem stuck in a face-off, making me feel unbalanced. Maybe what I should do is listen to my gut. If only I can figure out what *it* is telling me.

I need to get out of here for a bit.

I grab my phone off the counter and look for my keys in my purse but they're not in there. I end up locating them on the hall table in the foyer, where I must've dropped them the last time I drove the big SUV. I think that was last week.

I rush out of the house, get in the Lincoln, and head for Williamstown and the pint of pistachio ice cream I'm craving all of a sudden.

Except there's a smell in the vehicle—a rather unpleasant one, like produce gone bad—that doesn't do much for my appetite. I'm trying to remember what could've fallen out of my grocery bags last week. To my recollection I wasn't missing anything when I put my purchases away.

I'm reaching behind my seat to feel around when Janey calls.

"Hey, are you sitting down?" she asks when I answer her call.

"I am. Why?"

"Lee and I did something..." she drawls.

My mind jumps to fill in the blank.

"You got married?"

She seems momentarily stumped by my guess.

"We did, but that's not why I'm calling."

"You got married? Secretly?" I realize I'm yelling.

"I guess, but we didn't want to make a big fuss."

"Wow. Okay, I suppose congratulations are in order."

I realize I sound bitter, petulant, and am instantly ashamed.

"I'm sorry. Of course I'm happy for you. Thrilled. You deserve all the happiness."

"Thank you, but that's not why I'm calling. I need you to talk me off the ledge. We got married for a reason, and I need you to tell me we're not nuts for doing this."

"What is it?"

Now I'm intrigued.

"It's Ricky, we're adopting him. That's crazy, right? He's a teenager, for crying out loud. I never wanted to be a mother, Raj. I don't even know if I'd be any good at it."

I chuckle, because Janey is one of those people who excels at anything she puts her mind to.

"You'll be great, and I'm so happy for Ricky. He deserves a loving family, and you're just the right people to give that to him."

"I have no experience," Janey whines, and I don't even try to hide my laughter.

"No first-time mother has experience, my friend, but the good news is, you won't be starting with an infant who can't tell you what they want or need. Your first child will be fully developed, and all he needs is some stability and a lot of love. Whatever you give him will be a vast improvement on what he had."

"I guess so," she mumbles.

I get another wave of that god-awful smell and crane my neck to peek in the back seat, but I can't see anything.

"God, my car reeks," I comment. "Like rotting food."

"Well, did you leave something in there?"

"Not that I know, unless something rolled under my seat. It's like hanging your head in a dumpster. Eww."

"Where are you going anyway?"

"I'm heading to Williamstown to pick up a few things."

A bit of a stretch of the truth. What I'm really doing is getting some comfort food for reinforcement, and avoiding Jacob at the same time. But I can't tell Janey that, I promised not to.

I'm only really delaying the inevitable anyway. I know I have to face him at some point, but I need to make sure I'm clear on what I want, how I want to proceed.

"Why don't you simply stop and check?"

Of course, logical Janey would suggest that.

"I would if I could. There are no shoulders on this stretch of road, just steep embankments down to the trees."

I keep my eyes peeled for a driveway, or even a widening of the narrow strip of grass on the side of the road.

"Well, hope you figure it out. I need to get back to work, thanks for the boost. I'm not quite so panicked anymore."

"I'm glad. There's no need to panic, you've got this. Besides, you've got Lee—"

The words get stuck in my throat when I feel something moving over my foot. I jerk my foot as I try to see what it is, but a distinct rattle has me freeze. I'm shocked at how loud it is in the enclosed space.

"Raj...what is that sound?" Janey's disembodied voice asks.

I open my mouth to answer but not a sound comes out.

"Raj?"

Right then I catch sight of a second snake in my peripheral vision, sliding across the center console.

"Snakes..." I can just manage.

The next moment the Lincoln suddenly tilts sharply to the right, and my eyes snap to the road, except all I see are trees. Before I can make any corrections, the SUV rolls, and I feel myself tossed around as it flips over and over, down the steep embankment.

EIGHTEEN

JACOB

I was just coming around the front of the house when I caught the back of the Lincoln disappearing down the road.

Clearly still avoiding me, but she'll have to come back at some point. In the meantime, the farrier has gotten back to me and is scheduled to come Thursday morning, and I spoke to Rob who was going to email me a few contacts he has in this area.

I'm just reading his email when I see a call coming in.

"Pearl, what—"

"I need your friend's number. Something's happened to Raj," she cuts in, grabbing every bit of my attention.

"What do you mean something's happened to her?" I snap, tossing my laptop in the back seat as I get out of the passenger side.

"I think she crashed. I was on the phone with her

when she said something about snakes, and the next thing I know I could hear sounds of some kind of impact—glass breaking, metal groaning. Then the call was cut off."

"*Call 911*," I yell at her as I get behind the wheel.

"I did, but I couldn't give them a precise location. I need time to pinpoint where she is. All I know is she said she was on her way to Williamstown. I thought it might be faster for Hamish to find her. Isn't he at the farm?"

"*I'll take care of him. You get to work on her location. Call me when you have something.*"

I'm already flying past the house and turn onto the road with squealing tires. There really is only one direct route to take from Four Oaks to Williamstown.

I firmly shove any self-recriminations aside and focus on the road ahead. Plenty of time to blame myself later. Instead, I replay my conversation with Pearl, getting stuck on something she said.

Snakes?

I shake my head to clear it, and keep my eyes peeled for any sign of the dark SUV. I almost miss it, there aren't even tire tracks on the road. My eye catches on a churned-up section of grass along the side of the pavement, and I slam on the brakes. The vehicle is upside down at the bottom of the embankment, leaning against the thick trunk of a tree.

My heart lodges in my throat as I scramble out of the truck and run to the edge, yelling her name. The moment I hear a faint response, I virtually throw myself over the edge, barely able to hold on to my footing as I slide and tumble down the steep slope.

"Raj?"

The driver's side is propped up against the tree, the front and side windows shattered and the side panel safety bag bulging out. I can't immediately see her. I push the bag aside so I can poke my head inside, when I hear her from somewhere in the back.

"Please be careful. I don't know how many are in here in total."

"What are you talking about?" I ask as I ease my head in.

Immediately, I pull back when I hear an ominous rattle coming from the vicinity of the steering wheel. A timber rattlesnake is coiled up on what is supposed to be the underside of the steering column.

"Are you hurt?" I inquire as I do a quick scan of what I can see inside the vehicle.

"Just a little banged up, nothing serious, provided I don't get bitten."

I spot her with her back wedged against the intact rear window behind the third row of seats. She has blood running down the side of her face.

"You're bleeding."

She shakes her head. "A few small cuts, that's all," she assures me.

Then I catch movement from the corner of my eye and notice three more snakes, slithering along the ceiling of the Navigator.

"What the hell? Tell me you haven't been bitten."

Because she'd be in trouble if that were the case. The

timber rattler is one of the more venomous snakes in Kentucky.

"Not yet, mainly because I haven't moved since I landed here."

"Give me a minute, I'll get you out," I promise, although I'm not sure how to go about it.

I could try to get the snakes out, one by one, but I don't really have the equipment to do that, so I'd have to improvise and risk startling them or pissing them off.

The easiest would be to break the rear window and get her out that way.

"Raj? I have to grab something from my truck, okay? I'll be right back."

"Okay."

Her dark eyes are wide and panicked, despite the calm facade she tries to maintain.

"I promise, sweetheart. Two minutes."

I don't wait for her to answer before I start clambering up the steep hill, cursing when I slide back a few times. I need my tool bag, which is in the back of the truck, otherwise I wouldn't have left her behind.

Luckily, going down is a lot faster. I quickly poke my head in to let Raj see I'm back. Then I drop my bag and dig around for a Phillips screwdriver and a hammer.

"Cover your head with your arms. I'm going to break the back window," I warn her. "Move slowly."

I watch to make sure the snakes keep their distance while she tucks her head down and crosses her arms behind it. Then I walk around, put the tip of the screwdriver against the rear window as far away from where Raj is pressed against the glass as possible.

I have to put some force behind it when it finally shatters after the third try. First, I knock as much of the glass aside as I can, before I reach inside and slide my arms around Raj from behind.

"Ready?" I ask, my lips brushing the shell of her ear. "Use your feet to push back if you can. Speed is key."

"I'm ready."

I brace one foot against the bumper and make sure my grip on Raj is secure.

"On one. Three...two..."

As I pull, I can feel her propelling herself backward, the force landing me on my ass, with Raj on top of me. I immediately slide her off me so I can check her out.

"You okay? Did they get you?"

"I don't know. I don't think so," she answers, her voice shaking as her body starts to tremble. "Where are the snakes?"

I look around but don't see any sign of them.

"Hopefully, still in the vehicle."

I pull up the legs of her jeans and run my hands over her skin. No bites visible. Then I grab her shaking hands and look at her face. Her eyes are almost black, her pupils large. Head wounds are notorious for bleeding, I know that, but it's still unsettling to see her face covered in it.

"Hey! Is everyone all right?"

An officer is standing at the top beside my truck, a sheriff's department cruiser parked behind it.

"Do you have rope?" I call back.

"Yup. I'll grab it," he confirms.

I have a feeling Raj may need some assistance getting up that slope, and if she doesn't, I might. I'm feeling a little shaky myself.

I return my attention to her and cup her stained face in my hands.

"Promise you're good?"

"Yeah," she whispers.

"Fuck, I was scared," I admit.

"Yeah, me too."

I lean in and kiss her hard on the lips.

"You're okay."

Onyx

I refuse to leave, even after I was checked by the EMTs.

I passed on the ambulance ride, which did not make Jacob happy. Neither did my refusal of a ride home from him.

"At least sit in the truck while we wait," Jacob insists.

I allow him to help me up, recognizing his need to hover. I'd be the same way.

We're waiting for Tri-State Wildlife Management to come and remove the snakes from the SUV. The tow-truck driver doesn't want to hook up the Lincoln until the snakes are gone, and I don't blame him.

I'd like to ask the wildlife officer whether it's possible those snakes came in from under the hood, which is what the officer suggested. He says snakes can make nests in warm places, especially when it gets colder outside.

I personally think although that might be possible for one snake, five is unlikely. All about the same size. That's a bit hard to swallow. Jacob didn't seem to buy it either, but he hasn't said anything.

In fact, he's been rather quiet since he and the officer hauled me up the embankment, handing me off to the EMTs from the fire department.

"I'm sorry about the SUV."

I'm talking to the back of his head as he keeps staring down to where the vehicle is still teetering on its roof.

"Don't apologize," he rumbles without turning around. "I was just thinking I'm so fucking grateful I bought a tank for you to drive around in. Any other vehicle and the roof might've caved in."

A shiver runs down my back. I know I was lucky, both coming away with just bruises and scratches, as well as managing to avoid a snakebite. I swallow hard. It could've been really ugly.

Ten minutes later, a wildlife management officer arrives and is immediately taken down to the SUV by the sheriff's deputy. It doesn't seem to take him long before he climbs back up, a moving canvas bag in one hand and some kind of grabber tool in the other. He heads straight for the back of his vehicle.

"I want to talk to him," I announce to Jacob, who is blocking my way.

He turns around.

"Why? What do you need to talk to him about?"

"I want to know if there is any way those snakes could've gotten in the car on their own."

"Highly unlikely," he reluctantly admits.

"I'd still like to hear it from a professional," I insist.

It's not that I'm purposely difficult, it's I have a hard time computing someone would willingly do such a thing, and why.

Jacob closes his eyes and sighs deeply.

"Fine. You stay right there. I'll ask him."

He turns on his heel and marches away.

I'm not a fan of being ordered around, but now that the adrenaline is wearing off, I don't have the energy to argue.

"Ma'am? You wanted to talk to me?"

He's a young guy, early to mid-twenties at most.

"Yes, thank you. I wanted to know what the likelihood is those five snakes found their way into my car."

"Five, ma'am? I removed seven in total."

Seven?

I slap my hand over my mouth.

"And I'd say it would be very rare for one snake to find their own way into your car, let alone seven. Someone had to have put them there. I'm sorry, ma'am."

I try to say thank you but can only manage a nod.

The next thing I know, Jacob is in front of me, leaning down and putting his hands on my shoulders.

"I'm taking you home now, okay?" he announces. "Swing your legs in and buckle up."

I'm grateful he doesn't say much else once we're on the road, giving me time to collect myself.

Someone put seven fucking poisonous snakes in my car. I have to assume someone means me harm. Why? Who does that? Who could do that?

By the time Jacob turns into the driveway, I'm already full-on pissed. Then he parks the truck, kills the engine, and turns to me.

"I need you to pack your bag, you're off the case. You're coming home with me tonight."

Wrong thing to say to me right now.

"Like hell I am," I spit out, my blood instantly boiling.

"You damn well are. You could've been fucking killed," he barks with force.

But he doesn't intimidate me in the least.

"I'm aware, thank you," I counter with as much sarcasm as I can muster. "However, taking me off this case makes no sense at all. You don't know if this has anything to do with the damn case." I'm so worked up I can't seem to stop my volume from going up, or waving my finger in his face. "And even if it does, it means we've succeeded in rattling someone's cage and you'd be an even bigger idiot taking me off!"

He leans over the center console, invading my space.

"Did you just call me an idiot?" he growls.

I'm not sure what possesses me, but I bring my face just inches from his.

"You're damn right I did."

Next thing I know, his hand shoots out, hooking me behind the neck, and his mouth slams down on mine.

The kiss is raw, it's angry, and I'm one-hundred-percent here for it. Which is why, when I can feel him pull back, I grab on to the back of his head and take over the kiss.

I throw everything into it, every last bit of pent-up frustration, anger, and need I've been hanging on to these past few days. I'm not shy about exploring his mouth with my tongue, or sinking my teeth into his lush bottom lip. I love the way he growls down my throat when my nails scratch his scalp.

He reaches for me with his other arm, and attempts to pull me over the console and onto his lap, but I'm still strapped into my seat belt. My battered and bruised body protests loudly.

"Ouch," I yelp, and he immediately releases me and surges back.

"Jesus, God...I'm sorry. I'm..." he mutters.

Then he shakes his head and jumps out of the truck, while I unbuckle my belt. My door is opened and he reaches in a hand to help me get out.

"Did I hurt you?"

"I'm fine," I assure him.

He clearly doesn't believe me when he lets go of my hand and begins walking to the front door. He may think he's going to leave me hanging again, but the seal is off now, and I have no intention of letting him bow out this time.

I follow close behind him as he opens the door. I'm

not surprised he has a key and the code for the alarm. Nothing about him can surprise me anymore.

He gestures for me to go inside ahead of him. I wait until I hear him close the door and reset the alarm. Then I swing around and crowd him, forcing him with his back to the door.

"Rajani," he mumbles with his hands up.

"Jacob."

I mimic his tone as I grab his wrists and pull his arms to the side. Then I fit my body against his, rise up on my toes, and kiss him like there's no tomorrow. I feel his body's response against my stomach, and press up to him a little harder.

It only takes a moment for him to cave and wrap me tightly in his arms. Then his hands slide down, cupping my ass, and I smile against his lips.

That's what I'm talking about.

NINETEEN

Holy hell.

That went from zero to sixty in no time at all.

We barely made it inside the house before she cornered me, and frankly, I didn't waste much time resisting. Why resist when I'm holding my fucking dream in my arms? Especially when she seems as hungry for me as I am for her. I could blame adrenaline, but the truth is, we've been working toward this moment for years. I'd like to believe the outcome was inevitable.

"Rajani..." I mumble when she abandons my mouth and runs her tongue along my jaw and down my neck.

She works her hands under my shirt, but I stop her before she can get very far. Grabbing her wrists, I spin her around and press her back against the door as I stretch her arms over her head. I pin them with one hand while mapping her body's contours with the other.

Ducking my head I nip her collarbone, dip my tongue in the hollow at the base of her neck, and inch my way down to the swell of her breasts. I love the taste of her skin, the feel of her soft curves in my hand, and the small sounds she makes in the back of her throat as I explore her body.

"You're teasing me," she complains.

"I know," I admit, as I lift my head and take her mouth again.

She manages to free one of her hands and slides it down the back of my jeans, grabbing on to my bare ass. Guess she doesn't like being teased.

Before this goes any further though, we should move from this foyer.

I release her mouth, step back and, holding on to her one wrist, begin to move in the direction of her bedroom.

"Where are we going?"

"Your bed," I tell her firmly. "This is not going to happen up against a door."

I assume she's on board with that when I hear no objection.

Her bedroom is much like the woman she presents as on the outside: classy, balanced, and comfortably serene. Who knew there was such passion looming under the surface? I hope the king-sized bed I put together can hold up.

I pull Raj to me, turning her so her back is toward the bed as I kiss her. Slipping my hands under the back of her shirt, I locate and release the closure on her bra.

"Arms up," I mumble against her lips.

As soon as I feel her lifting them, I bunch up her shirt and slip it, and her bra, off in one move.

My throat is instantly dry when my eyes take her in, standing in front of me. Strong shoulders and prominent collarbones, sloping down to generous breasts with dark brown areolas against her glowing, dusky skin. The gentle dip of her waist makes the flare of her rounded hips more pronounced.

I'm momentarily stunned.

Everything about this woman is perfection; from her gorgeous classic features, to her hourglass figure, but nothing is as beautiful as the look in her dark eyes aimed at me right now.

The next moment she reaches for me and flings herself back on the mattress, pulling me down with her. My mouth finds her breast, closing over her nipple and tugging deep. Her hips lift off the mattress in response, and I go straight for her pants, fumbling slightly to get the buttons undone, before sliding my good hand inside.

I dip my fingers between her legs, finding her warm and slick, and I groan against her skin. My cock strains against my zipper and I press my hips into the mattress.

"Jacob, yesss," she hisses when I roll her clit underneath my fingertips.

All I can think of is burying myself to the root inside her wet heat, but I'm determined to make her come first.

She grabs on to the back of my shirt when I press my thumb on her clit and pump first one, then two digits inside her. She rocks against my hand, undulating her hips unapologetically, and it's the sexiest fucking thing I've ever seen.

When she comes, her entire body tenses like a bow as she plants her heels in the mattress and presses her head back into the pillow. She collapses with a deep groan. Then her eyes find mine and a satisfied smile stretches her tempting mouth.

"I want you inside me."

Hell, yes.

I grab the waistband of her pants and, along with her panties, pull them down over her hips and off. The neatly trimmed patch between her legs glistens with the remnants of her orgasm, and my eyes are instantly drawn there. It's not until I take in the whole of her gloriously naked body, I notice a large bruise just starting to form on her hip. Then as my eyes travel up, I see another mark along the side of her ribs.

Raj props herself up on her elbows and looks down her body to where my eyes are fixed.

"Oh no. No, no, no. I'm fine," she insists, sitting up. "Don't you dare stop now."

I'm about to assure her—even if I wanted to—I don't think stopping is an option, when I hear Opal's voice call out.

"Raj? Where are you?"

Shit.

Raj is already scrambling to her feet, grabbing for a robe draped over the chair beside the bed.

"Go," she urges me, gesturing furiously for me to get out of her bedroom.

"Really?" I return.

Then I point at my crotch and my prominent erection, which will clearly need some time to subside.

"For Pete's sake," she mutters. "I'll go."

Then she pulls open the door, only to reveal Opal standing right outside. Her eyes zoom in on me like a homing beacon before they flit to Rajani.

"Are you okay? Janey called me and told me something happened to you, but I couldn't get a hold of you."

"The SUV rolled and my phone flew out somewhere. It must've broken. I'm okay, though," Raj responds.

"You still have some blood on your face," Opal points out.

Raj lifts a hand to her hairline where medics didn't quite clear away the blood.

"I was just about to have a shower."

"You should wait for those cuts to properly scab over."

"I'll be careful," Raj assures her friend.

Then she ducks into the bathroom, leaving me standing by the foot of her bed. Opal is still in the doorway, grinning at me.

"Well, well...Hamish. This is an interesting development."

Last thing I want is the third degree from Opal, so I use her words and redirect them.

"Yes, it was. Someone put seven rattlesnakes in her SUV. She's lucky she didn't get bitten."

"Seven? I didn't know *that*. Janey just mentioned a snake."

I called Pearl when Raj was being looked at by the EMTs, but I should have given her an update after we talked to the wildlife guy. I need to get my head in the game and stay sharp. I can't afford to be distracted.

"Does Jacob know?" Opal asks, stepping aside as I walk out of the room.

"He does." I stop at the front door and turn to her. "Do you plan on being here for a bit? I need to pick up a few things but I won't be long. I'll be staying here until this is sorted out."

"I'm curious, did you pass that by Jacob?" she inquires with a smirk.

"No, but I will."

Onyx

I close my eyes and let the warm water run down my body, forcing myself to relax.

I'm starting to feel the impact of the rollover on my body. My muscles ache and my energy is drained. Although, I can't blame all of that on the accident. I'm sure the orgasm Jacob gave me contributed to my current state.

I'm never going to hear the end of it from Kate, especially once she finds out it was actually Jacob she caught in my bedroom, so I'm not in a hurry to get out of the shower.

But I should've known she wouldn't let me hide out here very long.

"Raj? Are you drowning in there?" she calls out, accompanied by loud banging on the bathroom door. "Jacob just messaged, he's calling a meeting in five, so get your ass out here."

As I turn off the water and grab my towel, I find myself curious how he's going to pull off a meeting. Knowing how observant Kate is, she might notice him sitting in his truck down by the stables and wonder what the hell he's up to.

"Your boyfriend left," Kate announces, unapologetically leaning against the doorpost while I get dressed.

"Oh?"

"He's gone to grab some stuff because he plans on staying here. With you," she adds with emphasis.

I shrug, feigning nonchalance as I bend over to put on my socks. In my mind I'm processing the information, wondering whether he is being overprotective, or if he intends to finish what was so rudely interrupted by Kate. I guess time will tell.

"Come on, Raj, give me something," she pleads, making me laugh.

"You're incorrigible," I admonish her as I bump her aside.

She's on my heels when I walk into the kitchen.

"So is this serious?" she tries again, but this time the ringing of her phone saves me a response.

She answers, puts the phone on speaker and lays it down on the island between us.

"Onyx, are you there? How are you feeling?"

The temptation to roll my eyes is great. He knows better than anyone how I'm *feeling*.

"I'm okay, it left me a little achy, but I'm sure an early night in bed will bring some relief."

I suppress a satisfied smirk when I hear Jacob clear his throat.

"Right. That's good. So...seven rattlesnakes, someone isn't messing around."

"Wheeler?" I hear Mitch ask. "Because he hasn't left Grandview. We've been monitoring."

"He wouldn't get his own hands dirty," Lee contributes.

"And besides all that, I haven't met him face-to-face yet," I remind them.

"He might have seen you though. I'm sure he has security cameras on the property."

Of course, but even if he saw me, it doesn't mean he recognized me. I wasn't the one who held his interest all those years ago. I was no more than a prop in his sick control games. Not that I feel I can bring that up, it would almost be like a betrayal of Nathan's memory.

No one knows what happened in that kitchen, no one but me and David Wheeler.

"One more thing," I add. "The SUV has been sitting

idle. Hamish has been driving his truck almost everywhere. So it likely happened right outside."

"I already started checking the video feed from the security camera at the front of the house," Pearl volunteers. "Unfortunately, the camera only catches part of the passenger side."

"Who else would have reason to harm you?" Mitch asks.

"I have no idea, but perhaps instead of looking for a motive first, we should be looking at who had access to my keys and the vehicle," I propose.

"Or who might have seven freaking rattlesnakes, for that matter," Kate adds.

"What's that trainer guy's name again, Hamish? What about him?"

I almost laugh out loud at Lee's suggestion but keep my mouth shut as I wait to see how Jacob is going to get out of that one.

"It's not him," he states firmly. *"He didn't even know Onyx before I contacted him. He has no reason whatsoever to want her hurt."*

"Actually," Kate pipes up. "I think Hamish is getting to know Onyx quite nicely but I agree, it's highly unlikely he had anything to do with this."

"Didn't you hire two stable hands?" Janey brings up. "What do you know about them?"

"I only just met them a week or so ago as well. They don't have access to my keys or the house, and there's no reason for either of them to be involved."

But even as I say it, I'm trying to remember if there

might not have been a time where one of them could have had access to both.

"*Still*," Jacob says. "*Pearl has a point. We should look at everyone. In the meantime, keep the alarm engaged, even when you're inside, and don't go anywhere alone.*"

I bite my lip. I'll save my thoughts on his brusque orders for when we're alone.

"I can stay here," Kate volunteers.

"No," I jump in. "There's no need for that."

"*I agree. I already spoke to Hamish earlier and he'll be staying. He's there most of the time anyway. Also, I might need you in the field, Opal.*"

Jacob asks if anyone has anything else before instructing us all to check in with him first thing in the morning.

"Does Jacob know..." Kate lets the sentence trail off.

I try to ignore her and dive in the fridge to see what I can scrounge up for dinner, but she will not be deterred.

"Because, you know, he might not be so happy about his friend encroaching on his turf."

"His turf?" I echo incredulously, standing beside the open fridge door. "Is that supposed to refer to me? Because last time I checked, I wasn't a piece of property to be claimed."

"Oh relax, will you?" Kate dismisses me. "This is me talking. And you're avoiding my point."

I close the door and face her, planting my fists on my hips.

"How very perceptive of you. Yes, I am avoiding it,

because frankly, I haven't had a chance to figure out what is happening here myself."

"So you admit something is happening?"

I throw up my hands.

"Oh my God, I give up."

She grins wide in response.

"You're so easy."

TWENTY

J ACOB

"I need you to pack me my toiletries and enough clothes for a week."

Bernie is silent for a pregnant moment on the other end.

"And a good afternoon to you to," she finally returns with a hefty side of sarcasm.

"Hey, Bernie," I correct, effectively scolded. "An attempt was made on Rajani's life and I —"

"Wait. What? What do you mean? Is she all right? What happened?" she interrupts me with a rapid-fire of questions.

"She's all right," I reassure her. "Bumps and bruises. I'll have to tell you about it later, but the short of it is, I'm staying here to keep an eye on her."

"Of course. What do you need?"

In the distance I see the lights are already on at the

farm. The days are getting shorter and dusk has set in. It makes me think of Bernie alone at the house in the mountains and I don't like that idea.

"Remember I asked you to look into a short-term rental or something near here? Any luck with that?"

"I narrowed it down to a few places. A couple in Williamstown and a cottage right outside Falmouth. I haven't had a chance to pass them by you."

Falmouth is just ten minutes up the road. I like that one is close.

"Book the one in Falmouth."

"For how long?"

"Secure it for a month if available. Tomorrow, I'd like you to pack up my stuff and enough for yourself to last a week as well. I want you to temporarily move into the Falmouth place."

I turn into the driveway.

"Will you be picking your stuff up, or did you want me to drop it off at the farm?"

"If you wouldn't mind dropping it off?"

"You mean I get to meet Rajani?" she asks, excitement evident in her voice.

She's known about Raj for fifteen years and has a healthy dose of curiosity.

"May as well, since she knows who I am, and who you are to me." I pull up to the house. "But I've gotta go. Shoot me a message when you leave."

When I walk in it's been only an hour since I left, but it feels like half a day has passed. In fact, this entire day feels long. I'm carrying a bag of Mexican takeout and I picked up a few necessary things at the Walmart in Williamstown. Going home would've taken at least three hours and I didn't feel comfortable leaving Rajani that long.

The women are in the kitchen, sitting at the island with a teapot between them.

"Oh, great. Food," Opal observes, as she slips off her stool and snatches the paper bag from my hand.

I'd called from the parking lot of the Mexican restaurant so they could put in their orders. To my surprise, Raj jumped at my suggestion of takeout. I guess today's events have taken their toll on her.

"Tea? Or if you prefer, I think there's more beer in the fridge," Raj indicates, grabbing plates from the cupboard.

"I'll grab a beer."

I'll just have the one, I want to stay sharp, for more than one reason.

We have dinner at the table, and conversation is at a minimum. I occasionally steal glances at Raj, who is sitting across from me, but keep catching Opal glancing at me. I'm not sure whether it's because she found me in her friend's bedroom earlier or something else has her curious, but her expression is quizzical.

I wait until after Opal has left and Raj is finishing her tea, while I clean up the dirty dishes.

"A heads-up; Bernie is coming by tomorrow to drop off some of my things. She's going to be staying at a cottage in Falmouth."

"Why?"

I turn to face her, wiping my hands on a towel, and leaning back against the edge of the counter.

"Because I don't want her up in the mountains by herself."

She tilts her head. "Is that where you live? In the mountains?"

I feel my honesty is being challenged, so I look her straight in the eye.

"Yes. I have a house near Moreland."

"Just a house or a property? I mean, do you have horses, for instance?"

I notice she's tearing her napkin in strips and I wonder whether it's nerves rather than curiosity that has her asking me these questions.

"I have a few acres." Two hundred and sixty-three to be precise. "No horses though."

"You do now," she points out. "What are you going to do with them when this is over? Are you going to get rid of them?"

"No, I don't plan to, but I haven't decided what that's going to look like."

I push off from the counter and begin moving toward her. She glances up and watches me approach, biting her lip.

"I believe we had some unfinished business," I warn her.

If for some reason she changed her mind between this afternoon and now, she has plenty of time to stop me.

But she doesn't.

When I hold out my hand to her, she grabs on and

allows me to pull her to her feet. Then I slip my arms around her waist.

"Is there anything else we need to discuss before this goes anywhere? Anything more you'd like to know?"

She shakes her head.

"Any reservations or regrets?"

"Not a single one," she whispers, sliding her hands up my chest and around my neck.

I think it's safe to say she's on board, so I pull her flush against me and take her mouth.

Kissing Rajani is as good, if not better, than I recall. Or maybe it's simply that I'm in control now—in the moment—and savoring every responsive stroke of her tongue. She tastes like cardamom and star anise, an intoxicating combination.

This time it's Raj who ends the kiss and begins to walk backward, pulling me along to the bedroom. Once there, she grabs the hem of her T-shirt and starts lifting it up.

Guilt has me stop her.

"Wait," I tell her. "Before you do that, I want you to know what you're in for."

It's my turn to be nervous. I haven't exactly been a monk, but intimacy was never a goal before. It is now, with Raj. This is about trust, giving it, and earning it back.

I reach behind me and grab a fistful of my shirt, pulling it over my head. Other than medical staff or Bernice, I have not taken my shirt off in front of anyone. It isn't that I have anything to be embarrassed about, but maybe I wasn't ready to share that much of me.

I feel ready now, which is why I don't hesitate kicking off my boots and stripping my jeans down.

Rajani's eyes scan my body, not betraying any emotion. I know what she sees, my right side is a gnarly web of scars running down from my shoulder to my hip. I occasionally look in the mirror, it's not pretty.

She surprises me by reaching out, letting her fingertips move up my arm to my shoulder and trail down my torso to my hip. A shiver runs down the length of my body.

Her eyes dart up to my face.

"Do they hurt?"

"They get itchy sometimes, but rarely hurt."

She nods and proceeds to blow me away when she holds my eyes and slowly sinks down to her knees. Hooking her fingers in my boxer briefs, she pulls them down to my ankles. Then she taps first one foot for me to lift and then the other, helping me out of my socks and briefs.

Her eyes follow her hands as she runs them up my legs, and wraps one of them around my erection. Looking down, all I see is her beautiful eyes, lifted up to me as she leans in and runs her tongue around the crown of my cock.

I'm afraid to move for fear of scaring her off, but she doesn't seem scared. With infinite patience she slides her gorgeous mouth down my length, until I see tears form in her eyes when I hit the back of her throat.

Beauty and the fucking beast.

———

Onyx

He moves me to my core.

I see his gesture for what it is, exposing vulnerability as an offer of trust. Rather than tell him his scars have no impact on my attraction to him, I feel showing him will be a more effective way to get that message across. In return, I offer him something I've never given voluntarily.

I know he's enjoying my mouth on him; his jaw is slack as groans reverberate deep in his chest. Hell, I enjoy the effect my mouth has on him. I may be on my knees but I've never felt so powerful.

Suddenly, Jacob bends down and hooks me under my arms, abruptly lifting me to my feet and leaving me a little stunned.

"I want to be inside you and feel you come around me. Then I plan to look you in the eyes when I let go," he promises in a deep rumble I can feel down to my toes.

He wastes no time at all helping divest me of my clothes. Then he eases me back on the bed and follows me down. Brushing the hair from my forehead, he traces my face with his eyes, and it feels like the softest touch.

He kisses first my mouth before traveling down my neck and chest, while his hand explores the rest of my body. Special attention is paid to my breasts, as he switches sides, pulling each nipple between his lips.

When his fingers glide between my legs, he groans deeply.

"So wet," he mumbles against my skin.

"So ready for you," I disclose.

"Yeah?" he asks, lifting his head so he can look at me.

"Oh yeah."

One side of his mouth curls up and he moves his body over mine. I open my legs, making room for him, when all of a sudden he gets off the bed.

"Don't move."

I watch him walk out of the room, gloriously naked, and I note his ass looks as fantastic as it feels. A few seconds later he's back, carrying the Walmart bag he came in with. He reaches in and pulls out a large box of condoms.

"Such a Boy Scout," I tease him.

"Family-sized," he states with a grin as he produces a foil packet and rips it with his teeth.

I watch with interest as he rolls the condom down his length before climbing back in bed, lowering himself on top of me. I immediately wrap my legs around him, savoring the weight of his body on me. Impatience has me tilt and roll my hips, until I can feel the crown of his cock brush through the slick between my legs. My mouth opens and my eyes close, as I wait for him to slide inside me.

"Look at me, Rajani," he mumbles.

I do as he asks and find his hazel eyes only inches away, beautiful golden flecks making them look lit up from the inside. A warm feeling of homecoming washes over me when he enters me in one, confident stroke.

He sets a steady pace, but soon I find myself sliding my hands down his back, and grabbing on to the firm globes of his ass, encouraging him to move faster and deeper.

He reads me well and in no time, he is powering inside me, hitting spots that have my eyes roll back in my head.

"*Rajani.*"

When I try to focus on him, my gaze slides over his shoulder, and for a brief instant, I get a flash of steel-blue eyes before Jacob draws me back.

"Look at me," he grunts.

I zoom in on him as I feel my release build inside me. Our bodies are slick with sweat.

"Come for me, sweetheart."

He slips his hands under my knees and pushes my legs back and open, hammering inside me. I feel every inch deep inside me as I spasm and clamp down on him.

I ride the aftershocks and can't manage much more than a whimper as I watch him reach for his own release.

He collapses on top of me and I immediately wrap him up in my arms. I don't know how long we lie like that, breathing each other in as we catch our breath. It's not until I feel him soften inside me and finally slip out that he raises his head and brushes my lips with his.

"I'll be right back."

He leaves the bed and heads to the bathroom,

presumably to get rid of the condom. When I hear the toilet flush, I get out of bed myself to get cleaned up.

Jacob catches me with one arm around my waist in passing, bending his head to kiss my shoulder before he lets me continue. This gentle side of him is not something I expected. The Jacob I thought I'd gotten to know is an opinionated, authoritarian slave driver, and yet I still managed to be drawn to him. Now that I've seen this other side of him, it'll be hard not to fall completely.

I finish up in the bathroom, wash my hands and my face, and brush my teeth. It's still early, but I'm exhausted and I don't want to think about snakes, how they got in my car, or who has it out for me. I'd rather just go to sleep and worry about all of that tomorrow.

Jacob is sitting on the edge of the bed, sliding his jeans on, and I feel a pang of disappointment. I had visions of sleeping snuggled up to him, but I guess that was wishful thinking. I reach past him to grab my nightshirt from under my pillow, but he grabs my hips and pulls me between his legs.

"Hey, are you okay?"

"Fine," is my knee-jerk response.

His fingers tighten on my hips.

"Sweetheart, I want to know if I hurt you." He shakes his head and levels his eyes with my belly button. "That was a long time coming, it was fucking amazing, and I totally blanked on the fact you were in an accident today. Plus, I should've pulled out sooner."

I cup his face in my hands and tilt his head up.

"You didn't hurt me, I agree it was fucking amazing,

and I don't want to be reminded of the accident," I inform him with a smile.

"As for your last point, I appreciate your concern, but just so you know, pregnancy is not a concern."

His eyes slide down my body as he reaches out and runs a finger along the thin white line bisecting my lower belly.

"It's a hysterectomy scar," he observes.

I confirm with a nod.

"Guess you hadn't heard that?"

"Heard what?" he asks.

I run my own fingertips along the scar as I respond, "This is how they made sure there couldn't be any accidents."

"They?"

I look him in the eye.

"This was compliments of Transition House."

TWENTY-ONE

Jacob

I watch as Joey leads Moon back into the stables to rub her down. Steam comes off the horse's back in the cool outside air.

Putting Arion's Moon through her paces has given me a chance to stay close to the barn so I could observe both Jose and Joey this morning. I may be barking up the wrong tree, but one of these two could've had an opportunity to put the snakes in the SUV. I don't know why they would, but I'm hoping Pearl has had a chance to look a little deeper into their background. In the meantime, I'm going to see what I can find out.

Following Joey and the horse inside, I catch sight of Jose cleaning out Murdoch's stall. Both companion ponies are grazing in the field behind the barn. Joey will be occupied with Moon for a bit so I focus my attention on Jose.

"How are things?" I ask, leaning my elbow on the half-door.

He glances over his shoulder.

"Good, good."

"I meant to ask you, did you notice anything unusual in the past week or so? Maybe unscheduled visitors, or strange vehicles pulling up to the property while Ms. Baqri and I were picking up the horse?"

"Here?"

I notice he darts a glance past me where I know Joey is grooming Moon. Curious.

"Yeah, around the stables or the house," I clarify.

"Can't say I have," he responds. "Did something happen?"

"You could say that. Someone tried to harm Ms. Baqri with rattlesnakes in her vehicle."

"I'm sorry, I didn't see anything," he states, turning his attention back to his work.

No reaction to the mention of rattlesnakes, which I find interesting. It's not exactly common to purposely harm someone with snakes. I'd at least have expected a raised eyebrow.

Maybe I should be asking Joey what she's seen.

She has Moon's halter clipped to two leads between stalls on either side of the aisle. I place a hand on the horse's rump so I don't spook her as I move around to her side.

"She did well," I comment.

Joey pops her head up on the other side.

"She did. Although she was lagging a bit around that

last corner. But there was plenty of gas left in her tank on that final stretch."

"I noticed she lost a second or two there. What do you figure it was?"

"I'm thinking it could be the track, the dirt seems a little looser there."

"Okay, I'll see if Jose has time to run the track conditioner sometime today."

"Thanks."

I run my hand along Moon's neck.

"I meant to ask you; did you notice anything unusual around here since you got here?"

She stops brushing and glances at me.

"Unusual, how?"

"Someone messing with Ms. Baqri's SUV, to be specific." I keep a close eye on her reaction. "Someone who might have dumped a bag full of rattlesnakes in her vehicle?"

The shock on her face is instantaneous and seems genuine.

"Rattlesnakes? I hate them," she squeaks with a visible shudder. "Oh my God, is she okay?" follows immediately after.

This is the kind of reaction I would expect.

"She rolled her SUV, but was lucky to get away without serious injury or snakebites for that matter."

"That's crazy. So you figure someone put them in her car?"

"Chances for seven adult snakes to find their way in are slim to none."

"I guess so. Well, I haven't really seen any strangers around, but then again, most of my time is spent in the stables or the guesthouse. I don't get out front much." She shrugs and begins brushing Moon again. "The only person other than you I've seen around is Jose."

"Okay. Let me know if you notice anything," I encourage her.

Of the two reactions, Joey's seems the more genuine one, but for all I know she could be a talented actress. If that's the case, her portrayal of an aversion to snakes should be considered an Oscar-worthy performance. In that same vein, Jose's feedback could simply be the result of being less socially savvy.

On my way back to the house, I stop to check in with the contractor, who tells me the work should be done by Friday. His crew didn't start until this Monday, which makes it a bit unlikely one of them could've been responsible, but I ask him a few questions anyway.

I walk away, none the wiser, five minutes later and go in search of Raj.

This morning I left her asleep in bed. Last night I'd gone outside to move my truck so it was in full sight of the security camera. Then I made sure all doors and windows were locked properly, before I rejoined Raj in bed for round two.

It was well after midnight by the time she settled against me, satisfied, and fell asleep. I was awake for hours longer, trying to wrap my head around the fact I had the object of my desire curled up in my arms.

I didn't get a lot of sleep, but I feel more energized and alive this morning than I have in years.

I find Raj in the office. She puts a finger to her lips just as I hear a girl's voice start talking. Then she flashes me five digits, so I back out of the room and head for the kitchen.

The coffee is all gone so I prep another pot. I could probably use the extra shot of caffeine to make it through the day.

No word from Bernie yet, but I suspect she'll be here sometime mid-afternoon.

"Hey."

I turn to find Raj walking into the kitchen. She doesn't stop until she's plastered against me, and my arms automatically hold her there. It's amazing how natural this all feels right away.

"Hey," I rumble back, looking into her deep brown eyes.

"Sorry, I was just checking in with Amelia."

Amelia Sherwood is a teenager my team was able to rescue back in the early summer. She'd been lured from West Virginia to Columbus, Ohio, where she was abducted and groomed to be auctioned off to wealthy pedophiles. We were able to take down most of the group responsible—that's when Jesper Olson was taken into custody—except for who we believe the mastermind to be, David Wheeler.

"How is she doing?"

"She's hanging in, focusing on schoolwork, still seeing

her therapist, as are her parents apparently. Still, she likes New Mexico. She's making new friends."

"Good to hear."

Rajani provides aftercare and counseling for some of the kids we manage to rescue from the hands of predators. Even if their day-to-day care is in the hands of other professionals, she tends to stay in touch, keeping a finger to the pulse.

Suddenly Raj turns her head toward the front of the house. Then I hear it too; the crunch of wheels coming up the driveway. She swings around—forcing me to let go—and starts moving to the foyer.

"It's probably the security company I called this morning to install more cameras," she shares.

We briefly discussed upping our security at some point last night. Clearly, Raj didn't waste any time, confirming to me she was more rattled by yesterday's experience than she cares to let on.

"Or," I suggest, following her. "Bernie is early."

Onyx

"What a lovely place."

I follow Bernie, who is finding her own way to the kitchen before I have a chance to show her around.

As it turned out, Bernie and the security company

arrived at the same time. After a brief introduction, Jacob went with the security guy to show him what he wants done, leaving Bernie with me.

The older woman loaded me up with a couple of cooler bags she pulled from the back of her vehicle, before she grabbed a large pot of some kind from the back seat.

"It's Scottish beef stew I've had going since J called last night," she indicates, setting the pot on the stove.

Then she turns to me and takes the cooler bags from my hands, placing them on the kitchen counter.

"I also baked some biscuits earlier, and put together a quick lasagna this morning. You can freeze it, or it'll stay good for a few days in the fridge."

"Wow. That's...amazing. Thank you," I manage, a little overwhelmed by the quiet, but determined, force this woman radiates.

She pulls containers and oven pans from the bags, stacking them on the counter. I swear there's enough to feed a battalion. There's no way we'll be able to eat all this. I can't even figure out how she was able to throw all this together since yesterday afternoon when Jacob mentioned he contacted her.

"Oh..." Bernie looks surprised when she opens my fridge. "You actually have proper food in here."

I chuckle. "I like cooking, and I like eating even more," I share with her.

She shakes her head and seems to be laughing at herself.

"I'm so sorry. I assumed, like J, you wouldn't have the

time or the inclination to cook. I didn't mean to insult you by bringing food."

She begins packing up the lasagnas again, so I stop her.

"Are you kidding? I haven't had lasagna in years, and that stew smells mouthwatering. I do enjoy cooking, but that doesn't mean I want to do it all the time. Having someone else create something delicious is such a treat."

I take one of the oven pans and fit it in the freezer. The other one I stick in the fridge. Bernie is smiling when I turn back to her. I feel like I've passed a test.

"You brought food?"

I didn't hear Jacob come inside so his voice startles me. His focus is on Bernie though.

"I did," she confirms, almost defiantly. "I wasn't sure whether you'd been eating or not."

Apparently, Bernie is very serious about looking after Jacob.

"You don't have to worry about me eating," he reassures her, draping his arm around my shoulders. "I've been feasting on Rajani's Indian and Pakistani cooking. You've gotta try it, Bernie, you'd love it."

I elbow him in the ribs.

"What?"

"I'm not sure it's proper manners to gush about someone else's cooking to the person whose beef stew you will be eating tonight."

Bernie bursts out laughing.

"Oh, I like her already," she shares, beaming at Jacob.

Then she grabs her bags and heads for the door.

"Aren't you staying?" I ask.

"Oh no, I should check into the Airbnb, and I have a container of stew for myself in the car."

I gesture to the hallway going to the guest room.

"We have extra rooms here you're more than welcome to."

This time I get a warning from Jacob by way of his hand grabbing onto my upper arm firmly.

Bernie starts laughing again. "If only you could see your face," she mocks Jacob. Then she addresses me. "I appreciate the offer, but I'm afraid J here will put me out to pasture if I were to accept. Besides, the Airbnb has a fancy hot tub I'm dying to try out."

I nod my defeat. "Ah, well, a hot tub, I'd pick that too. Then maybe once all this is over, I'll have a chance to return the favor and cook a meal for you."

"I'd love that," she returns before turning to Jacob. "Walk me out? Your things are in the car."

I watch the two head outside, smiling at the contrast between the short, pleasantly plump, elderly woman and the tall, bald, and marred man. Jacob may look intimidating, but I'm willing to bet Bernie holds the strings in this relationship.

I glance at the microwave clock and see it's almost noon. Kate will be summoning us into a conference call shortly. We're meeting a little later than originally planned because Mitch and Janey were busy with something this morning.

Grabbing a couple of mugs from the cupboard I quickly pour us each a coffee, just as Jacob walks in.

"I'll put these away later," he promises, indicating the two suitcases he left in the foyer. "Opal will be calling soon."

He takes his coffee into the spare bedroom while I return to the office. We don't want to risk anyone hearing either of us in the background of the other.

"Sorry for this morning," Janey starts when we're all present. "We had some movement during the night we wanted to check out."

"*And?*" Jacob prompts.

"Yesterday afternoon there was quite a bit of activity around the guest cabins. Looked like staff hauling stacks of linens, boxes with supplies, and cleaning materials. Then we caught a helicopter landing on the field at the front of the property a little after midnight last night," Mitch describes. "I could see three figures getting out before the chopper took off again. Janey was already on the grounds to adjust one of our trail cameras and was able to get a closer look."

Janey takes over.

"The three headed straight for the lodge. I noticed one was walking behind the other two. It looked like he was holding a weapon aimed at the others."

"Could you tell if they were kids?" I ask. "Girls?"

"I'm pretty sure they were both male, and young," she clarifies.

"*Wheeler favors boys,*" Jacob contributes.

A chill runs down my spine, right at the moment I hear a click on my phone line, indicating an incoming call.

"Guys," I interrupt. "I have to go. It's Oliver Doyle calling."

I switch to the new call.

"Mr. Doyle, what can I do for you?"

"Ms. Bariq, I am actually relaying a message. You have been invited to a soiree at Grandview Estate this coming Friday evening, with apologies for the late notice."

It takes me a second to register what he's saying to me.

"Let me get this straight, are *you* inviting me? To accompany you?"

"No. I'm merely passing on the invitation. Mr. Ackers has asked me to extend his apology for missing you last Saturday, and would like for you to join him and a select number of other guests for a light meal and some refreshments at the lodge."

"I'm afraid I'm not sure who Mr. Ackers is," I feign ignorance.

"Morton Ackers is the owner of Grandview. I'm sorry, I thought you knew," he apologizes.

"I had no idea. I don't think his name was ever mentioned. The only name I knew was Pegasus GLAN."

"My oversight. Can I tell him you will be in attendance? Cocktails at six."

"Please tell Mr. Ackers I would very much enjoy that," I assure him.

I'll have a chance to meet Wheeler face-to-face. I can't wait.

"He will be delighted. Oh, and one more thing, Ms. Baqri. This is not a plus-one event."

Shit. That means I can't bring Jacob as my date. Not

sure how that's going to go over, but this is the opportunity we've been working toward, so I can't turn it down.

"Of course. I'm looking forward to it."

Five minutes later I have Jacob yelling in my ear, and am grateful for the great room separating us.

"Absolutely not, I won't allow it!"

His outburst is followed by a pregnant silence. I guess everyone is taken aback. I was afraid this might happen, which is why I mentioned it in the conference call, instead of saving it to tell Jacob alone. I'm counting on the team to pipe up, which is why I'm not saying anything.

"Forgive me if I point out the obvious, but wasn't this the whole purpose of this exercise?" Lee is the first to observe.

"It's too dangerous for her to go in without backup."

"She has backup, Mitch and I are already here," Janey mentions.

"And I'm going to drive up with her," Kate contributes. "The whole team will be backing her up."

I can almost hear him grind is teeth.

"Jacob, you're the one who wanted me on this case," I remind him gently. "I can handle it."

The line falls silent again while everyone appears to wait for Jacob's response.

"I'm aware, but that doesn't mean I have to like it," he finally shares and Lee makes a casual observation.

"I swear, you almost sound like a protective boyfriend."

TWENTY-TWO

JACOB

Fuck.

I watch Rajani walk away from me. She came in after we ended the call to tell me in no uncertain terms she would not put up with my authoritarian attitude. She didn't even give me a chance to defend myself.

This is ridiculous. I've kept it together for years, and now I'm so close I can taste it, I end up hindering my own cause.

Luckily, Opal was able to steer the call back on track after I overreacted and Lee called me out on it. She crisply went down a list of updates we needed to cover, giving me time to pull myself together.

Pearl reported she'd made a start doing a more thorough background check on Jose and Joey, but was pulled away because of the developments at Grandview. I told her if she could send me what she had, I'd take over.

Opal was able to tell us she'd been in touch with the Kentucky State Police to get an update on their investigation of the crash. The Lincoln had been towed to their compound and would be processed for fingerprints and signs of tampering.

I'm still waiting for Lee to get back to me on the catering company that was seen entering the Grandview property. He got the name of a caterer from one of the neighbors and was supposed to meet with their event manager this afternoon.

Part of me wants to smooth things over with a clearly upset Rajani. However, the loud slam of her office door a few minutes ago suggests it might be wiser to give her a chance to cool off before I attempt an approach. Instead, I check my email, discovering Pearl has already sent me the information she has on Joey Vernon and Jose Cantu.

There isn't a whole lot, a few social media links and some family history on Joey, whose background isn't that difficult to piece together and fairly uneventful. I can't find anything that raises a red flag.

The only thing I have for Jose Cantu is a record of entry into the U.S. dating back to 2008 when he was just fourteen years old. He arrived here alone, which strikes me as a little odd, since generally for immigration purposes eighteen is the age of consent. I can't find any records of him from before he landed in the U.S., except he's originally from Colombia. The only way a young kid like that could've entered the country by himself is for the purposes of reuniting with relatives, or if he was adopted into an American family.

I run his name through several different search engines and am still not able to find any concrete information on Cantu. No school records, no evidence of any kind of memberships to sports clubs, but I do come up with an old address along US Hwy 41A in Hopkinsville, Kentucky.

Before I have a chance to pull up a map, my phone rings.

"The Posh Palate," Lee announces when I answer his call. "They're basically on retainer for any and all events taking place at Grandview Estate."

"Good. Any particulars?"

I jot down the name of the catering company on a scrap of paper.

"Their event manager was pretty talkative. Apparently, he's not a fan of those repeat jobs. They're only allowed a skeleton kitchen crew on the premises, while Grandview has their own serving staff they prefer to use. They're also restricted to the use of the kitchen only. They cook, plate, and load everything on carts they leave just outside the kitchen. Other than the security person who shows them to the kitchen and out again once they're done, they don't see a single person while at the lodge."

"Sounds a little paranoid," I observe.

"Yes, it does. It makes you wonder what the hell goes on there to require such strict security. Especially since Posh Palate is scheduled to work the event there this coming Friday night," Lee announces.

The event Raj plans to attend, with or without my

support, as she has made perfectly clear. Maybe there's a way to use this knowledge.

"I need you to get me on that skeleton crew," I inform Lee.

He scoffs. "Do you have any kitchen skills I could sell them on? Otherwise, that might be a tall order."

"Get me the owner's information. You try with the manager; I'll see if I can exert pressure from the top."

If need be, I have money to make the proposal a bit more attractive. I'll pay whatever it takes to get me inside that lodge. I'll feel moderately better about Rajani attending this thing, if I know I'll be under the same roof.

I jot down the name of the owner Lee mentions and assure him I can find a number for the guy.

"One more thing," I add. *"I'd like you to keep this to yourself."*

"I was wondering if you were going to ask me that," he remarks. "You realize you're asking me to lie to my wife?"

"No need to lie, when you can just avoid the subject," I point out.

"I must've been close with my earlier guess," he continues. "You care enough about Raj to finally come out in the open. It makes me wonder why it was necessary to hide your identity in the first place."

It doesn't really surprise me Lee brings it up. Especially not after his comment earlier today.

"You're going to have to curb that curiosity a little longer," I inform him. *"And as for my request to keep this to yourself, I don't want any distractions on or before Friday, because you're right, I care a great deal about her."*

"Fair enough."

I breathe a sigh of relief he's letting it go. I really don't want to waste time trying to explain my motivations, when we should be focusing on getting safety measures in place for Friday night.

"Good."

I'm about to end the call when Lee obliterates my cover.

"Oh, tell Raj I said hi, Jacob. Or should I call you Hamish?"

That fucking guy.

I don't bother to respond and end the call. Then I go in search of Rajani, she should probably know I've been found out.

The door to her office is still closed, so I knock, only to be left waiting for a few minutes. I'm annoyed, and about to show myself in when the door opens.

Her eyes are suspiciously shiny.

"You'll never guess what I just found."

Onyx

Whatever annoyance I may have felt has disappeared when I pull Jacob into my office.

"Check that out."

I point at my screen, which shows the address on a hospital bill.

"Help me out here," he says, confused. "What am I looking at?"

"That's the address Britta Olson listed at the time she gave birth to Jesper."

"Okay..."

I drag the image of the invoice to the side to reveal a map of Somerset. One of its more affluent neighborhoods, in fact. I switch to street view to show the actual house Britta listed as her residence.

"Seems a big house for a young, single mom," Jacob comments.

"Considering she was barely eighteen when she had him," I fill in. "Which had me look into the actual owner-ship of the house at the time Britta lived there."

I pull up the property's history and Jacob leans over my shoulder to see the document up on the screen.

"GLAN Industries," he reads out loud. Then he turns to me, a half-smile on his face. "Are you thinking what I'm thinking?"

"That Jesper may well be related to Wheeler? Yes, I am," I admit. "It fits. Olson was being groomed to follow in Daddy's footsteps."

"Isn't Olson's hearing in front of the circuit court this coming Friday morning?" Jacob brings up.

"It is."

"What if this impromptu party at Grandview is somehow connected?"

When it hits me, I grab Jacob's arm.

"You mean like a father celebrating the homecoming of his prodigal son?" I conclude.

He confirms with a nod.

"This is crazy."

I watch Jacob pull out his phone and make a call.

"Lee? Listen, I want you in the gallery of Judge Severino's courtroom for Jesper Olson's hearing on Friday."

I listen open-mouthed as Jacob explains to Lee what we discovered.

Without using his voice distortion app.

His eyes are on me when he ends the call with Lee.

"He knows."

"He knows?" I parrot. "How?"

Jacob shrugs. "He's a journalist, figuring stuff out is what he does. I was actually just coming to fill you in."

"You already talked to him?"

"He called me earlier to let me know he found the catering company, but I don't want to talk about that right now."

I don't resist when he reaches for me and pulls me close.

"I made you angry," he states matter-of-factly.

I don't see the point in lying about it, especially when he brings it up himself.

"You did. Although perhaps angry isn't the right word. You can be annoyingly confusing. One moment I feel like you trust me, and the next you say or do something to make me think you don't. And yet you expect me to put my faith in you. It's infuriating and frankly, a bit hurtful."

When I look up, I notice his gaze has drifted off somewhere over my shoulder, and he almost appears to be struggling with something.

"I'm going to try and get into the lodge as part of the catering crew," he suddenly announces, his eyes locking on mine. "And I wasn't going to tell you."

"Why?" I blurt out the first thought in my head.

I'm not quite sure how else to respond to that.

"Because I don't want you distracted, thinking about what I might be doing when you should be paying attention to what's going on around you."

"If that's the case, why tell me now?"

"Because you're right. I—"

Jacob is interrupted by the doorbell.

"I'll get it," he announces, as he releases me and moves into the hallway, but I follow on his heels.

It's Joey.

"Hey," I bump Jacob aside. "Is everything okay?"

She gives me a little smile but it doesn't reach her eyes, they look concerned.

"I was wondering if you'd seen Jose," she asks, her eyes darting between Jacob and me.

"Jose?" Jacob echoes. "I was talking to him a couple of hours ago, while you were grooming Moon, right before I came to talk to you."

"I know, but he left the barn right after you did. It's funny because I spent most of the afternoon thinking I should've just mentioned something to you, but decided I would ask Jose about it first." She glances at Jacob a bit sheepishly. "I checked the grounds and he's nowhere to be found. His truck is gone, and when I checked the staff quarters just now, I noticed all his stuff is gone too."

I feel tension radiating from Jacob.

"What were you going to ask him about?" he asks sharply.

"When you asked me earlier if I remembered seeing anything or anyone out of place, it honestly didn't register at first. Not until I had some time to think about it, but I wanted to give him a chance to explain before I mentioned anything."

"Explain what, Joey?" I prompt her, before Jacob loses his head.

I can hear him grinding his teeth beside me.

"It was Saturday morning; you had been gone for a couple of hours. I'd been into town to pick up a few supplies. When I returned, I could've sworn I saw him ducking around the side of the house. I kind of dismissed it. Then after I'd put my groceries away, I walked to the barn and that's when I saw him stuffing some kind of burlap sack in the toolbox in the back of his truck. It seemed a bit odd, but didn't make too much of it. Not until I started thinking about what you asked this morning."

Jacob turns to me.

"I need you to pull up—"

"I know," I interrupt him, already in motion.

I rush back to my office and open the security software that allows me to check the individual cameras.

Now we have seven, thanks to Jacob's vigilance, but back on Saturday there were only three cameras. One of them aimed at the front of the house, one pointed down the driveway, and a third one in the rear, directed at the paddock and the stables.

That last camera is the one I'm interested in. I access the file for last Saturday and pull up the archived feed, fast-forwarding until I see Jacob's truck pull the horse-trailer away from the stables.

"Slow it down," Jacob says behind me.

I resist the temptation to roll my eyes. The man can't help himself.

I play the video at regular speed until I see Joey get into her old RAV4 parked on the far side of the barn, where I can just see the rear of Jose's truck. Once the SUV is out of the image, I pay even closer attention.

We don't have to wait long before Jose comes walking out the barn doors and goes around the side toward his truck. Barely a minute later, he appears again with a burlap sack in his hand. It looks heavy.

"Son of a bitch," I hear Jacob mumble.

On the screen, Jose walks out of view of the camera when he gets close to the house. Five minutes later he reappears, running, the sack clearly empty in his hand.

It doesn't take us long to confirm that yesterday, shortly after Jacob came into the house, Jose loaded up his truck and hightailed it out of here. He's not even trying to hide anything, which tells me he's not planning on coming back.

Warm lips brush my ear.

"Call the state police, sweetheart. Give them what we've got. They can pick him up."

"And what will you be doing?" I ask, tilting my head back so I can look at him.

"I'm gonna talk to Joey. See if she has any connections." He presses a hard kiss on my lips before straightening up. "Looks like we'll need another stable hand."

TWENTY-THREE

ONYX

My eyes are still closed when I slide a lazy hand over my breast and down my belly.

My fingertips brush the bumps and ridges marring his scalp, as his mouth and tongue wake up my body. When I peer down, his hungry eyes are blazing up at me.

"Morning," I mumble breathlessly, only to lose my voice completely when his fingers join the magic his mouth is creating between my legs.

When he hums against my highly sensitized flesh, the deep vibrations cause my hips to buck off the bed. He capitalizes on the moment by sliding his hands under my ass, lifting me to his mouth like I'm his personal breakfast buffet.

Not that I'm complaining—far from it—as his fingers spread me open for his tongue to explore. With one hand clamped on the back of his head, I use the other to play with my breast, plucking at my nipple when I feel the tension coil low in my belly.

I've never been devoured quite like this before, voluntarily relinquishing all control over my body to the man who is making it sing. Right now, Jacob holds all the power and I'm perfectly okay with that.

When I come, it's a full body experience: heart-stopping, mind-blanking, limb-shaking, and breath-stealing. The French call it *la petite mort*—a little death—which seems appropriate as it feels for a moment like I'm leaving my body.

My eyes snap open when his cock fills me in one smooth stroke, and I see his hazel ones only inches away. The gold flecks in his eyes sparkle, and his labored breath fans my face, while he pumps inside me. I watch him lose control, his mouth going slack and his eyes glazing over, as his hips buck erratically.

When Jacob finally pulls from my body, I feel bereft, like losing a part of me.

I'm falling in love with him.

I've probably loved him on some level for a while already. Although, that was more intuitive, without the benefits of my senses. Having now touched, heard, seen, smelled, and tasted him, only confirms what I somehow knew instinctively.

There was only once before I've felt this deeply connected to someone, this visceral sense of belonging. Only one time when I looked into another set of hazel eyes and saw my own soul reflected.

There have been a few unfiltered moments where I

allowed my mind to drift unchecked, and decades-old memories would begin blending with current experiences. But then I force myself back to reality, where those memories are nothing more than ashes, spread out over the grounds of a building long since burned down.

"Are you coming?"

Pulled from my thoughts, I turn my head to find Jacob leaning against the doorpost to the bathroom. I hear the shower running in the background.

I fling back the sheets and swing my legs out of bed. "Coming."

LAST NIGHT WE DID ALL WE COULD DEALING WITH Jose's abrupt departure.

We filled the authorities in on what we discovered, and provided them with copies of the video files. Then we asked Joey to join us for some of Bernie's outstanding lasagna so we could discuss short-term solutions and long-term options for the stables.

Jacob wanted to get that out of the way, so we could put it out of our mind and spend today and tomorrow concentrating on the upcoming event at Grandview Estate.

I'll admit, my first thought this morning of what might be waiting for me in Russell Springs had my stomach in knots, but I recognize it's lack of strategy and planning that makes me nervous. We're going to change that today by gathering as much information as we can, making a plan of attack based on that knowledge, and then creating several alternative strategies as a back door.

Kate had offered to come here but, at Jacob's urging, I convinced her to work from the office instead. I suggested we might need her to collect some of our tech equipment, depending on what we end up planning. Having her here would make things complicated for Jacob.

He is currently on the phone with Lee, hammering down details on how he's going to get inside the lodge with the catering crew.

I've been reviewing some of the trail camera feed Janey sent us, along with satellite images of the property, to get a feel for the grounds. I've paid particular attention to the cabins, but there doesn't seem to have been more activity than what Janey had already reported. She did mention this morning she hadn't seen any sign of whoever the three were who arrived by helicopter earlier in the week.

It makes me sick to think of what might be happening to the two brought to the property at gunpoint. Wheeler is a deviant, a pervert of the worst kind, and I have no doubt a murderer too.

For many years I'd believed him dead as well, perished in the fire that took down Transition House, along with his two equally sick accomplices. Except—as we've discovered in recent years—they didn't die in that fire. None of them. I suspect Jacob has somehow always known.

I, on the other hand, had been living under the impression the man who took more from me than any other whose uninvited hands had violated me, was already doing his penance in the afterlife. For me it had been a form of closure; a lock on the box of memories I no longer had the power to influence or change.

Discovering he is still breathing the same air I am, hearing his voice, has brought everything to the surface. The fear, the anger, the pain, but also the need for justice and even revenge for what was so brutally taken.

I wasn't equipped back then to stand up for myself, but I am now, and I have Jacob to thank for giving me a chance to take my power back. With force, if need be.

"I'd love to know what is going on in that mind of yours right now."

I swing my desk chair around at the sound of his voice.

"I'm not too sure about that. I'm imagining all the things I'd love to be able to do to Wheeler."

"Are you kidding? Revenge fantasies used to be one of my favorite pastimes," he jokes with a grin.

I raise an eyebrow. "Used to be?"

He nods as he pushes away from the doorway and steps up to me, bracing himself with his hands on my armrests.

"Touching you, kissing you, watching you...those all are now at the top of my list."

Jacob

Over the course of the day, as the plans are coming together, I can feel the tension building for the whole team. Myself included.

At my request yesterday, Mitch contacted Matt Driver, his former boss and the commander of the Child Abduction Rapid Deployment team. We've worked with Mitch's former team a few previous times, but in those cases minors were missing. We're not actively searching for any missing kids this time, but after Janey described what appeared to her to be two young males being led at gunpoint, I wanted to have the CARD team at least alerted.

The truth is, we don't have anything concrete to tie Wheeler to at this point. Hell, we can't even prove Morton Ackers is, in fact, David Wheeler. What we do have are suspicions, so this whole operation is nothing more than a fishing expedition. Not interesting to law enforcement perhaps, but GEM works with much different standards. We aren't limited by the letter of the law and tend to apply our own criteria and measures.

"Is that the guy?"

I follow Raj's gaze out the front window where I just catch sight of a pickup truck driving past the house.

"Looks like it," I tell her, leaning over to brush her lips with mine. "I'll head over to the stables."

I leave Raj sitting at the dining table, where she's sewing a small microphone and transmitter into the trim of a colorful kimono she's decided to wear to the soiree.

The fall air is cool and refreshing when I step outside. I use the walk to the stables to get back in the role of Hamish, the horse trainer. These past few days it's been harder and harder to keep the two identities separated. Another reason why I'm eager to bring this to an end, because I'm bound to screw up sooner or later.

That said, I feel we're in good shape for tomorrow.

I'm driving to The Posh Palate in Richmond early in the morning. Jeremy Lancaster, the chef and owner, has agreed to let me come as part of his crew, but insisted I be at his kitchen to help with the prep at nine in the morning. Since he can only bring a skeleton crew as it is, he wants to make sure I can at least pull my weight in the kitchen. Not exactly my comfort zone, but I'm willing to do whatever it takes if it means I can be in close proximity to Raj.

I'll be hitching a ride in the catering van with Jeremy to Grandview Estate.

My only concern about this arrangement is that someone at Grandview might recognize me. I will need to alter my looks as best I can. I'm afraid a baseball cap won't cut it, so Bernie is going to be here just after dawn to help me with some makeup and a wig. I'm not exactly looking forward to it, even though Bernie was almost giddy at the prospect.

Mitch is on his way back here and will rent a suitable vehicle, since the Lincoln is a write-off. Then tomorrow he'll be driving Rajani and Opal down to the Marriott hotel in Somerset, where Raj booked a suite. They'll check in there and use the room for Raj to get ready for the evening, but will actually be sleeping in adjoining rooms at the Holiday Inn down the road under a different name.

Anyone who might be trying to find out where Onyx Baqri is staying will be sorely disappointed. The subterfuge is probably not necessary, but it'll help me sleep better.

I haven't quite figured out where Lee is going to be, he's been rather close-lipped about his plans, but I have no doubt he'll be close. Lee has his own reasons for wanting to see some justice come to Wheeler. He firmly believes Wheeler is guilty of killing his mother.

Needless to say, motivation is high for everyone, even though not all for the same reasons.

The woman standing next to the silver pickup with Joey is a surprise. I could've sworn she mentioned her friend's name was Hunter Sinclair. I guess it's my mistake for assuming Hunter referred to a man, especially since we already have a female Joey.

"You must be Hunter."

I brace myself for her reaction to my appearance, like I always do. Although these days it's more of an annoyance than it is hurtful.

To her credit she barely flinches.

"That would be correct," she returns, offering me her hand.

She's older, with a helmet of short gray hair, and a heavily lined face. I'm a little concerned this work may be too physically demanding for her.

"And I can assure you I'm up to the job," she adds with a smirk.

She must've picked up something in my expression.

"I have no reason to believe otherwise," I concede, taking her hand. "I'm Hamish."

I take Hunter into the stables, observing her as she seems to check the building out carefully. She approaches the horses with a casual ease that betrays the level of comfort you'd expect to find in someone who has spent a lot of time around them.

She honestly answers my questions about her work history, and admits she has left several places of employment as a result of what she considers to be workplace harassment. I don't doubt her claim of harassment. I imagine as a woman in a role more commonly associated with men, you get all kinds of feedback, and little of it positive.

And here I am, no better than anyone else silently questioning her abilities. However, in all fairness, that was more about her age than her gender.

"I'm used to working with women in different roles," I share. "I don't care about your gender as long as the job gets done."

"Sounds reasonable," she replies, nodding.

Next, I confirm she's okay working with Joey in charge, which she is. Then when I lead her back outside, I ask her about her availability, to which she opens the gate of her truck, revealing a couple of duffel bags, a saddle, and a collection of small appliances.

"I took a chance," she says with a grin. "Joey

mentioned you'd need someone right away. I figured if things worked out, I'd save some time."

"Give me a moment with Joey."

I gesture for Joey to step aside with me for a moment.

"You're sure you're good working with her?"

She nods. "I am."

"Okay, because we're not going to be around for the next day or two, and I'd feel better if there are two of you here."

Fifteen minutes later I walk into the house, leaving the women to move Hunter's stuff into the staff quarters.

"And?" Raj asks as she looks up from her handiwork.

"Turns out Hunter is a woman. I think she'll work out —Joey seems to think so—but I guess time will tell."

"Of course," she scoffs. "Now that the changes to the staff building are done, we don't need them anymore."

The contractor left less than two hours ago.

"I'm sure the second bathroom is welcome regardless," I point out.

"I guess."

Raj gets to her feet and shakes out the kimono before slipping it on over her clothes.

"Can you see anything?" she asks.

I step closer and check the seam along the neckline.

"No."

It's not until I run my fingers along the edge, I feel a slight bump. Not enough for anyone to notice.

"It looks good. Are you done? Ready?"

I grab the other side of her kimono and pull her close.

"I just need to pack my stuff, but that'll take two minutes tomorrow morning. What about you?"

"Yeah, I think I'm ready. I feel a lot better knowing we're not leaving Joey in a lurch."

I slide my hands under the kimono and around her waist.

"I know we've had our hands full," Raj brings up. "But we haven't really addressed Jose, or his motivation for wanting to get rid of me."

"I have," I admit. "I've been in touch with a private investigator I've worked with before, and asked him to put surveillance on Gordon Chen."

She leans back and eyes me with a hint of disbelief.

"You really think Chen has something to do with it?"

I pull up my shoulders. "I'm not sure, I can't see what Chen's beef would be, other than he's pissed at you for showing him up at the auction, but...he's the one who put Jose in contact with you. I'm not ready to brush that off as coincidence and besides that, he's the only connection we know about. I feel better knowing he has eyes on him."

I tug her toward me again, locking my hands in the small of her back.

"Is that everything? Nothing else on your mind?" I inquire. "Because I think it's time to relax a little."

She grins up at me, sliding her hands up my chest.

"Relax? We haven't even eaten yet."

"We can—"

"Is that Bernie?" Raj interrupts me, looking over my shoulder out the window.

I groan and turn my head. Sure enough, there's

Bernie walking up to the front door with, if I had to guess, more food in her hands.

Swallowing a curse, I reluctantly let go of her so she can rush to the door and open it.

"Are those your cinnamon rolls?" I hear Raj ask.

Of course, she shows up with those. There's no way I can send her packing now.

So much for my relaxing plans.

TWENTY-FOUR

JACOB

"A beard too?"

I glare, first at Bernie, who is not in the least impressed with me, and then I swing the office chair around so I can glare at Raj, who is laughing even harder than she already was.

"Shouldn't you be getting ready?" I suggest to her.

"I'm done. I'm ready to go. Besides, I wouldn't miss this for the world."

To demonstrate, she leans against the doorway and crosses her arms over her stomach.

My eyes return to my reflection in the mirror. The makeup Bernie caked on my face feels unnatural and itchy, but it looks pretty good. It seems to have smoothed out some of the scarring on my skin, it's less obvious now.

"Let's worry about your wig first," Bernie announces.

She produces a roll of transparent tape and cuts off a length.

"This is two-sided and will keep the hair in place."

"How did you learn how to do this?" Raj asks her.

"I spent the last twenty-five years of my career in the various burn units, and this—fitting wigs for burn victims —is something I learned to do on the side," Bernie explains as she affixes the tape to my skin.

"Tell me there's an easy way to get that stuff off," I grumble.

"Yes, relax." She holds up a small bottle. "It's an alcohol-based solvent. Just dip a cotton ball and dab it along the hair-line. You should be able to peel the hair back, tape and all."

Next, she pulls the wig from a bag. It looks to be close to the hair color I used to have; a dark brown. It even looks wavy, like mine was.

Somewhere in the house a phone rings and Rajani pushes away from the doorpost.

"Shit. Left my phone in the kitchen," she mumbles as she darts out of the room.

"Sit still," Bernie admonishes me as I crane my neck to catch a last glimpse of Rajani.

Then she begins to fit on the hair, starting in the front, agonizingly careful, and therefore annoyingly slow. With the wig hanging in front of my face, I don't see Raj coming in, but I can hear her, and she sounds annoyed.

"That was Kate. She says they're a little ahead of schedule and she wanted to make sure I was *decent* this time."

Bernie snickers. "Sounds like there's a story there."

"You could say that," Raj answers at the same time as I say, "There isn't."

That only makes Bernie laugh out loud. "It's gotta be a good story, then."

"Anyway," Raj steers away from the subject. "I just wanted to give you a heads-up, she says they'll be here in twenty minutes or so."

Obviously, I'd like to avoid them seeing me at this point.

"How long do you figure, Bernie? Just skip the whole beard idea."

"If you can find a way to sit still, I can be done in less than ten minutes."

"I won't distract you, then," Raj announces, and I hear her footsteps disappear down the hall.

True to her promise, it's not that much later when Bernie swings my chair around in front of the mirror. I haven't seen the face staring back at me in over fifteen years.

"Jesus," I mutter. "You made me look like me."

"I'm not sure what you mean," Bernie responds, looking confused.

I realize she probably doesn't, since she never knew the old me. There are no pictures in existence, other than a few grainy snapshots Hamish still has of our time overseas.

And now I have a dilemma.

I can try and duck out of here without Raj seeing me,

but then I run the chance of her catching sight of me at Grandview, which could end in disaster.

My other option is using the next ten or however many minutes I have left before Mitch and Opal get here, to try and explain myself in that limited time frame.

Fuck. This is a lose-lose situation. Either way, she's going to be upset, and feel betrayed, and likely never want to see me again.

"I have a favor to ask," I address Bernie. "I need you to send Rajani in here, and run interference with Opal and Mitch when they get here. Keep them occupied until Raj comes out."

Which may be sooner than I'd like.

As Bernie leaves to find Raj, I take another glance in the mirror. It's amazing what the hair and a little makeup can do.

"What's—"

Raj stops right inside the door, her eyes fixed on the mirror and my reflection.

"No..."

I surge out of the chair and grab hold of her arm, pulling the door shut before she can dart out.

"Rajani, let me explain."

Her face is pale as she shakes her head.

"I can't believe I didn't see it. It's so obvious now. How is this even possible? I don't understand."

"They lied to you. To me. Threatened you and the others would pay the price unless I complied." I'm rambling, I know I am, but I can't help myself. I feel pressured to make her understand. "So I did. I never resisted, thinking I was protecting you, and later... Later I convinced myself it was better you didn't know the truth."

"Better?" she scoffs, twisting out of my hold. "You decided it was better for me to live life with a hole in my heart? Is that what you're telling me?"

I knew this wasn't going to be easy, I just didn't expect it to be quite this hard.

"I thought I'd be bringing back bad memories." As much as that is true, it's not the main reason I worked hard to keep my identity hidden to this day. "I also promised I'd come back for you and the girls, but when I finally was able to get there—thirty-nine months, two weeks, and four days later—you were already gone. That's when I—"

I stop myself when I hear voices coming from the front of the house. Raj hears them too and darts past me out of the room. Not much I can do but watch her go.

All I can do is hope she'll give me a chance to explain later. There's so much more to unwrap. The fire—my failed attempt to eradicate the memories and the people responsible for them—my escape into the military, the attack, my recovery, and the dreams of vengeance.

I need to tell her how I finally tracked all three of them down, hoping to find them happily married, with families of their own. Instead, none of them seemed to have fulfilling lives, none of them had put down roots of any kind, and no one had formed any meaningful relationships.

That's when I realized I might still be able to have a

positive impact on their lives. That's why I formed GEM. For these three women: Kate, Janey, and Rajani.

I've been trying to fulfill a promise.

Onyx

"Are you sure you're okay?"

Kate twists in her seat to check me out in the back seat.

"I'm fine, I had a bit of a rough night."

More like a rough morning, but I keep that to myself. I'm still processing it.

"Why don't you close your eyes? Get some rest," she suggests. "It'll be a couple of hours on the road."

"Maybe I will."

I doubt I'll get any sleep, but I'll have plenty of time to sort my thoughts and feelings. Both are all over the place right now.

Part of me wants to deny this is even possible, but another part feels like it shouldn't be a surprise. There are things that make a lot more sense now—like my almost instant draw to him—but there is still so much I'm unclear on.

What I do know, and with absolute certainty, is I'm angry. Probably for more than one reason. I've wasted twenty-four years basically pining for this man, I feel betrayed, and I'm hurt, to list a few.

And yet, there were some things he mentioned that made me sad too. Like threats made to him, they sound identical to the threats issued to me. The younger girls would suffer unless I complied. I heard that more than once. Or when he suggested he was counting the days until he could return, only to find us gone. That definitely struck a chord.

Thirty-nine months, two weeks, and four days. Over three-and-a-half years later. By that time, I would've been on my own for a couple of years already, and living in North Carolina. I was working every shift I could get at the restaurant to pay for college, which I'd just started.

That was the same year Transition House burned down, and Kendrick, Sladky, and Wheeler were reported to have perished.

I inevitably wonder who might've been responsible for that fire.

My bet is on Nathan Ramos.

But mostly I'm trying to figure out where he may have spent those almost four years.

I have to remember he was just as traumatized and abused as we all were. Seared in my mind is the apology in his eyes when we were forced to have sex, and moments later his shock and pain when Wheeler mounted him from behind. Even while Nathan was being violated, he was trying to protect me. He pleaded with me to look in his eyes, holding me there, just him and me, detached from what was happening to our bodies.

Even years later, whenever nightmares would revive that bad memory, or one of the many others, it would be the memory of those eyes that brought me comfort.

What boggles my mind is that those eyes were not a dead giveaway. I guess the possibility never even occurred to me since Nathan was dead. I'd lived with that reality for too long, and he looks nothing like the boy I remember.

At some point I must've fallen asleep because when I open my eyes, Kate is hanging over the back of her seat, shaking my shoulder.

"We're here."

I sit up and glance out the window, noting we're stopped in front of the Marriott's main entrance. I've slept for hours.

"Fluff your hair," Kate instructs me. "And you have a little..." she gestures to the corner of my mouth.

I quickly wipe and fluff, hoist my fake Chanel backpack over my shoulder, and climb out of the vehicle while Mitch holds the door open.

"I've got the bags," he assures me.

Kate walks slightly in front of me, as we enter the lobby and head straight for the front desk. By the time I've checked in, Mitch has joined us with the bags. When we get to the suite, he drops the luggage inside before heading back out. He plans to keep an eye out on who comes in and out of the hotel, while Kate keeps me company.

We have a couple of hours to kill before I need to get ready for the party, so we end up finding a movie on TV for distraction, and ordering room service. The movie can't hold my attention, but I force myself to eat something, knowing it'll be even harder to get something down tonight.

When my phone rings two hours later, I know it's him before I even look at my screen.

"I'll just take this in the bedroom," I tell Kate.

"Hamish?"

I nod. I'm not sure what to call him anymore.

"Who is Jacob?" I ask him the moment I answer the call.

He doesn't hesitate, "My middle name."

"And Branch?"

"The English translation of Ramos."

All very logical and painfully obvious, if you know what you're looking for. I get this weird feeling in the pit of my stomach at the sound of his voice. Even that sounds so familiar now. Deeper, a little more mature, but now I know it belongs to Nathan, I can actually hear it.

"What am I supposed to call you? I don't even know."

"Sweetheart, I don't give a rat's ass. Whatever feels most natural to you right now."

Shit. That's a really good answer, and it actually helps me clarify something for myself.

"Jacob it is."

Because Nathan may not be dead but he's gone, in his place is a grown and fully formed man. When it comes down to it, the same is true for me; I'm not the person I was then. I've evolved, grown, strengthened.

It suddenly gives me some insight into what Jacob's

objective with GEM may be. Why he got all of us involved, why he assigned this particular case to me.

Jacob is trying to give us our power back.

"Good by me," he accepts, before getting to the purpose of his call. "I wanted to let you know I should be at Grandview in about half an hour. We just stopped for some gas."

Knowing what I know only ratchets up my concern for him. What if Wheeler recognizes him? But I guess the same is true for me, probably more so because I haven't changed as drastically as Jacob has.

"Be careful," I urge him, despite not wanting to admit I care that much.

I know it's stupid, probably immature, since he already knows better, but I feel I've been through the wringer, and hanging on to my anger for a bit keeps me alert.

"You too. Your safety comes first. Any sign of trouble and you give the signal. If you find any evidence he's still exploiting kids, document it, and alert us so we can get Matt and his team in there. And, Rajani? Remember he can't hurt you anymore."

"I know that."

"I've got to go, but one last thing," he adds. "Lee just sent me a message; Olson is out on bail."

"Figures."

If anything, that news makes me even more determined. It's about time someone puts a stop to these people.

For good.

TWENTY-FIVE

ONYX

I adjust the thick side-braid hanging down my shoulder.

It hides the earpiece keeping me connected to the team.

I'm wearing a skintight, black tank dress under my kimono. The dress hits me mid-thigh and barely hides the thin switchblade I have strapped to the inside of my thigh, but the kimono goes all the way down to my ankles. Janey picked the outfit. According to Janey the little black dress is sexy, and the kimono gives the outfit class. Kate assured me no one will suspect I'm armed.

All I know is that my hands are sweating as Mitch drives me down the long, winding driveway to the lodge. It's already getting dark, the sun set fifteen minutes ago, and as we leave the trees behind, I can see the fences, stables, and lodge are all lit with strings of outdoor lights.

The grounds should look beautiful but, given what may be going on behind closed doors, it only looks creepy. Like the opening scenes of a horror movie.

"I can hear you almost hyperventilating from here," Mitch warns me.

He's right, I'm breathing like a steam engine. I mindfully adjust my breathing and attempt to center myself.

A young man wearing a burgundy vest stops us, instructing Mitch to drop me off at the base of the steps. After that he's supposed to park the vehicle by the garage, which is on the other side of the lodge from the stables.

A second valet is waiting at the base of the stairs and rushes up to open my door when Mitch pulls up.

"I've got your back," he relays softly.

I give him a curt nod before I get out of the car, tugging the ends of the Pashmina wool shawl I added to my outfit to ward off the cold. I'm pretty sure Janey would not approve, but I have no interest in freezing my butt off.

"Ms. Baqri, may I?" the young man asks, offering me his arm.

He's almost pretty, fine-boned and smooth, no sign of any manly stubble. Little more than a child.

"What's your name?" I ask as I take his arm and let him lead me up the steps.

He seems a little taken aback at my question, but still answers, "Stefan," in that soft voice.

"Stefan. That's a lovely name. Have you been here long, Stefan?"

We've almost reached the top of the stairs and I'm doing my best to slow down our progress.

I catch his glance up to the portico, held up with two massive log columns.

"Two years and five months," he mumbles as we step onto the landing.

There he steps aside and my hand slides from his arm. "Ma'am?"

His voice is louder as he gestures to the front doors where a girl, dressed in a black mini-dress with a white lace apron, is waiting. The only thing missing is the white collar and black bow tie to complete the Playboy bunny look.

As I walk toward her, the earpiece crackles to life with Lee's voice.

"Olson just turned up the driveway."

Instinct has me turn my head to look behind me before I can stop myself. The vehicle I see pulling up to the stairs does not hold Jesper Olson though, but a couple around my age or a bit older who look vaguely familiar. I don't want to be caught gawking so I swing back to the door where the girl is still waiting.

"Ms. Baqri, can I take your wrap?" she asks politely.

I will eat my shoes if this girl is older than eighteen.

The fact these kids address me by name makes me feel physically ill. What do they see when they look at me?

I slip my Pashmina from my shoulders and hand it to her.

"What's your name?"

She looks as surprised as the other kid did, but it's important to let them know I see them. I have no proof, but I also have no doubt, these kids are not here voluntarily.

I remember all too well how the process of conditioning started by stripping me of my identity. I was made to feel like no more than a piece of chattel. My name was never mentioned, I was moved around and arranged like a piece of luggage, and most of the time I was blindfolded when I was used.

To the point I became as anonymous as I was being treated.

So yes, it's important for me to know their names.

"Heather," she finally answers, as if it took her a while to remember.

I smile at her. "Thank you, Heather. I appreciate it."

"Cocktails are past the stairs to your left," she indicates.

I glance around the foyer and my eye catches on the door to the powder room. It gives me a chance to check in with the team and, if I time it right, maybe I'll be able to intercept Jesper Olson when he walks in.

"Thanks, I'll just use the facilities first."

I duck into the bathroom just as the couple arriving behind me steps into the foyer. I'm curious to know who they are.

"Janey? Do you have eyes on the gate still?"

"*I do.*"

"Did you run the plates for the vehicle that came in right behind me? It's a couple, they look familiar."

"*Car's registered to Frank Galloway. Church of Abundance.*"

"That's who it is."

I occasionally see ads for the televangelist, promising a life of prosperity and promoting family values. Some of the advertisements feature his wife.

"Including Olson and myself that makes six guests so far, correct?"

"Correct."

"Any news on the identity of the first guy?"

Janey kept us up to date with any arrivals before me. There'd been two. The second one a news anchor for a national network Janey recognized, but we haven't figured out the first one yet. The problem was he didn't arrive in his own vehicle but a limousine.

"A Hollywood plastic surgeon for the rich and famous. Flew into Lake Cumberland Regional Airport in a private jet."

My first thought is it must be nice to be that privileged. Then I remember, by measure of dollars, Jacob belongs to the ranks of the privileged as well. But I know better now. His path to wealth has been all but privileged, it was painful and traumatic.

"Guys, hang on," Kate interrupts. *"Someone is coming in by boat as we speak. Docking at the back of the property. One person getting off. It's too dark and I'm too far to see a face."*

Kate has found a spot in the trees on the edge of the water near the cabins. From there she's able to see the stables and the rear of the lodge, as well as the water.

I almost jump at the sound of a knock on the bathroom door.

"I have to go," I whisper, quickly running water in the sink.

"Ms. Baqri, are you all right?"

The voice is male and cultured, but I don't recognize it. I turn off the water and unlock the door.

I've never seen the man standing on the other side.

"My name is Barnaby," he introduces himself. "I'm the majordomo here at Grandview Estate."

That's a somewhat elevated descriptor for a butler, but it suits him, surprisingly.

Barnaby looks like he's straight from a British TV show. Slim, with an ascot tucked into the neck of the dress shirt he's wearing under his V-neck pullover. At first glance he looks to be in his thirties, but on closer examination I see the fine lines in his face and the slight waddle under his chin, which makes it more likely he's in his fifties.

"It's a pleasure to meet you, Barnaby."

I shoot him what I hope is a pleasant smile, but I'm a little distracted when I see Jesper Olson walking right past us. Instead of heading left, he turns right on the other side of the stairs. From what I remember that's where, among other things, the office is located.

"Could I escort you to a cocktail?" he offers.

"That would be wonderful."

Barnaby leads the way, but when I expect him to turn left, where the girl instructed me to go, he turns right. The same way Jesper went.

"Are we not joining the others?" I purposely ask, so the team knows what's going on.

"Absolutely, but Mr. Ackers wanted an opportunity to welcome you himself."

I expect the man to lead me to the office at the end of the hall, but instead he opens the door to the room with the dark paneling and the pool table in the center. It's empty except for a cart with a selection of liquors.

"What can I prepare for you?" Barnaby asks, standing by the bar cart.

"I would love a Negroni, if you have the ingredients."

I've only had a Negroni once in my life, but it's the fanciest thing I can think of to order.

"Of course."

I look around me while Barnaby mixes my drink. Why am I in here? And if Ackers wanted to meet me so badly, where is he?

"Mr. Ackers had one last thing to finish up," he explains, as if I'd posed the question out loud.

He turns to me, holding out my cocktail, complete with a slice of orange. He looks at me expectantly, so I take a quick sip.

"Perfect," I compliment him, at which he beams.

"Excellent. He will be with you shortly."

Barnaby nods and backs out of the room, closing the door behind him.

I feel distinctly uneasy and almost jump out of my skin when I hear Janey in my ear.

"Where are you?"

"Room with the pool table."

Everyone has studied the blueprints of the lodge, and

I'd been able to fill in some more of the layout after my last visit here.

A sharp click sounds behind me and I swing around to see a panel in the wall open up.

I hold my breath and steel my expression, when David Wheeler steps into the room.

Jacob

I'm frustrated.

I thought it would be easier if I knew I was in close proximity, but I have no freedom of movement here.

The view from the few windows in the kitchen look out on the water, and all I can see of the house is one side window to the living room, which appears to have been treated with reflective material, and a section of privacy screen blocking a view of the outdoor patio.

There's no way for me to keep an eye on what's going on.

The catering van was directed to a set of stairs at the rear of the lodge leading up to a back entrance directly into the kitchen, bypassing the rest of the lodge altogether.

The only person we've seen is some guy named Barnaby, maybe a personal assistant or something, but he appears to be in charge. He only communicates with Jeremy, ignoring Marcel, the sous-chef, and myself.

So far most of what I've been doing is dishes to the point my fingers are pruned. Bernie would say for lack of practice, since it's not something I do much of. I've listened to what little radio traffic there's been, while working, but I haven't turned on my mic since the others don't know I'm here. Besides that, I wouldn't want my voice to throw Raj off.

Now I've graduated to plating a goat cheese salad. Again, not exactly my wheelhouse, but with a bit of instruction and an example to work from, I seem to do okay, sliding each finished plate onto the cart.

I can tell Raj arrived at the lodge a few moments ago because she was interacting with some of the staff, making small talk. Now she's in the bathroom, talking with the team, when I hear knocking in the background. Suddenly Raj whispers she has to go.

I listen intently to Barnaby introducing himself, but the hair on my neck stands on end when Raj asks why they're not joining the others. When I hear the explanation Wheeler wants to meet her alone, every alarm bell goes off in my head and my feet are already moving.

I'm halfway to the door when Jeremy stops me, blocking my way.

"Where are you going?"

"Something's wrong."

I reach around him for the door.

"You open that door, I break my contract and I won't get paid," Jeremy warns me. "You'd better be sure."

"I'll fucking pay you double," I growl.

Right then the door opens and Barnaby walks in.

"We're ready for the first course," he announces.

"One minute," Jeremy tells him, giving me a stern look as Barnaby nods and backs out of the kitchen.

So far, all I hear in my earpiece is a calm, male voice. I can't quite make out what he says, and I hope to God if Raj was in danger, she would be vocal. I quickly finish plating the last of the salads and as I'm placing them on the cart, I hear Raj say, "That would be lovely."

Jeremy hands me the bread baskets and then, before anyone can stop me, I grab hold of the cart and use it to push open the door to the hallway.

Barnaby is waiting right outside, looking startled.

"You're not supposed to be out here."

"I'm sorry, I was under the impression you were in a hurry," I tell him innocently.

Then my breath hitches in my throat when I catch sight of Rajani, still in one piece, and walking past the kitchen, side by side with the man for whom I still feel such hatred, it makes my blood run cold.

I could swear he feels my energy when his head snaps around and those dead blue eyes lock on mine. One perfectly arched eyebrow inches up as he holds my gaze until he disappears down the hall.

There is not a single doubt in my mind he knows exactly who I am.

TWENTY-SIX

ONYX

"Ms. Baqri, it's a pleasure to finally meet you."

His voice, although still recognizable, is cloaked in a layer of fake, soft-spoken charm that makes my skin crawl. Still, I manage to plaster a smile on my face and resist pulling my hand back when he presses a kiss to my knuckles.

"Unfortunately, I couldn't be present when you came to collect Arion's Moon, but I hope you'll allow me the honor of introducing you to some of my friends."

Struggling to find words, I simply nod and take his offered arm, letting him lead me out of the room.

I hear Jacob's voice before I see him. A brief glimpse to my right reveals him and Barnaby standing in the alcove leading to the kitchen. I force my eyes forward, but notice Wheeler keeps his attention on the two men as we pass. I hold my breath, waiting for him to recognize Jacob, but he stays silent as he leads me into the living room where a group of people is gathered.

I'd already seen the televangelist, Frank Galloway, and his wife, and the plastic surgeon is easy to pick out with his smooth skin and fake tan, although that could be the news anchor as well. The other single man is leaning casually against the fireplace, his elbow resting on the mantel, but he looks vaguely familiar, which would probably make him the news anchor.

Wheeler aka Morton Ackers leads me around, introducing me to the others.

The televangelist sandwiches my hand in both of his, smiles piously, and deigns to call me *dear*. When his wife, Margaret's limp hand and lowered eyes are next, it becomes clear which way the wind blows in that household. I feel a strong need to wash my hands.

The doctor is introduced as Troy Stone, a name I'd want to bet is as fake as his tan and hairline.

"You have gorgeous skin," he gushes, building me up before dropping me back down to reality with, "Too bad the wrinkles are taking over, I can help you with that."

"Behave, Troy," our host chides him. "Some of us prefer to age gracefully."

The plastic surgeon does not seem at all impressed and barks out a laugh.

"Surely, you're not counting yourself among them? You've probably had more work done than the rest of us in this room combined."

Wow. Troy apparently does not hold back. I glance furtively at Wheeler, who smiles at his friend tightly.

Interesting. It makes me wonder whether Troy was the one who did the work on him. I'm not sure whether his face was damaged in the fire, or whether the work was done to hide his identity, but other than his eyes and voice, Wheeler looks nothing like he did before.

Dick Corzone is the anchor, and the next person I'm introduced to. Rather than a handshake, Corzone shoots me a perfunctory smile and nod, before letting his eyes drift over my shoulder. I've clearly been deemed uninteresting and dismissed, which suits me just fine.

Then Wheeler turns us around to someone sitting in one of the wingback chairs facing the fireplace, and I'm rattled by an unexpected surprise.

"I believe you've met my dear friend, Gordon Chen?"

It takes everything out of me to keep shock off my face and grab Chen's extended hand.

"Of course, Mr. Chen, it's good to see you again."

It's actually very unnerving, since he was more than likely behind the attempt on my life, but I can't let that show.

"I understand you gave Gordon a run for his money at the auction?" Wheeler brings up.

"She certainly did," Chen says with what appears to be a disarming smile.

He doesn't seem too annoyed with me for bidding him up. I never really thought that could be an incentive to get rid of someone, although you never know. People have been killed over less.

But no, if Chen indeed was involved in the attack on me, it must've been for other reasons. Depending on how deep his connection is with Wheeler, that might be a better reason, but it also implies they know who I am.

And that would suggest I'm being toyed with.

I need to watch my back.

"Dinner is served!"

Barnaby opens the sliding doors, revealing a massive dining table set for eight, which would mean someone is still missing. Probably Olson, I haven't seen him yet. Luckily, I've never actually met him face-to-face, so at least I don't have to worry about him recognizing me.

I'm being led to the chair to the right of the head of the table, where I assume Wheeler will sit. He steps aside to say something to Barnaby, who nods, before he takes his seat. Troy Stone is sitting across the table from me, and the Galloways beside him. Directly next to me Chen takes a seat, making me feel a little claustrophobic, and Corzone takes the last chair on this side. The only open seat is the one opposite Wheeler, but no one appears to comment on it.

Barnaby comes around, pouring wine. I'm the third one to be poured from the same bottle, which puts me at ease a little, but I still stop him at half a glass. Even though I barely touched my Negroni, other than that first tiny taste, I don't want to risk even the smallest impairment.

No sooner does Barnaby step out of the room when Wheeler claps his hands and gets to his feet, beaming.

"There he is."

I recognize the tall, blond young man who walks in from pictures.

Jesper Olson.

He looks like he just got out of the shower, droplets of water hanging off the ends of his longish hair. He's handsome, I can see how he'd be successful bait for teens.

I sit back and watch as everyone stands to greet and hug the kid. They all seem to know him quite well, which gives me a really foul taste in my mouth.

"Son, I'd like you to meet Onyx Baqri. She's the lady I told you purchased Arion's Moon."

Steel-blue eyes, the same color of his father's, turn to me with curiosity when I get out of my chair and turn to greet him. I hold out my hand but am pulled into an unexpected hug.

"I'm a hugger," he says, his lips brushing the shell of my ear. "Especially of beautiful women."

My instinct is to push him away but I'm here with a job to do, so I force myself to play along and slip my arms around his waist.

"Nice..." he mumbles, his hold on me tightening.

Then he rolls his hips, and I have to swallow down bile when I feel his erection pressing against me.

"Save that for after dinner, Son," his father laughingly reprimands him, as collective chuckles go up around the table.

Holy hell, I can almost smell the pheromones in the room.

"Let's eat."

As if they were waiting for the announcement, the two valets and the girl who met me at the door walk in, carrying trays. Once again, I have to shore up my resolve when I notice not only the boys are bare-chested under their vests, but Heather, the only girl, is as well. The lace of her apron does nothing to shield her breasts from view.

I'm not surprised to see all three faces wearing an impassive, detached expression. They're here, but they're not. These three have been well-conditioned.

"Heather..." Jesper glances up at the girl when she serves him a plate. "I see you've settled in nicely."

She doesn't show any reaction when his hand slides up her leg and dips under her little black skirt.

"Patience, Jesper," Wheeler says sharply this time. "You'll see plenty of action before the night is out."

I hear a muffled curse in my ear, probably Kate, who is a bit more fiery, but it's a comfort to know they're close by, listening in. It would be so easy to let myself disappear to the same place those three kids have gone. A place I'm intimately familiar with.

Instead, I look down at my plate, wondering how the hell I'm going to get anything down when I feel like I'm about to puke. I surreptitiously slip a hand between my legs, needing to feel the security of the cold blade.

A throat clears beside me. I jerk my hand free and catch Gordon Chen dropping a pointed glance at my lap before winking at me. I don't even need to guess what is on his mind, these people are all perverts. I'm going to need to bathe in bleach after this.

I'm able to sit through dinner, even eating some of every course set in front of me. The conversation during dinner is surprisingly normal. Most of it superficial and fairly general in nature. No one really talks about themselves, which is fine by me, it saves me from making up stories.

Then Wheeler gets to his feet, leaning on his fists as he glances around the table.

"Everyone ready for dessert?"

Instantly my anxiety returns.

Jacob

That little, fucking punk. I'm gonna tear him a new one when I get my hands on him.

I could hear his voice, right next to her. Then Wheeler called him off, but he also gave us a good idea of what the rest of the night is going to look like. I could hear one of the others curse.

Things are moving much faster than I anticipated, and I feel I'm losing grip on what exactly is happening. First of all, I could've sworn Wheeler knew exactly who I was when he saw me in the hallway, but nothing's happened since and I'm starting to think maybe I saw something that wasn't there. Then there's Chen showing up at this party, which suggests the possibility Wheeler may have ordered the hit on Raj via his good friend, Gordon.

Finally, I'm pretty sure I know what kind of party this is going to be, but what comes as a surprise to me is that they'd invite someone uninitiated into one. There's no way for them to know if Onyx Baqri is into sick stuff like this or not.

Dinner is a flurry of activity in the kitchen until the cart with the main course is picked up by Barnaby and we start cleanup. I've been listening to boring table talk with half an ear. The whole time I've been trying to make heads or tails of what is going on and I keep getting stuck on one question.

Why would Wheeler risk bringing an unknown in?

None of it makes sense, unless...

When I hear him announce dessert through my earpiece, I jump into action.

"I've gotta go," I tell Jeremy, taking off the apron he gave me. "If anyone asks about me, tell them I'm putting stuff away in the van."

"Is something wrong?" he asks.

"Yeah, very wrong."

I open the outside door and turn on my mic as I head down the stairs, then I pull out my phone and put it to my ear in case someone sees me.

"Contact Driver, tell him to bring reinforcements," I snap, trying to keep my voice down as I find a vantage spot behind the van. "We've got problems. Raj, don't let yourself get separated from the group."

"Who the fuck is on this frequency?" I hear Opal bark.

"It's Jacob."

"Like hell it is," Pearl snaps.

"Actually, I can confirm it is," Lee jumps in.

Before this turns into a lengthy discussion about who knows what and why, I take the lead.

"There's something off. I think Wheeler knows who I am, or at least suspects it, and he's used Rajani to draw me out of hiding. He turned the game on us."

"How would he know you?" Mitch asks.

He must have found a quiet place and turned on his transmitter. It doesn't surprise me he's the one to hit me with that question. I'm about to tell him that's a question for later when I hear the crunch of gravel behind me. But before I can swing around, I feel the cold steel of a barrel pressing in my neck.

Goddammit. I knew it.

Without moving my body, I gingerly turn my head until I catch sight of the person holding the gun.

"Well, well, well, if it isn't Brian Haley. I guess you're not only his trainer, you're his muscle as well? Nice gun."

"On my way," Mitch's voice sounds in my earpiece.

I want to tell him to focus on Raj instead, but that would only alert Haley I'm still transmitting. I'm sure he will find my earpiece eventually, but the longer I can hang on to it and feed information to my team, the better it is.

"I knew you were a fraud," the trainer accuses. "Give me the phone."

"Everyone went down to the basement," I suddenly hear Rajani whisper. Water is running in the background. *"I'm in the bathroom, but Olson is outside the door, waiting to take me down there."*

Mitch is quick to respond. *"Good, stick close to Olson, he's so damn horny he'll be easy to manipulate."*

Haley gets impatient and jabs my neck with the barrel. I'm tempted to try and take him down, but I don't want to risk anything until I know Raj is safe.

I hand him the phone. He drops it on the gravel and stomps on it with the heel of his boot. I have a feeling he assumes that's what I was talking on.

"Lift your arms and don't move," he grumbles.

With quick sweeps of his free hand, he checks me for weapons. I'm not carrying one because I felt the risk would outweigh the benefit.

"Walk," Haley orders.

"Where to?"

"Around the side of the house. Basement door."

The basement.

Yes. That's where Raj is headed.

"Heard that," Mitch mutters in my ear.

I'm glad to hear he's taking charge. Not that I don't trust the others, but if difficult decisions or choices have to be made—if it comes to choosing to rescue one over the other—I'd rather it be Mitch making them. The girls are too close.

I figure Wheeler must've alerted his goon after he saw me, or maybe Haley was lying in wait for me the whole time. It doesn't really matter; the outcome is the same.

There's a keypad next to the door and I step out of the way so Haley can get at it, but he grinds the gun in my skin.

"How stupid do you think I am? The code is 917294."

Pretty damn stupid, since he just revealed the code to my team as well.

I punch in the numbers and pull on the handle when I hear the lock disengage.

The hallway he forces me into is dark. No light comes in from the door behind us and I can see very little ahead of me. The walls appear to be painted black, and only a faint crack of light is visible at the end of the hall.

"There's a door to your right," Haley points out.

The faint light reflects off the knob and I reach for it.

"Light switch around the corner," he adds.

I'm momentarily blinded by the overhead bulbs, but then the room comes into focus.

And my blood freezes.

TWENTY-SEVEN

ONYX

I swear, the only reason I'm allowing Jesper Olson to put his slimy hands on me and virtually drag me to the basement is because I know Jacob is down there.

Calling it a basement doesn't really do the space justice though.

Already the stairs going down give the impression of luxury, with deep burgundy paper in an embossed fleur-de-lis pattern lining the walls, which continues into a main room. The row of high windows on the far side ensure privacy but still provide an amazing amount of light into the space.

In the center of the room is a large seating area with a couple of semi-circular leather couches and some over-sized club chairs in a rich, golden brown where the rest of the party is already seated. All are facing what looks like a stage with a glass wall on either side.

As Jesper leads me closer to the rest of the group, I notice there are several narrow cubicles behind both glass walls. Six in total.

I struggle to keep my composure when I see each one holds a person. To the right of the stage, I recognize the two boys and one girl who waited on us earlier. Those three are standing, apparently unaffected by their nudity. That's not the case for the three individuals in the left three cubicles, however. Again, two boys and one girl, from what I can see. The girl and one of the boys are sitting on the floor, pressed against the back wall with their knees pulled up to their chest. The second boy is standing, his hands cupping his groin as he glares in our direction.

I don't know what these perverts see, but all I'm looking at are six teens, already traumatized in a way they may not ever recover from. Oddly enough, it bolsters my determination to do whatever it takes to shut these people down once and for all.

"Welcome to my playroom," Wheeler aka Ackers declares with a grand gesture.

"Impressive," I comment, deadpan.

I can see my response shakes him a little. He was clearly not expecting that. Good, keeping him off-balance serves me well.

But it doesn't last long.

"Why don't you take Ms. Baqri into the private room. Don't get started without me."

I don't resist when Jesper walks me to a barely notice-able door in the wall, across from the glass cubicles. I have to trust my team won't allow anything to happen to those kids.

"You won't need this anymore," he says as he moves up behind me.

He then proceeds to peel my kimono down my arms and tosses it carelessly in a corner. I don't even flinch.

"Much better," he mumbles behind me as he strokes his hands over my shoulders. Revulsion coils in my stomach at the feel of his clammy hands on my skin, but for those kids I can endure.

I feel a little bereft without the microphone, I'm not sure how much it can pick up from where Jesper threw it, but at least I can still hear the team. Plus, I have a little added security hidden on my body.

Jesper reaches around me and presses on one side of the door which must've been closed with a pressure latch, since it swings open easily. Seeing what's inside has me hesitate on the threshold, but only briefly.

Somewhere down here Haley is holding Jacob at gunpoint, which motivates me to step inside. I have a sneaking suspicion what Wheeler might have in mind, which would mean I'll probably see Jacob sooner than later.

The foam chaise with different adjustable or removable segments, as well as the blackout blinds covering the other side of a window, give it away.

I'm afraid when those blinds open, I'll see Jacob on the other side. It's exactly the kind of sick game Wheeler would play. There is no doubt in my mind Wheeler knows not only who Jacob is, but who I am as well. I think

Wheeler may well be aware Jacob set the fire at Transition House, and he intends to get his revenge by torturing Jacob.

Using me.

Our team is out there, I have faith in them, but getting the kids to safety has priority. Which is the way it should be, but it means Jacob and I will be on our own. With only the switchblade strapped to my leg between us.

Olson closes in behind me again, wrapping an arm around me and sliding his hand down to my lower belly. Then he presses in as he pushes his pelvis into my ass. His other hand cups my breast and I quickly cover it with mine.

"Didn't your daddy want you to wait?"

"Hmmm," he hums in my neck. "He won't mind if we have a little sampler. Tell me you don't want some of this."

He grinds his erection against me, breathing heavily in my ear as his teeth clamp onto my shoulder, like some rutting animal. What keeps me in this game—playing my part—is the knowledge that at the end of it, we'll have spared so many young kids from this trauma. I'm an adult now, I understand the power sex can have, and my ability to wield that power.

So, I push my ass against him and drop my head back, offering him my neck as I pretend to play along.

"Sure I do, but I have a feeling your daddy wouldn't be too happy with us."

"Nor will I."

My head snaps up at the tinny sound of a voice and

Jesper instantly lets go of me. The blinds roll up, revealing a smirking Gordon Chen on the other side.

But he's not the reason for my involuntary cry. It's the sight of Jacob, strapped down on a spanking bench, his eyes closed and body slack.

I barely recognize the shrieking as coming from me.

"What have you done to him?"

Chen turns around and smirks at the monster stepping into view.

"You're right, my friend, this is much more fun."

"And to think you went against my advice and almost had her killed," Wheeler responds coldly, both of them ignoring me. "That would've really foiled my plans. The real fun will start when dear Nathaniel here wakes up."

I can't believe they're talking about us like Jacob and I aren't even here

Chen is still focused on Wheeler and appears to shrug his shoulders.

"It seemed too much of a risk to let her walk around when she could've easily remembered me."

Remembered him? Was he one of the many anonymous strangers who used me? I made it a point too remember as little as possible, so I'd had no idea.

"How could she recognize you?" Wheeler asks. "Don't you always want them blindfolded?"

I guess it was too optimistic to hope maybe I'd been the only one.

"Yes, you know I have too much to lose."

"Your secrets are safe, my friend. I will make sure of it."

Yeah, I didn't think Wheeler was going to let us walk out of here. What I didn't expect was Wheeler pulling a gun and firing.

The shot is loud and so sudden, the expression of shock stays on Gordon Chen's face as he collapses to the ground.

"Jesus, Dad," Jesper mumbles behind me. "A warning would've been nice."

Jacob

"He was becoming too much of a liability."

It took every ounce of strength out of me to keep playing dead when the shot went off.

I took one look in this room, saw that damn bench, and knew in an instant what he had planned for us. By then it was too late. Before I could even launch an attack, Haley jabbed me in the neck with a needle. I'm not sure what it was he injected me with but it felled me like a goddamn tree.

Next thing I know I wake up, shackled to this bench in a pose that feels all too familiar to me, and the sound of Wheeler's voice in my ear.

Jesus Christ, the man is a lunatic. Of course, I already knew that.

I don't need to look; I know exactly what I'll see when

I open my eyes. Gordon Chen, dead on the floor, and my beautiful Raj will be on the other side of this window. I could hear every word she and that little prick, Olson, said. But I need to stall as long as I can, giving the rest of the team a chance to get a plan of rescue together. Therefore, I keep my eyes firmly shut while I try to find a way out of the leather straps around my wrists.

Sadly, it doesn't last long when suddenly the heavy weight of a body presses me into the bench and hot breath brushes my cheek.

"How does it feel to be back here, pretty boy? Except, you're not so pretty anymore, are you?"

Wheeler's voice grates on me, but I refuse to give him any kind of reaction, he feeds on that.

"Good thing your tight ass looks as firm as it always was, it's gonna feel like coming home."

My eyes snap open and, like a homing beacon, I lock onto Rajani's dark, empathetic ones through the window. I need her to anchor me because, by God, I'll do whatever it takes to get her out of here.

"You know I'd much prefer my boys younger, firmer, but I wouldn't mind tapping you once more for old times' sake. Tell me, has anyone been in there since my last time?"

He grabs a handful of my ass cheek and squeezes too hard.

"Don't you touch him!" Rajani yells on the other side of the window.

"Come on, Dad. You said I was first."

Like a petulant child, Olson whines.

"Relax." Wheeler pushes off me. "First I want Nathaniel to watch as you play with her."

I watch Raj closely and instead of flinching at Wheeler's words, she sets her jaw.

Then with her eyes on me, her mouth forms the words, "I'm sorry," and the next moment she slips the clingy black dress off her shoulders and down to her waist where it hangs precariously. Her breasts are barely contained by the black lace bra. Then she finally takes her eyes off me and turns her back to face the Olson kid, propping one hand on a hip as she takes on a sultry pose.

"Well, in that case, what do you say?"

I can't stop the growl low in my throat when I see the lecherous smirk on that sick punk's face. His father chuckles softly behind me. These people are depraved beyond belief, but it spurs me to work harder on my leather shackles.

"You have no idea how sweet this is going to be," Wheeler whispers too close to my ear. "I couldn't believe my luck when I saw you on the video feed. I thought Gordon was blowing smoke at first when he claimed he saw that bitch of yours."

I'm not even reacting to his words; my eyes are focused on the sickening scene on the other side of the window. I'm not sure how far Raj will let this go, but it's torture to watch this guy's hands on her, however briefly. Rajani slips from his hold and uses the square footage of the room to tease him. Lead him by the dick, so to speak.

"...was told you were killed, that I'd missed my

chance. But here we are, it looks like I'll have my payback after all. And trust me when I say I'll make it hurt."

I block out his taunts, watching closely as I see Raj playfully slap the kid's hands out of the way, before putting hers on his waistband and opening each button of his fly with great care. God, help me.

I'm willing to swear the kid's forgetting his own damn name with the way she's playing him. I catch her whispering close to his ear as she circles around him, putting her hands on his hips and pushing his jeans down to his knees.

My heart is starting to beat faster when I notice she has effectively hidden herself behind Olson. In the next moment the kid is on his knees in front of her, a sharp thin blade cutting into the skin at the base of his throat.

She glances at me over his shoulder, an apology in her eyes.

Rajani's eyes are focused and intense as they find Wheeler, who is just realizing what has happened.

"Let him go," she orders in a sharp voice.

"Like hell!" Wheeler yells back, pulling his gun and aiming it at me. "I will kill him first."

"A sure way to end your son's life," she returns, as cool as a cucumber.

Hell, my hands are sweating. We're in the middle of a standoff and I'm fucking useless, tied up like a Thanksgiving turkey.

"You won't get the chance," he threatens.

The little smile she sends him is chilling. I wouldn't want to be on the receiving end of that.

"It's more likely one of your bullets will hit your son first," she mocks him. "But why don't you try me?"

The next moment everything happens at once, a shot rings out, then a loud crash sounds behind me while I watch the window shatter in front of me. Then I hear another shot and a sudden commotion in the room, but I only have eyes for Jesper Olson's crumpled form on the ground. Blood is spreading from underneath his body, but from my vantage point I can't see Rajani.

I'm frantically yanking at the leather straps when Opal kneels in front of my face.

"You're bleeding."

"Get me the hell out of these things," I snap, trying to peer around her. "I need to get to her."

She moves to the side to undo the strap around one of my hands, giving me a view of the other room. I catch Pearl entering with Matt Driver right on her heels. They walk right over to where I can just see Olson still lying motionless on the ground.

"We need medics in here!" Pearl yells, as Driver grabs Olson's arm and pulls him off Rajani's prone body.

She's covered in blood and not moving.

TWENTY-EIGHT

JACOB

"Back off."

Mitch and Driver are blocking my way to the chopper, which is about to take off with Rajani.

"There's no room for you in there," Mitch points out.

"I fucking need to tell her something."

I want her to know I love her before it's too late.

"You're just gonna hold them up," he insists. "She needs to get to a hospital."

I can see the helicopter take off from the field in front of the lodge. Too late now. I drop my head and hunch my shoulders. I'll never fucking forgive myself if something happens to her.

She looked bad. By some fluke the bullet had broken the window, missed Olson, and ended up in Rajani's chest, right below her left breast. I heard someone say her lung had collapsed.

Jesper Olson may have escaped the bullet, but he did not survive the deep cut in his neck. It's uncertain whether that had been intentional or by accident.

"Let's get you looked at and then we can follow her to the hospital," Mitch suggests.

I want to object but suddenly all the fight is gone from my body. I'm exhausted. My hand comes up to the back of my head, where Wheeler's bullet apparently grazed me. At the time I didn't even feel it, but my head is throbbing now.

I watch with a weird detachment as Wheeler is brought out in handcuffs by one of the CARD members, limping slightly as a result of having been tackled to the ground by Opal. He's placed in the back of one of the CARD vehicles. Next two body bags are brought out. One I know holds Gordon Chen's body, and the other Jesper Olson.

The EMT looking at me in the back of the ambulance a few minutes later tells me I'm lucky. I'd have gladly—and without hesitation—passed on any luck to Rajani. If by some diabolically cruel fate she does not survive, I'll wish myself dead, like I did fifteen years ago when I woke up in a military hospital in Germany.

All of this, all these years, would've been for nothing.

Things were unresolved after she discovered who I was, but even if there's no hope for us as a couple, I would want her to live with the knowledge she is loved.

She always was.

"So...Jacob."

I lift my head and meet Janey's eyes. It's no use hanging onto the aliases I created for them.

"What the hell is with the cloak-and-dagger stuff?" she snaps.

I'm glad someone broke the heavy silence that's hung in the hospital waiting room for however long we've been waiting here.

"Easy, Janey," Lee mitigates.

Her dark eyes snap to her partner. "Easy? I just want to understand why the secrecy. I don't get it."

"I do," Kate offers, her eyes narrowed on me. "Because we already knew him before he became Jacob, didn't we?"

"What are you talking about?" Mitch asks his spouse.

Her eyes never leave mine.

"It's Nathan, right? We were told you were dead. Raj was never the same."

Janey jumps to her feet. "Nathan? Are you kidding me?"

Mitch throws up his hands.

"Will someone please the fuck explain what is going on?"

"I can," I volunteer. Time to pay the piper. "My name was Nathan Ramos when I was at Transition House and Rajani Agarwal was my girlfriend. I was—"

"Yeah," Janey scoffs, "and then he disappeared, apparently faked his death, and left all of us there in that hellhole."

"Janey, let the man explain," Lee suggests, I'm sure motivated by journalistic curiosity.

She huffs in response, but stays quiet.

"I was taken from Transition House by Wheeler, and kept prisoner in his house for almost three-and-a-half years."

"Bullshit," Janey mumbles.

"I wish," I react. "Raj and I were leaving. We had a plan to make our way to Lexington and find someone who would believe us. We knew we couldn't trust local law enforcement, but wanted to get help for everyone at the house. Wheeler intercepted us in the kitchen. We were so close."

"How come Rajani never told us?" Kate questions.

"I hope with all my heart you'll get a chance to ask her that," I reply. "But my guess is he threatened all of you if Raj told anyone, just like he threatened to hurt all of you, if I did not comply with his wishes."

"We were already being hurt," Kate reminds me.

"He told me he could get a good price for you abroad," I convey. "I thought you'd stand a better chance here in the U.S."

"Why would Wheeler want to keep you a prisoner?" Lee asks.

I glance at him.

"Because he prefers boys. I didn't resist when he took me. I thought I was keeping the girls safe. He led me to believe he still had control over them. Then one day he brought me back to Transition House. Other than Josh Kendrick, Elsbeth Sladky, and David Wheeler, no one else was there. I overheard them talk about the sale of the property, and the need to clear out the basement."

"That's where the conditioning was done," Kate explains to Lee and Mitch. "I remember there were different apparatuses and even toys down there, I can see why they'd want to clear that out."

"*Fucking hell,*" Mitch hisses.

To which Janey comments, "Yes, it was."

"I set the fire when they were down there," I admit. "I guess after three plus years under his control, Wheeler didn't think I'd step out of line. He was wrong. The moment all three of them were down there I locked the door, pulled the hall tree and any other furniture I could get my hands on quickly in front of the door. Then, with fuel siphoned from the vehicles outside, I set the whole damn pile ablaze."

It's like, now I'm free of the burden of anonymity, there is no stopping the purging of secrets.

"Good," Mitch grumbles. "Too bad they didn't die there. How did they get away?"

"An old coal cellar I didn't even know was there."

I remember running out of the building and hiding in a tree on the grounds to watch the place burn down. I was convinced I'd killed them when I suddenly saw the ground move right underneath one of the kitchen windows. A door was flung open and I saw three figures crawling out, covered in black soot. It looked like something from a horror movie, three monsters crawling straight from the pits of hell.

I ran like I had the devil on my heels.

But for many months after I was plagued by nightmares.

"Rajani Agarwal's family?"

We all surge to our feet when a young man in scrubs walks into the waiting room, a face mask tucked under his chin. He looks around the room, appearing somewhat puzzled. I imagine we look like a motley crew.

"We are," Janey speaks up.

"Very well. Surgery was successful, I ended up resecting a small, damaged part of the lower left lobe and was able to remove the bullet. Of course, we'll also need to monitor the concussion she sustained. We will see in the next day or so, but she'll likely make a full recovery."

Relief has me sinking back down in my chair and I drop my face in my hands.

"When can we see her?" I hear Kate ask.

"She's still a little groggy and in the recovery room. I'll have a nurse come and get you when you can come in. One at a time for now though."

"Maybe Jacob should go first," Kate suggests when the surgeon leaves the room.

I shake my head and get to my feet. "No, you guys go. I need to go find Matt Driver."

I have to confirm I've done everything I can to make sure Wheeler will never see the light of day again. Plus, there's the matter of the other individuals the CARD team was able to pick up from the cabins at Grandview Estate. I need to tell them all I know.

"Can't believe you're leaving. Again," Janey grumbles when I pass her on the way out the door.

Her words stop me in my tracks, but I don't bother turning around.

"I'm leaving to finish the job, making sure all loose ends are tied. Make no mistake though, I love that woman more than life itself."

With that I walk into the hallway, only to feel a hand clamp on my shoulder when I'm waiting for the elevator. When I turn both Lee and Mitch are standing behind me.

"We're coming with you," Lee announces.

"You won't get very far without wheels," Mitch points out.

It's the male version of forgiveness.

I'll take it.

Onyx

The last things I remember are the knife in my hand, the shock of the window shattering, a sudden, immense pressure on my chest, and then falling backward.

Janey told me I likely lost consciousness when my head hit the ground. She also told me Wheeler is in custody and his son is dead. I assumed the same bullet that struck me had killed him, but I guess I was wrong.

"You mean he wasn't shot?" I ask Agent O'Neill, the federal agent who came in with Matt Driver.

O'Neill shakes his head. "No, both his carotid artery and jugular vein were severed."

My blood turns to ice.

"Are you saying his neck was cut?"

"Almost more like a stab wound, but yeah. You don't remember cutting him? I understand you had the knife to his throat?"

It sure sounds like an accusation. Please, tell me this isn't happening. Am I going to get charged?

"I did," I tell him honestly.

I'm not going to lie about it. If they want to charge me with something they can go right ahead. There is no way Jacob would let that happen. At least I'm guessing he wouldn't. I wouldn't really know, since I haven't seen him since I woke up in the hospital.

That was three days ago. I know he's been asking for updates, but he hasn't called or shown up. Of course, I haven't called him either. I'm still struggling with every-thing that has happened, and that includes seeing him so vulnerable, strapped to that spanking bench. Good God.

I would've done anything to spare him more agony.

"I didn't know I cut him, but I'm not going to apolo-gize for it. I had a knife to his throat in self-defense."

"You have nothing to worry about," Matt assures me. "We know it was self-defense. There are no repercussions for that."

He directs a sharp look at Agent O'Neill who seems annoyed, but changes his tone.

"I'm merely making sure I have all the details right. This is a large and complicated case that spans decades, involves a lot of suspects, victims, and locations. We need to be meticulous to make an airtight case against Mr. Wheeler."

O'Neill spends a little longer asking me questions and clarifying details, when we're interrupted by a nurse who wheels in a cart. When she announces the doctor will be by shortly to remove the drainage tube from my chest, both agents jump to their feet.

"We'll let you get some rest," O'Neill says, before leaving the room.

Matt walks over to the bed and grabs my hand.

"I don't want you to worry about anything, okay? You heal up and I'll be in touch."

The only thing I'll say about removing the damn tube is that I'd opt for a root canal any day, given the choice. Unpleasant, as the nurse warned me it might be, has to be the understatement of the year.

"Keep an eye on that," the doctor instructs me. "It can continue to drain a little bit the next twenty-four to forty-eight hours. If it goes on for longer than that, call my office. Keep up with your exercises, they're important, and I'll see you again for a follow-up in four weeks. Until then, you need rest, don't overdo it. Do you have someone to look after you when you get home?"

"I do," I lie.

I'll figure things out when I get back to my apartment. Janey and Kate will help out where they can. I'm sure one of them won't mind picking up a few of my things at Four Oaks to tide me over until I can pick up all my belongings.

"Can we call someone to pick you up?"

I smile at the nurse. "I have a friend coming. She'll be here any moment."

Kate said she'd be here at four, with something for me

to wear. I'm going to need it because I have no idea where my little black dress went. I'm assuming it wasn't salvageable.

"In that case, let me get your discharge papers together so you're ready when she gets here."

Fifteen minutes later, I'm confused when Bernie walks in, carrying a tote bag. I look behind her to see if perhaps she came with Jacob, but it looks like she's alone.

"How are you feeling, dear?" she asks, dropping the tote bag on the foot of the bed.

"Getting better, thank you." I smile at her, a little nonplussed. "I'm surprised to see you here."

"I offered to take you back to the farm. It made more sense, since I'll be looking after you the next few weeks anyway."

There is no way I can hide the fact I'm taken aback.

"You are? That's...um...that's very kind of you. I'm sorry, I had no idea."

"Of course you didn't. Jacob is so used to doling out orders, he sometimes forgets to communicate like a normal person," she says with a little shake of her head.

Then, as if it's the most normal thing in the world, she pulls a pair of my yoga pants, my favorite slouchy sweater, and a pair of underwear out of the bag. It's actually something I would've picked out.

"Are you okay on your own, or do you need help?"

"Um...I think I'll be okay, thank you."

I swing my legs out of bed and grab the clothes she pulled out, disappearing into the bathroom. I take my time, splashing some water on my face, putting on some deodorant, and brushing my teeth, while I ponder how I should proceed. I really don't want to upset Bernie—it's very sweet of her to do this—but somewhere in all of this arranging, someone forgot to notify me.

I shove my toiletries into the small bag Kate brought me a few days ago, and quickly dress in the clothes Bernie came with. It's amazing how much something so simple tires me out.

So much so, I don't complain when Bernie has a wheelchair waiting for me when I walk back into the room. She grabs my toiletry bag and gestures for me to take a seat. Then she places the tote in which she put all my belongings on my lap, and wheels me to the elevators.

I'll go to the farm with her and not complain, but only so I can address Jacob's highhandedness with him directly.

It's about time he and I had a good talk.

TWENTY-NINE

Jacob

"When will you be back?"

I take the call outside the moment I hear Bernie's voice.

"I'm flying back tomorrow."

"Will you be coming here?"

Here is Four Oaks, where Bernie has been taking care of Rajani at my request, and she's getting impatient with me. Bernie, that is. I haven't had any contact with Rajani, so I'm not sure how she feels about my absence.

I've kept my distance for a reason though. Rather than forcing myself on her, I want to give her a chance to work through things on her own terms. I've waited for her for years, a few more weeks won't kill me, but there will come a point my patience runs out.

A lot of years, a lot of pain, and a lot of deceit stand between us. Neither of us is the same person we were back then. I love her, that's never changed, and I'm convinced she loves me, but it's up to her to decide if that is enough. And of course, if she makes the wrong decision, or takes too long making one, I will have to use my powers of persuasion.

"I have to check on the horse and talk with Joey, but I'll stick to the stables. I'll be heading back to the cottage after that."

The Airbnb has come in handy this past week. With Bernie staying at the farm, I've used the cottage as my home and work base.

"I'm not so sure not showing any interest in her is the right way to go about this."

"Bernie, trust me, Rajani knows how I feel about her."

"If you say so..."

She lets her words drift off, probably hoping I'll bite, but I'm not going to. I have twenty-four hours to convince Hamish, but especially his wife, Laura, moving to Kentucky is a good idea. Hamish is okay, he's a U.S. citizen, but Laura is Canadian and will need a green card or a permanent residence status to work here.

"I have to go. Let me know if there's anything you need, otherwise I'll give you a shout tomorrow."

After ending the call, I finish getting ready to meet Hamish and his wife at the Club Restaurant at Woodbine Racetrack in Toronto. The venue was his idea, apparently, he still frequents the races, but these days as a spectator.

The racetrack is not too far from the airport or the hotel I'm staying at. I'm normally not a fan of big crowds, not with the way I look, but my ball cap and shades give me a bit of a shield. I bypass the casino on the main floor and head up the escalator to the grandstand level where the restaurant is located.

I pass by the line-ups in front of the betting windows. Evidently, there's already quite a bit of traffic in anticipation of the races. Down below, the thoroughbreds in the first race are being paraded onto the racetrack by their lead ponies.

For a moment I simply stand there, looking out the large windows, taking in the building excitement, and imagining what it'll feel like when I have my own horse in the race.

"Jacob?"

I turn to find Laura Adrian standing behind me, a hesitant smile on her face.

"Hey, Laura."

My friend's wife is a very pretty, pleasantly plump blonde with sad eyes. It probably has something to do with the fact they're still childless after trying for many years to get pregnant. Of course, then Hamish had his accident and all her attention was focused on his recovery. Now Laura simply dotes on her husband. She's a good woman.

I bend down to kiss her cheek.

"We already have a table," she indicates, pointing at the restaurant. "It's trackside so you'll be able to see everything from there."

"Sounds good. Show me the way."

I follow her into the restaurant where a grinning

Hamish is sitting by the window. I greet him with a hug, and Laura encourages me to sit across from him while she takes a seat beside him.

We catch up while we decide on drinks and glance at the menu, but once we've put in our orders, Hamish turns the conversation to the reason for my visit.

"This sudden visit wouldn't have something to do with that horse you bought, Arion's Moon, would it?"

I grin. "It might."

"Then I'm guessing you've completed what you set out to do?"

Hamish is no fool.

"It does."

"You want us to come to Kentucky," Laura pipes up.

I turn my attention to her. "Yes, I do, and I recognize that might be a bigger ask of you than it is of your husband."

"It sure is, since I'd have to give up my practice to come to a place where I have no standing and can't work," she points out what I already know.

"I recognize that, and I've been thinking about it. I have a few contacts who might be able to help speed up the process of getting you a green card."

I'm letting her know I'm not blind to the obstacles, before pushing some of the selling points.

"The farm has a completely separate guesthouse where you'd be completely self-sufficient, so you wouldn't have to worry about housing. Hamish would get the time and opportunity to rediscover his training talents and skills. Then, if you were to decide to make it a permanent arrangement, we can talk about building a separate house with a little more privacy and some land. There's plenty of it."

The server approaches with a tray of drinks; beers for Hamish and myself, and a glass of iced tea for Laura.

"I see you rehearsed your sales pitch," my friend comments with a grin, once the server is gone. "Pretty compelling. What do you say, Laura?"

"He certainly makes it sound attractive," she responds. "But I still have a few questions."

For the next forty-five minutes—occasionally interrupted by a race and during our early dinner—they ask and I answer to the best of my ability.

"So, it'll be just you and Bernie living at the farm?" Laura wants to know.

A fair question, given I'm asking them to become very close neighbors.

"And Joey and Hunter, they live in the staff quarters. Both are women. Joey is an exercise rider and works in the stables, as does Hunter."

"That's it?" Hamish probes.

"Well, if I have my way, Rajani will be living there as well."

"Would this be *the* Rajani?" Laura asks.

Clearly Hamish shared some things with her.

"Yes, it would. So what do you say?"

They seem to share a pointed look before turning back to me.

"It's actually perfect," Hamish says, taking Laura's hand in his. "Because we're seriously looking at getting out of the rat race in the city. Also Laura is planning to put her career on hold for the foreseeable future."

"Oh?" I react with my eyebrows raised.

It's Laura who clarifies.

"I'm pregnant."

Onyx

The days are long.

Don't get me wrong, Bernie is lovely, and I'm really enjoying her company and kitchen skills, but I've missed my work, missed feeling useful.

I still get short of breath, but it's no longer every time I move. It's slowly getting better, but I can see why the doctor said it could be many weeks before I start feeling like myself again.

I'm going to need a ton of patience, and maybe a hobby or two.

I've been indulging in some reading, have watched a bit of TV, but those are sedentary activities and I miss being active.

So, this morning I thought I'd visit the horses and took a walk down to the stables. I got so lightheaded I was swaying on my feet, and Hunter forced me to sit on a bale of hay until it passed. She followed me like a shadow after that, hovering while I gave first Murdoch and Buck, and then Arion's Moon some loving.

Finally, she insisted on walking me back to the house where Bernie reminded me, I've been home barely a week and not to push myself. Then she urged me to lie down and rest for a bit.

But I've been up for a while now, staring at the ceiling, getting all emotional because I'm wasting my time in bed, thinking about Jacob.

Kate and Janey have been by, so I know he talked to them in the hospital when I was having surgery. Janey's still pretty pissed after his revelations, but she is someone for whom everything tends to be black or white.

Kate has a more moderate response, more understanding of what drove Jacob to make the decisions he did. It doesn't mean she's not affected, but for her it's more shock than anger.

My own feelings tend to vacillate, almost dependent on who I'm with. It's exhausting. I wish I could just pick one emotion and run with it, that would be so much less stressful than this constant yo-yo.

Here's the kicker though, when I'm in this room, in this bed, all I feel is a deep sadness he's not here. No anger or trauma, no confusion or pain, just a feeling of emptiness only he can fill.

I love him. After all this time believing he was dead, all the deceit and scheming, that hasn't changed.

But he's not here. I thought for sure I'd catch him here at the farm, but I haven't seen him since I got shot, and for the life of me I can't understand why. Is he back to hiding in the shadows? Behind technology?

I wipe my eyes with my sleeve and swing my legs out of bed. Enough moping around.

After splashing some water on my face, I head for the kitchen where I can hear Bernie moving around. Amazing smells greet me when I walk in.

"Fresh tea in the pot, and I'm just getting the banana bread out," she says as she opens the oven door and reaches in.

"Smells really good."

She straightens up and slides two loaf pans on top of the stove to let them cool.

"It's Jacob's second favorite," she shares.

"Second favorite?"

"His top favorite is my cinnamon buns, but I'm ticked at him so he's not getting those."

I know this is leading somewhere, with the way she drops little nuggets for me to grab on to, but I'm curious enough to indulge her.

"How come you're ticked at him?" I ask the question I'm sure she wanted me to ask.

"Because he's being a stubborn mule," she mutters, before adding, "In any event, he's back in the country today and he'll know I'm annoyed when he sees the banana bread."

"I wasn't even aware he was out of the country," I point out.

Bernie looks at me, bulging her eyes.

"Exactly, therefore he's a stubborn mule," she reiterates.

"So...the banana bread, does that mean he's coming here?"

I realize she has me right where she wants me when I see the little smirk she's attempting to hide.

"Well, if by *here* you mean the house, then no, but he did mention he'd pop in at the stables today to check on the horses. I guess I'll have to take him the banana bread."

"I'll take it to him," I offer, noting this time she doesn't bother hiding her smirk.

"Good. That's going to work out just fine then," she comments, rubbing her hands together.

"You know, Bernie, you could've simply told me he was coming without the whole...buildup."

She shrugs her shoulders, but her eyes sparkle.

"Now, what would've been the fun in that?"

———

I'M KEEPING HALF AN EYE OUT THE KITCHEN WINDOW while cutting vegetables for the chicken pot pie Bernie's decided to make for dinner, when I catch sight of the familiar dark green Dodge Ram rolling down the path to the stables.

"That's him," I announce, dropping the knife and quickly rinsing my hands in the sink.

"Now, don't go running down there," Bernie warns me. "Or you'll be out of breath before you can get a word out."

"Okay," I agree distractedly. "Where is the banana bread? Should I pretend to bring some over for Joey and Hunter? No, I'm not going to go there. No deceit, no pretense, no lies."

Bernie lets me ramble without interruptions as she cuts a few slices of the banana bread and wraps them in plastic wrap.

"Oh, I thought you were going to give him the whole loaf."

She smiles and shakes her head. "Then he wouldn't have a reason to come back here for more."

Good point, and yet another indication of Bernie's cunning.

She presses the package in my hand and shoos me out of the house.

I go slow but walk with purpose down the center of the path to the stables. I don't want to give him an opportunity to avoid me. He'll have to drive over me if he thinks of taking off.

I don't see him when I get to the stables, but I can hear voices coming from Moon's stall. I walk up and peek over the door, seeing Joey and Jacob bent over one of the horse's hooves.

The farrier was here earlier in the week to reshoe the horses, which is probably what Jacob's checking up on.

Joey is the one to spot me first.

"Hey, back again?"

"This time a little slower," I tell her with a smile, finding I'm still a bit winded.

"Should you be down here?"

I glare at Jacob, who straightens up. That's the first thing he has to say to me after shutting me out for over a week?

"Yes, since this appears to be the only way to get you to talk to me."

"And...that's my cue," Joey observes, looking between us before she moves to the door.

I step aside to let her out, but keep my eyes on Jacob, who remains standing beside Arion's Moon.

My heart beats faster just from looking at him. God, I've missed him.

"I'm mad at you," I start.

"I know," he responds, and for some reason that heats my blood.

"If you know, then why did you avoid me? Because that's what I'm mad about; you disappearing without a word."

He looks a bit puzzled as he takes a few steps closer.

"It is?"

"Yes. What did you think I was angry about?"

"My manipulations, my lies."

He's on the other side of the stall door and leans his arms on the top ledge.

"I was, for a moment, but then there was only confusion left and you weren't around to answer questions. *That's* what I'm angry about. Because if that's the way you always handle issues, by disappearing from the scene, we're going to have big problems going forward."

I turn my back, fighting the urge to open this damn door and throw myself in his arms.

Then I hear the latch open and feel his hand grab my arm, swinging me around. His eyes burn on mine.

"Going forward?"

"Yes, I have no desire to go backward. Do you?"

The growl comes from deep in his chest as he pulls me close, his arms wrapping around me like steel bands.

"No."

The next moment his lips take mine in a bruising kiss as his tongue plunders my mouth. I may have whimpered at the onslaught, but willingly give myself over to the wave of need and the feeling of completion. When he lifts his mouth, I'm literally gasping for air.

"I love you," I hear him rumble.

Then the world goes black.

THIRTY

JACOB

"One thing I'm still not clear on; why go to so much trouble hiding your identity?"

It's a question I've been asked more than once in the past week and although it's getting a little tedious, everyone deserves an answer. If anything, for the sake of full disclosure.

Lee does too.

"I didn't want past feelings, resentments, or disappointments to impact our investigations, or distract from the objective, which was to bring our collective tormentors to justice."

"Justice or revenge?" Lee wants clarified.

I shrug. "It's a fine line, and sometimes they're one and the same."

I keep my eyes on the road, even though I can feel him staring at me.

"Guess it is," he finally concedes.

We're on our way to the FBI's main Kentucky office in Louisville, where David Wheeler is still being held. It had taken a few favors from my contacts within the Bureau, but we've been granted access to the man. Officially, this is supposed to be an interview for a publication.

The real objective for Lee is to see his mother's killer behind bars. As for me, I simply want the man to know he may have kept me prisoner and subjected me to almost daily sexual assault and torture for three-and-a-half long years, but I'm also the one who will make sure he gets the punishment he deserves. I came out a victor, not a victim.

Agent O'Neill is waiting for us, along with Matt Driver. We're shown into a small meeting room, where O'Neill goes down a list of rules, mainly aimed at Lee.

"I mean it," he enforces with a glare for Remington. "This is an ongoing investigation and if you publish even a single word before we wrap this case up, I won't hesitate to throw the book at you with the full weight of this office behind me."

I get the impression O'Neill was not in favor of giving us access to Wheeler, but that's okay. He has nothing to worry about, we're not about to mess with his case.

"So noted," Lee acknowledges.

I give the agent a nod.

"All right then. Follow me."

O'Neill leads us into the hallway and downstairs to a secure area with holding cells and visitation rooms. He shows us into one of the rooms. The room is square, with doors on opposite walls. A steel table in the center is bolted down to the floor, as are the stools on either side. Not exactly an inviting environment.

"You have five minutes," the agent reminds us.

All I need is ten seconds.

The moment the door we came through closes behind us, the one on the other side of the room opens, and Wheeler is brought in. Dressed in an orange jumpsuit with ankles and wrists shackled, he looks like nothing more than a pathetic old man, but I know better.

He barely acknowledges Lee, but does a double take when he recognizes me. His eyes narrow on me as he's led to a stool on the opposite side of the table, chained to a ring welded to the surface, and told to sit his ass down.

He stares and I stare right back, until Lee finally speaks.

"My name is Remington."

Wheeler's eyes slide casually to Lee.

"You're the journalist. I know."

"I am," Lee responds. "But I'm also Kalisa Brown's son."

"Is that name supposed to mean anything to me?"

I can feel anger radiating off Lee, but to his credit, he keeps his voice calm and even.

"My mother was a housekeeper at Transition House."

I can tell the moment Wheeler realizes who the journalist is talking about by the brief clench of his jaw. Lee notices it as well and smiles as he gets to his feet.

He has what he was looking for.

I stand up as well, but put my hands on the table, leaning into Wheeler's space.

"Took me many years to find you. It won't take me nearly as long to make sure you get exactly what you deserve." I force a smile. "I promise the punishment will fit the crime."

Watching the color leach from his face is my reward.

Ten minutes later we stand outside in the parking lot with Matt Driver.

"I need a drink," Lee announces.

"Yeah," I mumble.

I feel weird; the sudden sense of being adrift is not what I expected. With Wheeler behind bars, I guess I've come to the end of my quest, but it leaves me in this strange vacuum. I'm not sure where to direct my focus next.

So yeah, I could use some liquid inspiration.

"Follow me," Matt suggests. "I know a place. I'll buy you guys a drink."

"NICE PLACE," LEE COMMENTS.

We're in the basement of the historic Grady Hotel, downtown Louisville. The bar/restaurant down here looks like a cross between a library and a wine cellar, with exposed brick, arched nooks and crannies, soft light, and burgundy leather seating. We got here just as the bar opened at four, so had our pick of tables. Matt chose one in a private alcove at the back.

I called Rajani from the road to let her know I might be a bit later than expected. When she asked how the meeting went, I mentioned I'd rather talk about it later. She didn't push.

She had entertained the idea of coming along to see Wheeler, but only for a moment before she decided she'd already gotten her pound of flesh by inadvertently taking his son's life.

"So, got what you needed?" Matt asks after the server takes our drink orders.

"I did," Lee claims. "Not sure if it's gonna impact my future, but it sure as hell puts a period behind the past."

I guess that's another way to look at it. I'm not quite to the point where I can put a period behind my past but that'll come soon enough, when I know Wheeler got what he has coming.

"I got what I wanted out of it," I contribute.

"Good. I'm pretty sure he's not going to see the light of day again," Matt shares. "This case is too high profile, given the others we arrested. A few of the ones we have in custody are spilling their guts, hoping for a deal. This is turning into a public scandal no one will be able to escape."

"What about the kids?" I inquire.

"That was a mess," the agent admits. "Four of them are addicted to opioids and not by choice. It's how they were controlled. A couple of them had been there for over a year, and two were just brought in a couple of days before we raided the place. Every single one of those kids is going to have a long road ahead."

Don't I know it. I think it's safe to say that road never really ends, it just gets a bit easier to travel.

Onyx

It's close to ten when I see headlights shining in through the front window.

Bernie retreated to her room half an hour ago, and I've been killing time watching some home improvement shows on TV.

I've been spending way too much time fantasizing about all the changes I would make if this were my place. For one thing, I would segregate the guest wing, where Bernie is staying, from the rest of the house with a door. Then I would add a separate outside entrance so she could come and go as she pleases. She'd also need some kind of kitchenette. We could turn it into a full guest suite, using the extra bedroom as a sitting room.

I'd also get a dog. This farm screams for at least one puppy, if not more. Maybe some rescue animals. Chickens for fresh eggs. I could probably keep going, I'd turn this into a proper farm.

That is, if I were actually living here.

For now, I've agreed to stay here until the doctor tells me I'm cleared for work. That appointment is two weeks from now. I'm looking forward to getting back to work, but I'm not sure how I feel about going back to my small apartment after staying in a place like this.

The subject hasn't come up between Jacob and me yet, but I don't want to run the risk of making assumptions, or leaving things to the last minute, so I'd hoped to bring it up tonight, right after I give him a proper welcome home that is long overdue.

Except it's already almost ten and I've been struggling to keep my eyes open, waiting for him to get home.

As soon as I hear footsteps approaching on the stone pavers outside, I get up and bolt for the front door. The moment it opens and Jacob steps inside, I launch myself at him.

"Careful, sweetheart," he cautions, catching me in his arms.

He moved his things out of the cottage they rented in Falmouth and back in here the night I confronted him in the stables. Or maybe I should call it the night I fainted.

That was embarrassing. The man I have serious feelings for tells me he loves me and instead of returning the sentiment, I blacked out. If not for Jacob holding me up, I would've hit the floor hard.

In my defense, I'd just walked down to the stables for the second time that day, and then had what remained of my breath stolen by that kiss. I was out for only a moment, but I guess it was enough for Jacob to decide he should stick around.

I've been sleeping in his arms every night this past week. Sleeping being the operative word. He hasn't properly kissed me since either, just a brief brush of the lips every now and then. Any attempts I've made for anything more were foiled instantly.

"I'm done being careful," I announce, adding with a bit of drama, "Kissing you has become a matter of life or death."

"Life or death?" he echoes with an eyebrow raised, as I pull him into the living room by the hand.

"My life, your death," I clarify. "Seriously, this abstinence is getting old."

I move him in front of the couch and give him a little push. The moment his ass hits the seat, I climb on his lap, and his hands automatically come up to rest on my hips.

"Two weeks isn't that long," he tries to placate me, but I'm not having it.

"I'm talking about kissing, Jacob. Maybe a little petting." I roll my eyes. "Hell, at this point I might just pass out from frustration."

He throws his head back and laughs. I know he's laughing at me but I love hearing that sound. He doesn't do enough of it, which I hope to change. When his eyes find mine again those golden flecks sparkle.

I reach out to cup his face in my hands.

"I love hearing you laugh, Jacob. I love *you*." Leaning forward I press my lips against his. "Come on, Jacob," I mutter against his mouth. "You're not going to leave me hanging after that, are you?"

He pulls back a little, looking up at me.

"Dammit, Raj, you make it impossible for me to resist."

Before I finish forming the word, "Good," his hand is

cupping the back of my head, his tongue is in my mouth, and his groan is vibrating through my body.

I give myself up to the kiss, reveling in the familiar taste of him, the feeling of safety in his strong arms. I don't care if I pass out again, there's no halfway when it comes to kissing Jacob.

"Damn, sweetheart," he declares when he lets me up for air. "No matter how careful I try to be, the moment I touch you, I ignite like a grease fire."

"Grease fire?" I scoff. "Is that the sexiest comparison you could come up with?"

His face splits into a grin.

"I'm a guy, grease is about as sexy as it gets."

I roll my eyes, then I slide off his lap and snuggle into his side. If anything, I'm wide awake now.

"Tell me about your visit," I ask him gently, putting a hand on his chest as I tilt my head to look up at him.

"I guess it was okay. Not quite the sense of relief or release I might have hoped for, but perhaps that's a good thing. Maybe that would've been giving him too much power again."

"That's actually not a bad way to look at it," I consider. "It kinda puts things in a better perspective."

"Hmm. Remington said something that got me thinking about what we choose to hold on to. The baggage we carry with us everywhere we go. It was poignant, even for Lee." He chuckles and gives his head a shake. "Sure had my mind going all the way home."

"What was it? What did Lee say?"

He shifts slightly, angling his body toward me. Then he lifts his hand and brushes my hair out of my face.

"Matt asked if we got what we needed from the visit. Lee told him he did, and that although he wasn't sure if it was going to change anything in the future, he felt it put a period behind the past. That resonated with me."

"It does with me too. We can't control what happened in the past, and sometimes we can't even help what impacts our present, but we can make a decision on what we choose to bring with us into the future."

He leans down and brushes my lips.

"Exactly," he whispers. "There is only one bright light from my past I happily welcome to the present, and choose to hold close for my future. That's you."

His face blurs a bit as my eyes well up, and my voice is a little hoarse.

"Does that mean you don't want me to move out?"

His eyes flash.

"Try, and see how far you'll get."

I guess I have my answer.

THIRTY-ONE

JACOB

The shower door opens behind me and Raj steps in, pressing her naked body against my back.

"Morning," she mumbles sleepily, sliding her arms around to my belly.

I'd left her in bed a few minutes ago, hoping she'd be able to sleep in a little. She needs it.

Her nights have turned restless ever since Wheeler's case went in front of a grand jury last week. We're waiting for the indictment which could come in tomorrow, or any time up to sixty days from the hearing. Unfortunately, since we found out it's in the grand jury's hands, Raj has been waking up from bad dreams nightly.

Rationally, she knows there is no way Wheeler won't be indicted, but she still worries. I hate to admit, not totally without merit. The man has better connections than I do, although he's known to make them through blackmail.

The public is already weighing in on this case though. The scandal has been widely reported on in the media already. It would've been impossible to keep the lid on a story like this, especially when there are so many well-known individuals involved.

Lee is finishing up his article, which is much more comprehensive than any other material out there, and will span the years from his mother's time at Transition House to the charges against Wheeler and his cohorts today.

He wants it ready for publishing, so when the grand jury comes back with an indictment, he can lead with that. He's agreed to keep GEM's name out of the article, referring to us only as an FBI support agency.

The last thing we want is to have our names or, God forbid, our faces all over the media. It would make our work very difficult, if not impossible. Anonymity is what allows us to get close enough to these sick predators to take them down.

Right now, I'm not thinking too much about work though. Not with Raj's hands lazily traveling down my abs. It doesn't take much for my body to respond to this woman and my cock is already hard as a rock.

Bracing my hands against the wall, I look down as her long fingers close firmly around the root, and slide up to the crown. With her thumb, she smooths the bead forming at the tip, and I grunt at the sensation.

Then she ducks under my arm, briefly kisses me with a quick swipe of her tongue, and then holds my eyes as she slides down my body. Letting my head drop between my shoulders, I stare at this gorgeous creature on her knees before me.

Every so often I look at her and am amazed she is right here. I never thought I'd consider myself lucky, but that's exactly how I feel these days.

Lucky.

A shiver runs down my spine when she slides her lips over my crown and takes me deep inside the heat of her mouth. Awash in sensations, my eyes want to close, but I force them open. I don't want to miss a second of the amazing view. That deep, coffee-colored gaze aimed at me, the rising swells of her breasts with each breath, and the movement of her right hand between her legs as she plays with herself.

The sight of all that, her mouth working my cock, and her other hand rolling my balls, has my ears ringing as all the blood rushes to my groin. I try to pull free, but she—quite literally—has me by the balls, and helplessly I feel the first streams of semen jet down her throat.

"My turn," I mumble in her hair, when she rises to her feet and wraps her arms around me.

I can feel her soft chuckle.

"Honey, you can barely stand."

She's not lying, my legs feel like rubber, and I'm gasping for air.

"Gimme a moment," I manage.

She cups my face and kisses me sweetly.

"You don't have one, Bernie will be here shortly, and the Adrians could be right behind her."

I groan, because she's right. Bernie, who moved into the guesthouse, could be in the kitchen as we speak, getting some kind of brunch together for when Hamish and Laura get here.

She tosses me a bar of soap, and turns her back as she starts massaging shampoo into her hair. I do a quick soap and rinse before stepping out of the shower.

The Adrians will be staying here tonight, but tomorrow—when the truck with their belongings arrives—they move to the Falmouth cottage. By their choice.

I've had quite a few phone calls over the past month and a half with the Adrians. After a bit of back-and-forth, they ended up opting for a short-term rental instead of moving into our guesthouse. Bernie was able to negotiate a six-month lease for them with the owner of the Airbnb she's befriended.

Hopefully that'll be enough time to get their new house move-in ready, because as soon as we can get the permits approved, we'll start breaking ground on the ten acres I've parceled off on the north side of the property. I'm supposed to take them there today. They've already seen and approved the plans I had drawn up in record time by a Williamstown architect.

We're only a few weeks from Christmas, and I'd love to be ready to go with construction the first week of January. With a bit of luck, temperatures will remain above zero to pour the foundation, but even if it ends up being colder, I've been assured the concrete can still cure, as long as we can keep it from freezing. According to the contractor I hired to oversee the project, we should be able to get the house finished before June.

I'm going to hold him to that, but I'll still push for sooner, because Laura is due the second week of June.

I dry off, toss my towel in the laundry basket, and pad into the bedroom. By the time I'm dressed, Rajani walks in, wearing her silky, little robe that shows off her long legs.

She snickers at my pained groan as she sits on the side of the bed, bending over as she removes the towel wrap she had tied around her hair. Then she grabs a brush from her nightstand and begins to pull it through the damp strands.

"Here, let me."

I walk over and take the brush from her hand, sliding behind her on the bed.

"You don't have to do that."

"I know," I tell her as I slowly start brushing her hair. "But it allows me to steal another few minutes with you."

She twists her head around and smiles at me.

"Careful, you're setting the bar high for romantic gestures. You're spoiling me."

I lean in and kiss her mouth before I resume my brushing. She should know by now there isn't a thing I wouldn't do for her.

Onyx

"I'm coming."

Bernie stops by the door and turns around.

"Well, then, let's go. The longer we wait, the busier it's going to get."

She might be right, it's Christmas Eve day so the likelihood is it'll be packed everywhere.

I grab my phone, shove my feet in my boots, and put on my coat.

"Alarm," Bernie reminds me when I'm about to step outside.

Right.

I turn to the keypad and punch in the code before following Bernie outside and closing the door behind me.

Jacob would have a fit if I didn't set the alarm while he's away. He had a hard enough time leaving me as it was.

A call came in four days ago. A missing twelve-year-old girl had separated from her friends in a Lexington movie theatre to go to the bathroom and never returned. Staff mentioned one of the emergency exits had been used around the same time the friends claimed Kayla went to the bathroom. Security footage from the theatre showed a man carrying a girl with long hair matching Kayla's description through the parking lot to an old white or silver Mercury Sable.

So close to Christmas, everyone wants to help on this one.

Even Jacob, who hasn't worked directly on a search

before, wanted to go with the team. I'm not ready for operations in the field yet, I still tire easily, which could make me more of a hindrance than an asset to the team. The last thing I want is to distract them, so I stayed behind. Jacob offered to stay back as well, but I could see he was itching to go.

They've been gone for four days, the weather's been really miserable, and I've done nothing but a bit of administration and answering calls. I'm ready to see some action, even if it is just the grocery store on Christmas Eve.

"Have you heard anything more?" Bernie wants to know when I buckle in beside her.

"Nothing."

This morning Jacob texted me they got a lead. A farmer spotted a vehicle by that description coming out of a dirt road at the edge of his property, which backs onto a golf course that is closed for the winter. They were heading there next.

"Is that snow?" I ask, leaning forward to get a better look.

"Sure looks like it. I didn't see anything like that in the forecast," Bernie states.

"Who knows, we might get a white Christmas," I suggest, eternally optimistic.

Sadly, it's already stopped by the time we get to Falmouth, where it takes us a frustrating ten minutes to find a spot in the grocery store parking lot. It's a zoo and I'm seriously regretting my decision to come.

That wouldn't be fair to Bernie though. It was my

idea to do a Christmas dinner here tomorrow, hoping like hell they will have found Kayla by then. With the whole team searching, it's unlikely anyone will have had an opportunity to pick up groceries or get organized for Christmas.

If they're not back by tomorrow, it'll just be Bernie and me, Joey and Hunter, and the Adrians, who we'd invited over before the girl went missing.

We start walking across the parking lot, trying not to get run over, when my phone rings in my pocket.

"You take that. I'm going in," Bernie tells me, tossing me her keys.

"Hey, Lee," I answer when I see his name pop up on my screen.

"Have you heard?"

I automatically assume he's talking about the girl.

"They found her?"

"Not that I know, but I just found out the indictment came through."

I blow out a breath, releasing all the tension I've been holding for the past two weeks.

"Relieved?" he asks.

"You can say that again. I didn't really think he'd be set free, but I feel better having it official."

"Understood. The courts are in recess over the holidays, so nothing will happen until after, but he's safely tucked away."

I feel a lot lighter a few minutes later when I walk into grocery chaos, and go in search of Bernie.

I find her in the dairy aisle, fighting with someone

over the last pint of heavy cream.

"HEY, SAWYER, I'M SO GLAD YOU COULD COME."

I greet Mitch's daughter with a hug and let her go ahead inside, to where most of the others are already gathered.

The team came back late last night.

They found Kayla—alive.

She'd been held in an old maintenance shack in an unused and overgrown section of the golf course. A new maintenance building was put up ten or so years ago, but the old shack was never taken down.

Her fifty-two-year-old abductor had been part of the golf course's maintenance crew for fourteen years.

Before Jacob crashed last night, he needed to unload, and shared they'd found evidence Kayla may not have been the first girl he held captive in that shack. It's possible we'll never know for sure, since the man died as the result of a car crash when he tried to run from law enforcement.

At least Kayla is safe and in the loving care of her family today, which means we have a house full of our chosen family for Christmas.

"Your house is gorgeous," Sawyer compliments, standing by the large Christmas tree Bernie and I decorated while Jacob was gone.

It's on my lips to tell her it's not my house, but I hold it back. It may not have been bought with my money, but technically my name is still on the deed, and I do live here.

"Thank you. We like it." I look up to see Jacob walk over. "Have you met Jacob?"

He loops one arm around my shoulders and shakes Sawyer's hand with the other.

"I haven't had the pleasure," she says with a smile.

"Sawyer," Jacob rumbles. "I'm so glad you could make it."

Mitch joins us when he catches sight of his daughter, giving her a hug and a kiss.

Kate is helping Bernie put out some appetizers in the kitchen, while Laura is sitting at the island, chatting with them. Hamish is deep in conversation with Lee at the dining table.

Janey ended up going to the stables with Ricky, Lee's daughter Yana, Hunter, and Joey to see the horses.

The house is full—overflowing in fact—and I love it. This is what I always dreamed of but never thought I could have.

"If you'd excuse us for a minute?" Jacob asks, grabbing my elbow. "I just want to borrow Raj for a minute."

"Of course. I'll get Sawyer a drink," Mitch offers.

Jacob leads me down the hall to our bedroom, closing the door behind us. I face him, a little curious what this is about.

"What is it?"

He takes both my hands in his.

"This isn't something I can share over Christmas dinner, but I can't wait for you to know."

I'd worry, but he doesn't seem at all upset or troubled.

"Know what?" I prompt him.

"Yesterday Wheeler was transported to the correctional facility in Manchester and accidentally placed in general population instead of solitary, where he was supposed to go for safety reasons."

The media hasn't stopped buzzing with this case, and yesterday's indictment would've only stirred that up. Some of that news has to have filtered into the prison.

"That was a serious mistake," I comment.

"Yes, it was. Holiday schedule, limited staffing. Wheeler wasn't found until early this morning in the showers. Dead. They figure he'd been there since last night."

"How did he die?"

"Trust me, you don't want to know, but you might have an idea, given what he was in there for. It wasn't pretty."

This is probably not appropriate, especially on Christmas Day, but I can't help feeling satisfaction at the knowledge he suffered.

"Am I an awful person if I say this Christmas is turning out even better than I could've imagined?"

"No," he says, tugging me close and wrapping me in his arms. "I feel the same way. I finally know what freedom feels like."

I wind my arms around his neck.

"I love you, Jacob."

He flashes that lopsided grin.

"Yeah, I know."

EPILOGUE

Onyx

Six months later.

"Oh my goodness, he's so tiny."

I'm a little nervous when Hamish hands me his newborn son. He's wrapped like a little burrito, and makes the most adorable little sounds as he settles in the crook of my arm.

We were going to visit them in the hospital but Hamish texted us to say they were already on their way home and to meet them there. They just moved into their new house three days ago, in the nick of time, as it turns out. Apparently, the baby was impatient and decided to arrive a couple of weeks early. Hamish assured us on the phone their son is perfectly healthy, albeit a bit small.

Laura is beaming and looks amazing for someone who gave birth just twelve hours ago. We've become good friends since they moved to Kentucky and see quite a bit of each other, so I've had the privilege of following along with her pregnancy up close.

"I can't believe they let you come home this fast," I direct at her.

Hamish snorts, shaking his head. "Don't think there was much choice involved on the part of the hospital. Nothing short of shackling her to the bed would've stopped her from leaving."

"I hate hospitals. Hate white coats. Hate the smell of antiseptics. I hate it all, it makes me anxious," she shares. "I've spent too much time around all of those for too many years during fertility treatments, as well as after Hamish's accident, but now that I have my healthy son..." She glances at Hamish, who looks at her with nothing shy of adoration. "*Our* healthy son," she corrects. "I wasn't about to stay there a moment longer than absolutely necessary."

"Understandable," Jacob mumbles, looking on from a distance.

I imagine he would, he spent a fair amount of time in hospitals as well when he was recovering.

I notice his eyes are locked on the little guy in my arms, and I can't help wondering if he ever dreamed of having kids of his own. Technically, he could, there's nothing wrong with him.

"Jacob." I nudge my head to call him over. "Your turn," I announce when he stops in front of me.

I kiss the baby's little head, inhale that delicious baby smell that tugs at every maternal cell in my body, and hand him over. My eyes well up when I see Jacob's strong hands cradling the tiny body and holding him up to his face.

"Does this little guy have a name?"

There is no immediate answer and when I tear my eyes away from Jacob, I notice Hamish and Laura looking at each other, both of them smiling.

"He does," Hamish shares, taking his wife's hand in his. "His name is Nathan Jacob Adrian."

My eyes instantly dart back to my man, who is staring at his friend in shock. Then he turns back to the little boy.

"Well, hello, Nathan," he croons, in a hoarse voice. "I like your name."

"And," Laura adds, her eyes shining suspiciously, "we would like to ask you both if you would consider being Nathan's godparents."

"Yes!" I blurt out instantly, and promptly burst into tears.

Clearly prepared, Hamish shoves a box of tissues at me, which I pass on to his wife, whose waterworks have been triggered as well.

I may be a blubbering mess, but when I look up and catch Jacob's warm, hazel eyes on me—crinkles and all—over that downy little head, I can't help but feel incredibly blessed.

If this is karma...she's been kind to me.

Jacob

I find Rajani sitting on the back deck, a glass of wine in her hand, and her bare feet propped up against the railing.

I know she's heard me come out when she murmurs, "Beautiful, isn't it?"

She points out the sunset, which is pretty spectacular tonight.

I sit down next to her and take her free hand, slipping my fingers between hers.

"The view is always good when you're sitting out here."

She turns her eyes on me and smiles. "You're really getting good at this romantic stuff."

I lift her hand to my mouth and kiss her knuckles.

"I have a little less romantic news if you're interested? It has to do with Gordon Chen's widow."

That poor woman. I remember finding out that man was married and feeling so incredibly sorry for his wife. What an incredible shock that must've been to find out your husband was a sexual predator with a penchant for children.

"I'm interested."

"Apparently, she was getting ready to put Chen's mountain property up for sale. She hadn't been there since last year. She wanted to make sure an old freezer Gordon kept in a shed for game was empty before having it hauled off, and discovered a body wrapped in garbage bags."

My mouth falls open and my feet hit the ground as I shoot up, the abrupt move sloshing wine over my hand.

"You're kidding?"

"Not in the least. Guess who?"

That doesn't require too much brainpower. There was only one person whose whereabouts had remained a mystery. The assumption had been he'd gone to Mexico, but apparently not.

"Jose Cantu."

He squeezes my hand.

"Got it in one."

I lean back in my chair and prop my feet back up, my eyes drawn back to the setting sun, which is making the sky look pink and purple.

"That's crazy."

"Hmm," he hums beside me. "So, what's new with you? You never told me how your meeting went today."

I had a Zoom meeting with Cassandra Wilson this afternoon. She first contacted GEM in March. I happened to take the call and would've hung up on her when she mentioned being David Wheeler's only surviving relative, had she not mentioned she got our number from Lee Remington.

Cassandra never knew she was related to the Wheeler family. Her grandmother was the older sister of David Wheeler's father. As the story goes, Cassandra's grandmother was disowned when she married against her family's wishes.

Ironically, her granddaughter—as the only surviving relative—inherited every last one of the Wheeler assets.

What had appeared an unexpected windfall at first, became a huge emotional and moral burden to Cassandra since. Lee had interviewed her for a follow-up story when he suggested we might be able to help.

"It went well. She already has a couple of horses and a few other animals at The Sanctuary. She's asking me to help her put together ideas for a program she could run for the kids that would integrate the animals. I was able to give her the name of a great assisted animal therapist in Libby, Montana I heard about. She runs a similar program at her horse rescue. Cassandra is going to get in touch to see if the woman would be willing to give us some pointers."

"Sounds like she's really committed to this plan of hers."

"She is," I confirm.

It took me a while to get used to her idea to turn what was Grandview Estate—a place that stirred up bad memories for a lot of people—into The Sanctuary. Her vision to combine a refuge for discarded and retired animals, with a safe haven for child victims of sexual abuse and exploitation, quickly gained ground with me.

It's perhaps another form of justice, a little more poetic, like growing flowers in cemeteries. Instead of destroying the place and pretending it was never there, her idea would build hope and light on its dark history.

A reminder of innocence lost as well as a promise of healing.

"Wheeler is rolling over in his grave," Jacob observes.

"Good. He deserves no rest."

We sit for a few more minutes watching the sun sink behind the hills. Another end to a great day. It won't be long until night sets in.

Jacob gives my hand a squeeze.

"Ready for bed?"

I turn my head and smirk at him. "Is that an invitation?"

He's on his feet in a flash, pulling me up with him.

"Goose!" he yells for our newest addition.

A three-legged dog we found at the shelter. He's an ugly mutt and his bark sounds more like a honk—hence his name—but he also has the sweetest disposition, loves us like crazy, and we love him right back.

His honk sounds from over by the guesthouse, where I suspect he's been begging for treats from Bernie, but the next moment he comes running across the yard and up the steps in his uneven gait.

With one last look at dusk settling over our own sanctuary, I follow Jacob inside.

I'm smiling.

ALSO BY FREYA BARKER

GEM Series

OPAL

PEARL

ONYX

High Mountain Trackers Series:

HIGH MEADOW

HIGH STAKES

HIGH GROUND

HIGH IMPACT

Arrow's Edge MC Series:

EDGE OF REASON

EDGE OF DARKNESS

EDGE OF TOMORROW

EDGE OF FEAR

EDGE OF REALITY

EDGE OF TRUST

PASS Series:

HIT & RUN

LIFE & LIMB

LOCK & LOAD

LOST & FOUND

On Call Series:

BURNING FOR AUTUMN

COVERING OLLIE

TRACKING TAHLULA

ABSOLVING BLUE

REVEALING ANNIE

DISSECTING MEREDITH

WATCHING TRIN

IGNITING VIC

Rock Point Series:

KEEPING 6

CABIN 12

HWY 550

10-CODE

Northern Lights Collection:

A CHANGE OF TIDE

A CHANGE OF VIEW

A CHANGE OF PACE

SnapShot Series:

SHUTTER SPEED

FREEZE FRAME

IDEAL IMAGE

Portland, ME, Series:

FROM DUST

CRUEL WATER

THROUGH FIRE

STILL AIR

LuLLaY (a Christmas novella)

Cedar Tree Series:

SLIM TO NONE

HUNDRED TO ONE

AGAINST ME

CLEAN LINES

UPPER HAND

LIKE ARROWS

HEAD START

Standalones:

WHEN HOPE ENDS

VICTIM OF CIRCUMSTANCE

BONUS KISSES

SECONDS

ABOUT THE AUTHOR

USA Today bestselling author Freya Barker loves writing about ordinary people with extraordinary stories.

Driven to make her books about 'real' people; she creates characters who are perhaps less than perfect, each struggling to find their own slice of happy, but just as deserving of romance, thrills and chills in their lives.

Recipient of the ReadFREE.ly 2019 Best Book We've Read All Year Award for "Covering Ollie, the 2015 RomCon "Reader's Choice" Award for Best First Book, "Slim To None", Finalist for the 2017 Kindle Book Award with "From Dust", and Finalist for the 2020 Kindle Book Award with "When Hope Ends", Freya spins story after story with an endless supply of bruised and dented characters, vying for attention!

www.freyabarker.com